WITHDRAWN

Ambassador of Reconciliation

A Muriel Lester Reader

Edited by Richard Deats
Foreword by Eileen Egan

New Society Publishers

Philadelphia, PA

Santa Cruz, CA

Gabriola Island, BC

Inquiries regarding requests to reprint all or part of *Ambassador of Reconciliation: A Muriel Lester Reader* should be addressed to:
New Society Publishers
4527 Springfield Avenue
Philadelphia, PA 19143

ISBN USA 0-86571-210-7 Hardcover
ISBN USA 0-86571-211-5 Paperback
ISBN CAN 1-55092-152-5 Hardcover
ISBN CAN 1-55092-153-3 Paperback

Printed in the United States of America on 50% recycled paper by Capital City Press of Montpelier, Vermont.

Cover design by Brian Prendergast.
Book design by Greg Bates.

To order directly from the publisher, add $2.50 to the price for the first copy, 75¢ each additional. Send check or money order to:
New Society Publishers
PO Box 582
Santa Cruz, CA 95061
In Canada, contact:
New Society Publishers/New Catalyst
PO Box 189
Gabriola Island, BC VOR 1X0

New Society Publishers is a project of the New Society Educational Foundation, a nonprofit, tax-exempt, public foundation. Opinions expressed in this book do not necessarily represent positions of the New Society Educational Foundation.

Dedication

To Jan

Acknowledgments

I began collecting Muriel Lester's writings after I first met her and heard her speak. Over the years numerous persons who knew her have sent me photos, letters, and articles pertaining to her life. Allan Hunter was especially helpful in the conversations we had about her and Armstrong Hunter generously sent me scores of letters and notes Muriel wrote to Allan and Elizabeth Hunter and to Stanley and Elizabeth Hunter. Sydney J. Russell and Neil Welsby, past wardens of Kingsley Hall, were very helpful in our correspondence, as has been A. M. Lucas, present administrator. John Anderson graciously spent long hours organizing and categorizing our Muriel Lester materials at Shadowcliff, the national head-quarters of the United States Fellowship of Reconciliation and Wilma Mosholder of the Swarthmore Peace Collection was, as always, most helpful. Gene Knudsen-Hoffman has been a perceptive and eager collaborator in this labor of love, as she works on a companion volume of the letters of Muriel Lester. Virginia Baron, editor of *Fellowship* magazine, was a constant encouragement.

Richard Deats
Lent, 1991

Foreword

Eileen Egan

The setting was Kingsley Cottage, the small home of Muriel Lester; Dorothy Day had just arrived from New York City. On our way to the 1963 Pax Conference, we spent time in the offices of the pacifist publication *Peace News*. The editor, Hugh Brock, asked Dorothy Day what she would like to do in London.

"The one thing I want to do is see Muriel Lester," was her reply.

Two revolutionary women, Muriel Lester and Dorothy Day. They were not only rebels, but prophets, having lived lives that pitted them against injustice, poverty, colonial oppression, racism, and above all, against war, preparation for war, and the vengeance that is the legacy of every war. They had both known the inside of prisons for their convictions and actions. Lester and Day, 79 and 66 respectively, were remarkably similar in looks: fine-featured with luminous, clear eyes. While some women's faces became saggingly indistinct, theirs were still sharply defined, their expressions eager and alive as they moved from the past to talk of their present hopes for the expansion of the peace movement.

On the mantlepiece of the simple living room was framed a letter. Lester related that Gandhi had written to her before undertaking one of his longest fasts.

"I had written to him telling him of my worries about his health," Lester explained. Gandhi replied asking her not to be concerned about his health nor even his survival.

Lester questioned Day about her most recent jail experiences. Day recalled how at the sound of a siren, New York City was ordered to come to a halt to simulate a nuclear attack by the Soviet Union. School children had to crouch under their desks and pedestrians were expected to dash for cover—any cover, even a nearby subway station. Local peace groups, seeing through the charade, responded with civil disobedience, sitting in front of City Hall instead of taking cover. The few who resisted in 1955 grew to thousands by 1960, and after 1961 the civil defense drills were called off. The longest resulting prison sentence was thirty days.

Hugh Brock, sitting with us, was at the center of the British peace movement. Sparked by Britain's decision to manufacture nuclear bombs, it was at its blazing height. A peace march on the Aldermaston military installation drew nearly 100,000 marchers, stretching seven miles from London to Aldermaston. Three decades earlier, Lester had led an anti-military march of protest at the Royal Air Force display at Hendon. It had consisted of twenty protesters raising their voices and holding high their placards in the face of 200,000 RAF enthusiasts.

As Lester and Day talked of campaigns lost and won, I found myself marveling at their vision and strength in challenging a tradition that had grafted itself onto Christianity—the tradition of the "just war." The "just war" tradition has become, through the centuries, one of the chief myths that men kill by. Every war declared by every nation is declared as a "just war." Lester and Day actively opposed every war, declared or undeclared, during their long lifetimes. They refused to take part in the contradiction of Christian teaching.

I realized how alike their careers had been. Their revolutionary convictions and activities had stemmed from the same root: the Sermon on the Mount. The Mahatma Gandhi, citing a Gujarati poem dealing with the beauty of doing good against evil, asserted that "the ideas which underlie the Gujarati hymn and the Sermon on the Mount should revolutionize the whole of life!"

The Sermon on the Mount, the very core of the gospel of Jesus, is sometimes seen as primarily a path to personal righteousness. Indeed, it does begin with the personal. But when it becomes a way of life for groups of people, even small groups, it can turn society upside down. Those transformed by it transform life around them.

This sermon, hardly over 2,000 words, revolutionized the entire lives of Muriel Lester and Dorothy Day. Through it, they found the courage to break with the values of their societies. As the Sermon on the Mount provided a way of life for Lester and her co-workers in peace time, it was unthinkable to jettison it in war time for an obviously contradictory way of life. At the outbreak of the First World War in Britain, Lester asserted, "We refused at Kingsley Hall to pronounce a moratorium on the Sermon on the Mount for the duration of the war."

Lester also saw the unbreakable connection between the Lord's Prayer (part of the Sermon on the Mount) and peacemaking. "We should stop praying the Lord's Prayer," she asserted, "until we can see that 'Our Father' means that we are tied to the same living tether not only with our fellow countrymen but with everybody on the planet." It was her conviction that we have no right even to use the phrase "Our Father," if we cannot accept that God intended the human race to be one family: each person equally a child of God. This attitude led Lester to voluntary poverty and opened her to all peoples of humankind, to their cultures, to their creeds, be it Hinduism, Islam, Taoism, Buddhism, Judaism, or any belief dear to part of the human family.

When in December of 1941, the United States entered the Second World War, Dorothy Day blazoned on the front page of *The Catholic Worker:* "We continue Our Christian Pacifist Stand." In her lead article, she proclaimed, "Our manifesto is the Sermon on the Mount."

Cleaving to the Sermon on the Mount in war time and to voluntary poverty at all times brought Dorothy Day much recognition and gave rise to a spate of articles and a few books about her and the movement she co-founded with Peter Maurin. Her own writing gifts were extraordinary, always devoted to the daily struggle for peace, justice, and human rights. A collection of her writings, prepared by Robert Ellsberg, helped make her witness known to a wide range of readers. But Muriel Lester, whose witness influenced countless lives, is largely unknown to younger people, even to those in the peace movement. Her work goes on, but her name is forgotten. There was a chance that Lester might receive public attention in Richard Attenborough's 1982 film *Gandhi.* Although Gandhi was invited to be a guest of King George during his three month stay in London for the 1931 Round Table Conference, he chose instead to make his home at Kingsley Hall with his friend and supporter Muriel Lester. Unfortunately, no mention is made of her in the film.

A recent event emphasizes the impact of Lester's witness on later history. When the Philippine people in 1985 were on fire to put down their corrupt and ruthless dictator, their resort to mass violence seemed almost inevitable. The moment of decision might have come when a man of peace, returning from exile to lead the forces of reason, was shot to death at Manila airport. The argument of that bleeding body seemed to many to justify violence and retaliation. But something stayed the hand of those ready for violence.

Hildegard and Jean Goss-Mayr, acting as Traveling Secretaries of the International Fellowship of Reconciliation like Muriel Lester before them, had been quietly conducting retreats and conferences on active nonviolence, as had Richard Deats, the editor of this book. These gatherings were attended by larger and larger groups of oppressed Filippinos.

The world saw the result on the television screens. Masses of people gathered to resist—by prayer. Religious sisters holding up rosaries stood in the front lines. To the soldiers sent to put down the protest they offered not taunts but cries of solidarity. A Franciscan priest in his long robe stretched out his arms, forming a cross before the approaching tanks. They were ready to accept but not to inflict suffering. In the end, soldiers capitulated to gestures of love, and a dictator was removed without blood-spattered streets.

The Philippine example of massive nonviolent resistance served as the forerunner of an international crescendo of nonviolent change in Europe—a crescendo that kept the world breathless with hope. As in the Philippines, the peoples of Eastern Europe poured into the streets in protest. Many prayed. All stood firm. Except in minor instances, the troops did not fire into unarmed masses, whose only power was moral.

The active nonviolence that prevailed among the people of the Philippines and the peoples of Eastern Europe was a revelation to the world. The idea that a revolution could be achieved by nonviolent means was an idea that many people thought would never come. Yet it has.

Those who prepared for its coming must not be lost to history. Their example is more necessary than ever as human beings are at last realizing, in the face of immeasurable violence, the immeasurable power of nonviolence.

Muriel Lester stands out as one who devoted a lifetime to preparing and growing the seeds of nonviolence in the hearts of men and women of vastly different cultures and creeds. At her death in 1968, it was said that the growth of the Fellowship of Reconciliation was due largely to her spirit. Countless people whose spirits are nourished by the International Fellowship of Reconciliation, and by allied movements, may not know how much they owe to the work of Muriel Lester.

Fortunately, Richard Deats has rescued this account of revolutionary love in action, bringing us the drama and power of Lester's own words linked by his own recreation of the events in her life. He is in a unique position to resurrect this precious legacy of peacemaking and justice-seeking that belongs not just to the Christian community, but to the whole human family.

Deats has allowed Muriel Lester to continue to give the message that the ministry of reconciliation has been entrusted to the followers of Jesus. How staggeringly different would our world be if Christians, across their own divisions, would take up the ministry of reconciliation to heal the divisions of the human family. How much closer would we come to the Reign of God if a larger portion of the Christian community decided to serve as the reconciling community for humankind.

It is this challenge that leaps from the pages of this book; a book important to all peacemakers, indispensable to Christian peacemakers.

Contents

Introduction

Richard Deats

I met Muriel Lester in 1951 when I was a student at McMurry College in Abilene, Texas. She spoke twice on the campus. At a morning assembly, she examined the cold war and the nuclear arms race from the perspective of the Kingdom of Heaven; that night she spoke on the meaning of prayer and its central importance in life. Afterwards I spoke with her at length about questions I was struggling with as a college student. My life was profoundly shaped by her visit to my campus. I read everything of Muriel Lester's that I could find, I joined the Fellowship of Reconciliation and I spent the next summer working in a refugee camp in Germany.

Over the years as I have traveled around the world in the work of peace, I have met numerous persons similarly influenced by the life and writings of Muriel Lester. But with her death in 1968 and her books going out of print and increasingly unknown, the conviction has grown in me, in recent years, that her writings should be made available again. She was a gifted writer and storyteller. For over half a century she lived a remarkable life in the midst of momentous historic events. Her witness and message are important for our contemporary world.

Raised in a wealthy home, she grew up with the opportunities afforded by a good education, frequent travel, and ample cultural experiences. First seeing poverty from a train window when going through the slums of London, her religious sensitivity stirred in her until finally she decided to give her life to the struggle against injustice. Moving into the Bow district of London's East End, she became a social worker and co-founded Kingsley Hall with her sister, Doris. The strain and

1

stress of such a life led her to see the absolute necessity of daily, disciplined prayer, and she began a lifelong quest to combine the inward and the outward journeys into a practical mysticism and a deeply grounded activism. It was the writing of Leo Tolstoy that led her to a pacifism that was to be repeatedly tested by the militant patriots and through bombings that shattered Bow, and Kingsley Hall, in both world wars. She protested war and injustice on the streets of London and from a soapbox in Hyde Park. She went into politics for four years, serving as the socialist alderman on the borough council of Poplar, an area with the highest child mortality rate in London. As chair of the maternity and child welfare committee, she organized the women of the area to start children's clinics and to distribute free milk to poor children, thus overcoming the opposition of the Ministry of Health in its austerity campaign. She was a lifelong advocate of the rights of women, whom she called "the most practical half of the human race." A relative of the Indian poet Rabindranath Tagore learned of her work and invited her to India to meet Tagore and Mahatma Gandhi in 1926, meetings that resulted in lifelong friendships, especially with Gandhi. She became a strong advocate of Indian independence and returned often to India. When Gandhi came to England in 1931 for the Round Table Conference, he made Kingsley Hall his home and base of operations for the entire three month period.

In time Lester turned over the leadership of Kingsley Hall to her sister Doris so that she could devote her time entirely to the International Fellowship of Reconciliation (IFOR), representing them first as their ambassador-at-large and later as traveling secretary. For over three decades, she traveled throughout the world, circling the globe nine times, speaking, writing, leading prayer schools, organizing branches of the IFOR and investigating injustices such as the drug trade in India under British rule and in China under Japanese rule. After a trip through Latin America during World War II, she was taken from an American liner when it docked in Trinidad and was interned for ten weeks by the British authorities for her pacifist activities. She was then returned to England and her passport was withheld for the duration of the war. She subsequently began traveling throughout England, Scotland, and Wales for the British FOR until the war was over, at which time she threw herself into the postwar efforts to assist the needy and to heal the broken international community. She resumed her work for the IFOR and continued her travels, even beyond her retirement in 1953 and almost to the time of her death.

Her voluminous writings—books, journals, articles, and letters—reveal a person with a pragmatic and forthright bent. As she put it, she had an "ingrained preference for facts that can be visualized rather than theories that can be discussed." When she saw the horrible effects of the drug trade coming into China in the wake of the Japanese invasion, she returned to Japan to talk directly with government officials about it. In China she picked up a piece of shrapnel beside a dead Chinese lad; when she went to the United States, she placed it on the desk of one of the scrap metal dealers in Seattle to confront him with the evil of fueling the Japanese war machine. Lester always tried to keep before the public the profound wisdom of the poor, such as she first learned on the streets of Bow, and was quick to point out the effect of public policies on people usually unheard and unseen—for example, the children who starved on the continent of Europe as a result of the Allies' food blockade during both world wars. She was openly self-critical and often admitted her own shortcomings in temperament, deeds, and thoughts. And she possessed a quick and ready wit, able to laugh at herself and to see the humor in even grim circumstances, such as her internment in the Caribbean during World War II.

In one of the issues of Gandhi's publication *Harijan,* Muriel Lester's—"Wanted: A Manifestation of Christ in Daily Life"—was reprinted. Gandhi noted in the preface to the article:

> Many persons have written like Miss Lester before now. The value of her conversation lies in the fact that she endeavors every moment of her life to practice what she professes and preaches in her writings.

This sums up perhaps the enduring significance of Muriel Lester. I hope that the pages that follow, taken from her books and other writings, will enable readers to make their own discovery of one of the twentieth century's unique persons.

Early Years

From Privilege
to Voluntary Poverty

Muriel Lester was a born storyteller. In her books, articles, letters, and reports, she recounted with warmth, humor, and insight the events of her fascinating life which spanned much of the twentieth century. From her birth in 1884 until her death in 1968, she lived an extraordinary life, whether she was working in the slums of London, meditating in Gandhi's ashram in India, traversing war-torn China, or sitting in a British prison in the Caribbean in World War II because of her pacifist activities.

Muriel Lester was born into a family of privilege near London. Life in an upper-class family shielded her for a while from the harsh realities of her time, but her family's religious sensitivity and her own wide-ranging reading, as well as her independent frame of mind, soon began to broaden her horizons dramatically. She tells her story in the first volume of her autobiography.

From *It Occurred to Me*

The railway route [from our home in Leytonstone] lay through this unsalubrious neighborhood of East London. Whenever we went "up West" for a party, a pantomime, or for shopping, we would close up the windows of the carriage with a bang and cover our noses to protect ourselves from the foul smell that pervaded the whole atmosphere of Bow. It came from the factories which produced sweet-scented soap out of bone manure. The West End enjoyed the pleasant perfumed delicacy. The East End perpetually reeked of its manufacture.

5

Dwellers in Essex, like ourselves, habitually commiserated with each other over the fact that their railway line ran through this malodorous area.

One day our train was held up for a minute or so on this part of the route. I stared down at the rabbit-warren of unsavoury dwelling-houses, gardenless, sordid, leaking. Being an innocent of some eight summers, I could not believe they were human habitations. I turned to the only grown-up, the nurse who was taking us home after a party, "Do people live down there?" I inquired, pointing. Perhaps she had orders not to let any of us become unhappy; I don't know. Her reply is clear-sounding in my ears still: "Oh, yes. Plenty of people live down there but you needn't worry about them. They don't mind it. They're not like you. They enjoy it."

On only one other occasion, a year or so later, do I remember considering the condition of the people. It was once more the sight and smell of this ugly bit of East London which prompted some forgotten query about the plight of the inhabitants. Once more a grown-up answered, promptly: "It's all right. They don't feel things the same way as we do. And even if they did, they've only got themselves to blame. They get drunk. That's why they're poor." One believes the grown-ups when one is under twelve.

*   *   *

The preparatory school we all went to was co-educational, advanced even for these days. We were encouraged to think. The Principal's wife, Mrs. T. B. Martin, was a vegetarian, and a number of us caught the habit from her and have kept to it.

On our walk to school and back, on excursions and picnics in the summer holidays, we were rarely our ordinary selves. One or other of our "talking games" was always in progress. Doris, Kingsley, and I each had our part in a perpetual play wherein we were all grown-ups and gloriously confident and capable, but it was when Kathleen was with us that the impersonations became heroic. She was King Harold, the rest of his brothers, brought up to date. We conversed interminably in modern English and didn't notice a tree, flower, bird, or view. We were in another world. During the long hours in which a child lies in bed awake on light summer mornings and evenings, I always impersonated the Duke of

6

Wellington or some other soldier, ancient or medieval. I would talk to myself in noble language, re-enacting wonderful exploits. Swords and dirks decorated the walls of my room. I trained my hand to leap to my sword-hilt at a second's notice.

Later on, when I discovered one could be quite as romantic about contemporary history, I became a miltarist patriot. On my bookshelf, next to the G. A. Henty books, were ensconced the *Life of Lord Roberts*, the history of Lord Kitchener avenging General Gordon in Khartoum, the account of the recent campaign of Baden-Powell among the Ashantis, the bloody story of the Soudan War. I bought a scrap book, covered it with khaki, and collected pictures displaying British prowess and native infidelity — any sort of native.

I was about twelve when a great treat was to be enjoyed by one of us children. Prince George [later King George V], the Duke of York, was coming with his wife to open the new Blackwall Tunnel. Mother and Father eventually decided that I should be the one to accompany them as they drove up to witness Their Royal Highnesses' arrival. Dressed in Sunday clothes, I was perched rather precariously on the little extra seat of the victoria, between its black-painted iron railing to which one clung when sharp corners were turned or when the wheel got caught in a tram line and had to be jerked out. At first the drive was jolly but soon we emerged into questionable streets. The houses grew squatter, less dignified, sinister. The roads filled with people who shouted for no apparent reason, waved paper hats and blew out ticklers. They had red faces and loud voices. They laughed a lot. With dismay I realized we had driven into the heart of East End, that rabbit-warren that years previously I had looked into with such horror from the secure vantage-ground of a first-class railway carriage. My parents, however, appeared completely at their ease and even gave orders to the coachman to draw up at the curb, whence a good view of the Duke and Duchess would be obtained. I can still feel the peculiar creak and crackle of white silk gloves suddenly drawn tight as I gripped the railing to control my fear. Etiquette forbade that I should betray it to my father and mother. How long should we have to wait for this Duke? Who cared about seeing him or any other royalty compared with the blessed security of home? I was in the midst of a sea of alien faces, creatures who cared nothing for me. I was bereft of all shelter and security, respect and consideration. How could any one call this a treat? Tense and wretched, I waited, not for the Duke to come but for him to go. As at last we drove away, I gave by rote the customary response to the query, "Well, dear, how did you like that?" But the thought flashed into my mind, "And there are some women who live as missionaries among these awful East Enders. What a fate!" I promptly put the whole horrible idea out of my head.

*   *   *

I left school when I was eighteen. ...There had been talk of Cambridge, but both elder sisters had married young, my parents had moved into the country, close to Epping Forest, and my father was nearing seventy. I wasn't really eager to go on trying to read Greek plays and translating good Latin into bad English. The prospect of spending the rest of the winter abroad charmed me. Mother and Father were easy people to get on with, quite apart from one's blood relationship, and they introduced me to their favourite haunts in Mentone, Bordighera, San Remo, Rome, Florence, and the Italian lakes. Italy is a grand place for any one trained in imaginative reconstruction by "talking games."

After ten weeks I came home to be a young lady at large. I played tennis, danced, took piano and singing lessons, visited school friends, helped Father while away his hours of leisure, did the housekeeping which I hated, took charge of a class of boys in the Sunday school, and spent hours a day sitting at the piano. Sometimes I played for my own pleasure. At other times I accompanied Mother's, Doris', Kingsley's, and my own songs, Kingsley's violin, one married sister's violin, and the other's cello. Kingsley was the sort of brother everyone wants, and he was rich in natural gifts. Doris, he and I had bedrooms with communicating doors. How satisfying is the memory of those well-worn jokes and stories with which we used to regale each other. We told each other some home truths, too.

I used to feel horribly afraid for Kingsley, the last child after four girls, lest when he grew up he should take to drink, fall into bad company, or lose touch with God. A sense of responsibility for him kept me worrying. When he was getting ready for Cambridge I imagined all sorts of pitfalls. Eventually I was delivered from my anxiety by discovering Tolstoi. In somebody else's house I found an old primly-bound volume of his *The Kingdom of Heaven is Within You*. It changed the very quality of life for me. A long chapter was devoted to the words of Jesus, "Judge not." As I eagerly devoured it, my burden of care-fraught ideas dropped from me. I saw that so long as Kingsley did what he thought right, I could honour him and enjoy him as much as ever. Another chapter on "Be Not Anxious" determined me to ignore once and for all those conventions and solicitudes, those pretences and fears, that cause so much friction. Another chapter tipped me right over into pacifism. That was a pretty swift transition for such an absurdly militarist young woman, but once your eyes get opened to pacifism, you can't shut them again. Once you see it, you can't unsee it. You may bitterly regret the fact that you happen to be one of the tiny minority of the human race who have caught this angle of vision but you can't help it.

*   *   *

"Would you like to come to a party in the East End?" inquired a friend one day. "The factory girls' club in Bow is celebrating next week. I'll take you along if you like."

The invitation seemed to promise a pleasant diversion, and I accepted. I had never come into contact with working people except as they served me — bus-conductors, porters, cooks, and gardeners. Like J.M. Barrie's elderly artist in *A Kiss for Cinderella*, who had cherished throughout his life a longing to see a policeman minus a helmet, a little uncertain whether that dignified appendage was, in fact, removable, I looked forward to the new sensation of meeting face to face, as separate personalities, the people who produced the cakes of soap, the boxes of matches, the chocolates, and the waterproof coats we all accepted as a matter of course.

As we threaded our way down narrow turnings and through murky streets, ill lit by occasional gas lamps, I reminded myself that this was the famous East End, in the public eye the disreputable haunt of thieves, drunks, and hooligans, the area I had gazed upon with so much distress as a child when the Great Eastern Railway train halted on its otherwise express run from London to my home.

The party marked an epoch for me. These girls, who danced with me, entertained me, made conversation to set me at my ease and plied me with refreshments, were just like myself; some of them, the same age, nineteen years old. Yet how experienced they seemed! How assured! What natural dignity! They were much more mature and more independent than I. Why were some of them pale, others thin, with bent shoulders? Compared with them, I was a pampered, sheltered, ignorant idler. Why should they go on working, producing pleasure and ease for such as I? For the previous five years, since they and I were fourteen, why had our lot been so different? For exactly that period I had been growing strong as a horse at an expensive and delightful boarding school, while they had been bound to a machine for ten and often eleven hours a day. Was this God's will? If so, God was certainly not admirable.

I came up to Bow next week, and the next and the next. I was avid to find out about these people, what their ideas were, how they felt about things. I longed to be asked into their homes and treated like one of themselves for a time. At length a dear old woman in a long-skirted black dress with a white crocheted collar told her daughter to "bring the new young lady in for a nice cup of cocoa before she sets out on that long journey to Loughton, being as 'ow this 'ouse is close to club and it's that cold in them trains."

Her daughter, Bettie, rather diffidently gave me this message. She was employed at Berger's starch works, aged nearly forty, shoulders bent, her little eyes almost invisible behind powerfully magnifying spectacles, her brochitic wheezing often an actual rattle in her throat. Tall and thin, she had no beauty of feature or garment to make her desirable; but like Bernard Shaw's Saint Joan "there was something about her." How can I fitly praise her? She had delicate consideration for others, integrity, fineness of judgment, courage. Her criterions were actually, not just theoretically, Christian.

Of course I didn't know all this when I started off with her that night, gleefully climbing the flight of stone steps that adorned the facade of her house. She didn't knock, but leaned over the railing, craned her neck forward over the area below, and called to the inmates of the basement. From behind its illuminated window there came an answering signal; a click sounded close to our ears and the door opened. "That bit of string of Mother's saves her old legs," explained Bettie as she turned up the gas-jet in the narrow passage cluttered with

10

bicycles and perambulator. At the far end was a dark winding stairway. Mrs. Pryke stood at the foot of it, holding a lamp. She led me through the scullery into the gayest and cosiest of rooms. Introductions were effected.

*   *   *

I was sorry when, my huge cup of cocoa emptied, I had to go to the train. Lodgers, married daughter, son-in-law, and three children had all helped Mrs. Pryke and Beattie entertain me.

This visit made me an addict. I set to work to learn the etiquette of the neighbourhood, its outlook, its syntax and the secret of its perfect, unhurried manners. I started coming to the club regularly. I read aloud and told stories, prepared and served penny teas, accompanied (inevitably) for the singing class, and otherwise began to serve my apprenticeship. ... [All the while] I learned a good deal about home life in Bow. ... Most of our talking was done on our walks. Pale-faced Hannah told of her father—how frightened she was of him when he was in drink; how her mother hid her away in a cupboard, but "some 'ow the old man always knew, sort of extra sense of something. He'd break out in perspiration and shiver and vow how there was some one about 'e couldn't see. Not 'arf queer!" I heard that the best way you could help an unemployed man was to give him a penny. Then he could go and sit in a public house with a glass of beer, and "as likely as not 'e'd get talking with a foreman or a chap who could speak up for 'im and find 'im a job." The girls explained to me how it often happens that men start talking about God when they're drunk. "Truth comes out in liquor. Men who'd never think of talking religious when they're sober can't 'elp it when the drink's in 'em. It's a pity men make such beasts of theirselves, but if you come to think of it, they must go somewhere in the evenings. There ain't nowhere else except the pubs. People don't go in because they're thirsty, but because there's good company to be found in them places. There's friendly words and no stiff ways; no fuss either, and no nagging. There's generally plenty of noise, what with so many people talking and the potman drawing the drinks, an' all, so you don't hear yourself speak; you don't even notice your boots squeaking: it's all free and easy and you don't never feel awkward in a pub."

11

*   *   *

It was a new experience for me to run up against suicide. Its frequent cause was indebtedness. To borrow ten shillings in some crisis, birth, death, marriage, or accident, is perhaps to put oneself in bondage for the rest of one's life. The rate of interest charge is often two-pence on the shilling, payable weekly. It works out at about 850% per annum. Loans of this sort are usually negotiated in the bar of a public house. Many lenders insist on being treated to a drink at the beginning and at the end of a transaction, some whenever a repayment is made. The borrower is often urged to drink also, for courtesy's sake or for the good of the house. If the debtor cannot keep up the weekly payments, a further loan is urged upon him. One of the blessed results of Lloyd George's Health Insurance Act was to lessen the occasions for borrowing. Illness and maternity are more or less provided for now.

*   *   *

Rosa Waugh Hobhouse brought the phrase "voluntary poverty" into common parlance. She denied that poverty was the right word to denote the condition of her neighbours in Hoxton or of mine in Bow. She said they were living in compulsory want. It was the great privilege of Christians to practice voluntary poverty. It was the precondition of serenity, the only means by which one could attain fellowship with the vast majority of citizens, limited and inhibited as they are by penury. These millions of dispossessed were our concern, not to be thought of as our field of activity or the recipients of our bounty whose ignorance we must dispel, but people better educated than we in the facts of life, whose faith had been tested by more fiery ordeals than ours, many of them with a surer grasp of the essentials, a more Godlike generosity of spirit, greater freedom from self-pity and a capacity to hope long past the limit of rationality.

*   *   *

As for myself, it was becoming ever clearer that I shared responsibility for those millions of dispossessed who have left the churches. The middle-class habit of draping the Eastern Carpenter in white Sunday clothes and putting Him in a coloured window instead of bothering to discover what the

Joiners' Union is doing for its members today, has much to answer for. That may well constitute our crisis at the Judgement Day. From our malodorous quarters among the goats we may challenge the Supreme Court as to the grounds of its decision, but surely we shall be reminded, as were the goats in the parable, that our downfall is due to our own romantic egotism which leads us to evade the stubborn practicality in Jesus' words about the "eye of a needle." If we had not shown such humorously indecent haste in protesting that the dilemma of the rich young man did not apply to our so different selves, we might be now be enjoying fullness of life without being haunted by fear, shame, and conscience pangs.

*   *   *

In 1921 Rosa Hobhouse, Mary Hughes, and I felt that the time had come to issue an invitation to the general public to consider the economic basis of their lives. Notices were sent to the press in the following terms:

> We know those who cannot obtain adequate clothing sheets and warm covering or necessary food for their children and themselves. The poverty which we refer to is commonly known as a state of privation or destitution. But we prefer to call this condition of their compulsory want, being brought upon them by force of hard circumstances. Our invitation to you is not into this enforced poverty, but into a very glorious alternative, involving a drastic readjustment in your affairs, called voluntary poverty.

We invite you into this condition, that the needs of others, whether in our country or abroad, generously be supplied by the overflowing of your treasure. We do not here wish to encourage the charity of patronage, but rather the large charity of God, which rejoices in richly providing. Nor do we desire to indicate the exact consequences of the step into voluntary poverty, into which we invite you. It will suffice to say we have many visions of possible blessing, derived from intimate contact with the sorrows of the oppressed. ...

[After an initial meeting and various inquiries] a number of people, eager to see Christ manifested in the economic sphere found a worthy leader in Bernard Walke, the rector of an old church in a remote village on the Cornish coast. He had been working out an idea of a brotherhood based on the economic significance of the communion table, where there is no specially favoured guest, no head or foot of the table, where Christ is the unseen Host of all who care to come. There is no lack or shortage, however many partake. The economists assure us that there is a plenitude in the world of everything we need, enough raw materials to supply food, clothing, and fuel for every member of the human race. We recognize this as God's gift, for all richly to enjoy. His gifts obviously are not intended for us to snatch and quarrel and fight over, but to be distributed sensibly. Is it anything but ridiculous to act as though the beneficent processes of nature were ordained to provide fortunes for a few individuals?

Some dozen of us East Enders who held these views formed a chapter at Bow under Bernard Walke's suggested title, *The Brethren of the Common Table.* We met once a month. We took no vows. We only promised to be honest and confess the measure of our greed and of our need. We found it the hardest thing we had ever done, so hard that we had to start with worship. Only through silent prayer during which we tried to think like God could we acquire the grace of straightforward, honest, direct statement. Among our number was an heiress or two, a curate, a writer, a teacher, a dog-biscuit packer, an out-of-work carpenter, a dock labourer, a young widow on relief and a journeyman printer. We each had to own up in turn as to how much we had earned or received during the past month and exactly how we had spent it. Those who had a surplus laid it on the table in front of us. Those who needed extra took it. It was *de rigueur* not to say "thank you," because we held that it was no longer the owner's property if he did not need it.

Therefore it wasn't a gift, but the proper possession of the needy. We took as our slogan, "The only Christian, the only rational basis for the distribution of goods is need."

The obvious thing happened to us. From very shame of confessing, one lowered one's weekly expenditure on self. After hearing an unemployed dock labourer's wife give every item of the family budget for the previous month, one noticed that fruit did not exist in their household, and vegetables were rarely seen. Milk was scarce and then only canned.

When I had worn out my accumulated stock of clothes and needed a new pair of kid gloves, it was distressing to contemplate reporting such a purchase. Obviously gloves were not needed in summertime. Yet to me it was unthinkable

14

to go down Regent Street without them. Could it be done? It took weeks to make up my mind to take this horrible step. Filled with a sense of crisis and feeling undressed, I strode down the street. No one seemed to have noticed. I soon learned to limit my expenditure on clothes to ten shillings per week, though it wasn't easy, as I am apparently unique in my ability to wear holes in stockings. Happily, however, darned and patched clothes don't trouble me. I soon found coats put me into debt for so many weeks ahead that I took to wearing a cape, which is an easy garment to get made and does not go out of fashion. After a little experimenting I found that the ten shillings a week could cover all personal expenditure, though this meant that I could give no more presents. I told my family and my friends to stop buying birthday and Christmas gifts for me. Subscriptions had to shrink to nothing, and soon I found myself looking forward to the arrival of parcels of cast-off clothes which long ago I had solicited from relations for sale among the Kingsley Hall members. It surprised me to find out how toothpaste, handkerchiefs, and shampoo powder ate into one's allowance. "Going to the hairdresser" became a luxury of extremely rare occurrence.

Those of us who had a surplus income soon got rid of it. It was jolly seeing the children of the group looking stronger. Now what about capital? A thousand pounds was put by one member at the disposal of a new international school in Switzerland. Another sum helped finance the election expenses of a labour candidate who afterwards made history, and that of a sort we did not care for. Another fairly large sum saved a labour newspaper from liquidation. One of its columns regularly abused Christianity, but its news service was good and it kept the public aware of what was happening among the people of other countries. Six hundred pounds was given to the treasurer of the newly formed "Save the Children's Fund," which was doing grand work for war victims all over Europe. Then came the consideration of jewels. There were a few lovely things in our possession, a string of pearls, a paste brooch supposed to have belonged to Louis Quinze. We decided that these should be enjoyed by us all. Violet Lansbury kept them for us at 39 Bow Road in a blue-velvet box. But when the Russian famine occurred a couple of years later [in 1921-22 following a severe drought and aggravated by the upheaval of war and revolution] we could not find it in our hearts to keep the precious things, and they were sold for food.

Probably the most important warning one can give is not to start with only middle-class people. Such tend to become too meticulous. On several occasions we middle-class members were saved from finicky particularism by the rough-and-ready sanity of the workingpeople. For instance, the curate, in reporting his budget one month, said, "And then I'm afraid I spent half a crown on a ticket for the Russian ballet." The poorest woman present leaned forward, and studied his face critically.

"Young man," she said, "why d'you say you're afraid you spent it?"

"Because I'm rather ashamed when there's such a shortage among the members," he answered.

"'But didn't you enjoy the ballet?"

"Very much indeed," he said.

"Well," she retorted, "now you can tell us all about it, and we can enjoy it, too."

The Brethren of the Common Table was by no means the only group launching out about this time on experiments in personal economics. Our friend Vera Pragnell decided that she had no right to her financial inheritance. With it she bought a well-wooded tract of land in Sussex, tore down the fences, the barbed wire, and the "Trespassers will be prosecuted" notices. She wrote up instead, "Free to the Public." Many a tramp was given new heart and hope by finding her cottage. She kept a light burning all night inside the open door leading to the guest-room. A tray of food and a drawer full of clean clothes were always ready.

Then "Neighbours, Limited" was founded by the economist, Jack Bellerbe. Neighbours do not keep for their own use more than the average income of an English citizen. The rest of their income, earned or unearned, goes into a common fund for educational purposes. Their own children may benefit by this; the country at large certainly does. The first Peace Ballot extending over selected typical London and country areas was financed from this fund.

Rosa Hobhouse used to say, "We're skimming the cream off the children's milk."

Saint Ambrose said:

That which is taken by thee beyond what would suffice to thee, is taken by violence....It is the bread of the hungry thou keepest, it is the clothing of the naked thou lockest up; the money thou buriest is the redemption of the wretched.

Kingsley Hall

"An Overdue Act of Justice"

Muriel Lester was nineteen when she began going to the impoverished area of Bow in the East End of London. As the years passed, she spent more and more of her time there. She saw herself as living in two worlds, the affluent world of her upbringing and the poverty-stricken world of Bow.

The Lester home was closed for several months each year while the family and servants went to the French or the Italian Riviera. Despite a warm and happy family life and all the privileges of travel and luxury, Muriel—along with her sister, Doris, and her brother, Kingsley—increasingly identified with the poor people of the East End. Eventually, in 1915, Muriel and Doris founded a social, educational, and religious center where barriers of class, color, and creed were not recognized. They named it Kingsley Hall in memory of their brother, whose life was tragically cut short by an unexpected illness.

From *It Occurred to Me*

Can one know a place unless one sleeps in it? Doris and I used to seize various opportunities for leaving home and living in Bow for a time. She was the first to do it, as a regular lodger in the house of a women's meeting member. The rest of us were in the midst of mimosa and orange groves, but Doris vowed she would like nothing better than to get rid of us all and settle down in Bow.

In 1912 Kingsley was getting interested in Bow. He had been in business but had decided to leave it and devote his time to Bow. He, Doris and I took a small house in a long row,

No. 60, had it deloused, papered, and started housekeeping together. ...

No. 60 became the centre of so much striving, such varied hopes, dangers and aspirations, that those who made it their Mecca for eleven years can never feel quite the same about any other place. It was somewhere near the middle of a long row of about fifty houses, the line of their ugly facades almost unbroken. According to local feeling, it is a distinguished road. It has a church at each end, a doctor at each end, and only one pub. Most of its houses have a battered railing and an iron gate, often with a broken spike or two. One gathered that our street door had once been brown. The varnish long ago had blistered and peeled off. The knocker was of iron too ancient and knobby to hold the black paint. Its walls were damp inside. It had mice, six small rooms and a wee garden wherein only one rose out of six survived its first year, a slightly higher mortality rate than the infants'. Our sitting-room measured twelve by fourteen feet. One could sit at the table, poke the fire, answer the wall telephone, open the window, and shut the door almost without getting out of one's chair. One just tilted it a bit.

*   *   *

"How to reach the Masses!" At interdenominational conferences this used to be a stock subject for discussion. It baffled the academic minds of even leading ministers. "How to reach the Masses!" I heard it well discussed by many public speakers. But no one suggested the simple expedient of going to live with them. In a street like ours a peculiar sympathy is set up among people who suffer at the hands of the same landlord, who compare notes as to which inspector is most likely to insist on the landlord making the roof water-tight, and which of them might be meeting the said landlord for lunch. Also, to demonstrate on each other's walls rival methods of delousing creates a bond of helpfulness that lasts.

Overcrowding reached the figure of twelve to a room. Let us translate the figure into terms of flesh and blood. See a room in your mind's eye. A father and mother, five adolescents, four children and a baby. There's a low built-in cupboard for dishes, cups, and saucers. There's possibly an alcove with a curtain hung in front, used for hanging up clothes, twelve people's clothes. There's a chest of drawers, a table, a stove. What if someone is ill? If one wants to study, to draw, play, take a nap? Where is the soiled linen to be put?

Suddenly I discovered trees. Of course I'd known they were there, that they were deemed worth driving out to visit when allowed to grow as they liked in forest. Browning had written a poem to a lady who loved them so much that he thought her ghost would walk among them. But as for me, I would stand still, politely camouflaging my boredom, while visitors whom I was supposed to be entertaining in the garden or the forest gazed round enraptured. Sometimes I would start counting the seconds to see how long the ordeal was lasting. Then one day in May, after a three-weeks sojourn in Bow, I went into the country. And it was like seeing everything for the first time—sky, grass, clouds, trees. I stared and stared. It was a new world. ...

The winter of 1913-1914 was memorable. I suppose most people who were grown up when the war broke out look back to that last Christmas of the old world with a peculiar tenderness. It has become vested with a strange sort of glamour. Something within one almost aches at the thought of it.

I was fortunate enough to spend the time in well-nigh perfect company. Kingsley had had appendix trouble. It started again rather seriously that autumn and he had to leave his work with his friend Ernest Dowsett to come home and be nursed. For his convalescence, Father, Mother, he, and I set off for the Riviera. Doris, as usual, said she would stick to Bow. Was she pretending, I wonder? Things always seemed to improve in my absence, and I took her at her word.

*   *   *

That winter I became more than ever disgusted with myself and with the contrast between conditions in Bow and on the Riviera. Evil was so deeply entrenched in the world that it was idiotic to fight against it with kid gloves on. ...

[Back in Bow after Easter, Lester started a men's adult school, meeting early Sundays with ample time for wide-ranging discussion.]

I suggested we should be strictly practical. Mere theories untested by experience would be useless. We had all spent a good number of years absorbing Bow atmosphere. We knew

21

the wretchedness inherent in the capitalist system. We had all been to countless meetings at street corners and in Victoria Park, where speeches were made by local orators, paid propagandists and volunteer devotees of various "causes." All described our miseries correctly. Some blamed the Church, some the rich, some the government, some original sin, some the devil. I suggested that perhaps we were a bit weary of hearing so many selfrighteous judgments. Even supposing all these were to blame, we might do no better ourselves were we in power. Let us be quite specific, then, in making up our minds what was the most needed thing in our neighbourhood. Of course we must each support our trade union and our political party, but we needn't wait for the final fulfilment of their program before we acted on our own responsibility. We might be dead by then. What could a group of individuals do to change the quality of life in a neighbourhood? Let us work out a practical plan.

This pleased them mightily. Not the next part of an adult-school program, the Bible study. Why drag that in? They knew that Christianity was my ground of hope, my source of happiness, the spring of my energy. They were content that it should be. But what relevance had it to them? I proposed we should study the words of Jesus for half an hour each Sunday morning. His own words, not what some one said about Him or what some one else thought He meant but actually what He Himself, the workman, said. I challenged their knowledge of Him. Had they ever read His life? While at school they had probably been set the task of learning a bit of the Gospels by heart and been rapped over the knuckles for failing to remember that passage correctly. His teaching was far in advance of our labour leaders. In it there was to be found the solution of every one of our problems, economic, social, personal, and international. I suggested that if, after ten weeks of study, we could not find in His teaching the answer to our local problems in this year of Grace 1914, we ought to start a campaign there and then encouraging people to shut up the churches. People expended an enormous amount of time, money, leisure, and energy in keeping them open, and it was utter waste if Christian teaching held no solution of the world's troubles.

At this the men brightened considerably. The momentary glimpse they had of themselves touring the country with me on a "shut the churches" crusade proved titillating. So we began one Sunday in May, the seven of us. They were as keen on music as I. We found songs and hymns to suit us in the Fellowship hymn-book. We had silence for our prayers. We soon found ourselves pooling our experiences of life, rubbing off each other's corners, making up for each other's deficiencies. We came to a common decision about the most desirable first step which, if we had the means, we would take to make life more interesting and pleasurable in Bow. It was to set up a teetotal public house, a sort of communal sitting-room, a place to meet one's mates in, to spend the evening in, a sort of people's house to be run by ourselves without profit or propaganda. But would the motive of the "common good" prove strong enough to produce adequate management which in ordinary pubs is paid for out of profits? Who would take on the unpleasant task of "chucker-out" [a slang term for the bouncer in pubs] the monotonous duty of serving the cakes and drinks at the bar, the thankless job of cleaning the spittoons, locking up at closing-time, keeping the furnace in order? Volunteers, they were convinced, would be available for every job. There were already seven such, anyway. Ah! but every night in the week? And after the novelty began to wear off? And when quarrels and jealousy started? I probed deeper. What about blackballing people? Should everybody be admitted? The drunkard, of course, but the thief, the prostitute? "Yes, so long as we keep our eyes well skinned," decided the men. Then what about the capitalist, the exploiter, the aristocrat, royalty? These might wish to visit us. "Yes, pore blighters, let 'em all come, if they want to. They'll learn a thing or two." This was the common decision. It found readiest expression when it had to be translated for clarity's sake into normal English, in the New Testament words, "Honour all men." "You can honour 'em as fellow creatures even if you can't admire 'em. You can 'ate the rotten things they do and at the same time see they can't 'elp theirselves. They was brought up that way. We've got to enlighten 'em."

The first day of the school we had collected enough New Testaments to start on the Sermon on the Mount from Matthew's Gospel. We each read as many verses aloud as we felt inclined, and then discussed their import. It took us months to get through those three chapters, so modern and revolutionary did they prove to be. One man was in the middle of reading when he looked up, surprised. "'pon my word, Miss" he said, "it do seem interesting, don't it, when you put your mind to it?"

The two parts of the school proved complementary when we came to the point of deciding whether the police were to be admitted to this hypothetical pub if trouble arose. The men were complete sceptics as to the incorruptibility of the police, would certainly not call them in, did not trust them nor their methods; moreover, they believed prison penalized the offender's children and increased his own criminal tendencies. We must depend for protection on ourselves, our common sense, on the good fellowship of the place.

"In case of war also?" I inquired. That gave them pause. We spent weeks considering Tolstoi's challenge to the Czar, and the Kaiser's speech to his recruits. ... A letter had appeared in the papers, "An Open Letter to the Czar of Russia from Leo Tolstoi." The old man appealed to the young Emperor to change his policy towards those people who had embraced the philosophy of non-resistance. The poor and simple peasants merited no persecution. He, Leo Tolstoi, was the one who should be punished. He was responsible for the spread of these ideas. He begged the Czar to take his life in lieu of theirs. It would be a most merciful act.

[This letter] reinforced the peculiar importance of doing Jesus Christ the honour of taking Him seriously, of thinking out His teaching in terms of daily life, and then acting on it even if ordered by police, prelates, and princes to do the opposite. I read them also the speech the Kaiser made in Potsdam to the new recruits of the German conscript army: "Soldiers, you are now mine. You have sworn the soldier's oath. Whatever you are ordered to do, that you must perform, even though it were to fire on your own kinsfolks."

We compared it with the Sermon on the Mount. Would the inherent kindliness and decency of ordinary human beings remain proof against a government mobilizing the nation's psychological as well as material resources for war? I explained my conviction that the practice of the Presence of God, as the Old Testament prophets caught glimpses of it, as Jesus knew it, as Brother Lawrence tested it out while performing his dull routine work in the monastery kitchen, was the only sure ground of brotherhood. It was the only adequate training for the attainment of that wisdom and disciplined courage that mankind must acquire before he finally overcomes the forces vested in imperialism, militarism, and capitalism. Man was always to be considered as man, God's child, never as one of a labelled crowd.

Thus we exercised our minds and stretched our spirits through those pleasant summer months, imagining that perhaps one day, ten or twenty years later, we should acquire this much-talked-of pub.

Then came August 4th and the pattern of the world was shattered. I took the news to Kingsley, who had just come home for the week-end. I found him in bed. He got up only to go to the hospital. There was one operation there, another at home six weeks later. And then he died. I was holding his hand. We talked a little, happily. His hand grew colder. I did not know death was near. I hadn't seen it come to any one before. "Muriel," he said, surprisedly, "it's getting dark." His breathing got slower. I turned to the nurse, beckoning her to give him a hypodermic, as had been done before. She shook her head. Kingsley had finished his twenty-six years of lovely living.

*   *   *

As the war days passed we were more and more thankful that Kingsley was neither being lionized for killing nor scoffed at for refusing to kill. Of physical pain he had his full share.

Doris and I had rearranged our room for his use during the illness. As no smallest detail of furnishing or decoration ever escaped Kingsley's eye, we inquired what picture he wanted to see on the wall at the foot of his bed when he awoke after the operation. "The one in the same position in my own room," he replied. So we brought in and nailed up Da Vinci's study of the head of Christ.

*   *   *

Kingsley had left in lieu of a will a sheet of notepaper specifying a few gifts to friends and leaving the rest of his money "to Muriel and Doris that the income from it may be used in their work among the people of Bow or wherever else they may go."

The Adult School men were gradually becoming the nucleus of a little group that could expand in bigger premises. Doris and I offered to rent the upstairs rooms next door if they cared to convert them into club premises, throw the two rooms into one, strip the walls and paint the woodwork. [And so Kingsley Rooms came to be. Some time later] Father said: "What better memorial for Kingsley could we have than that public house you and the men in Bow are always talking about? I think I'll buy a place for you if you can find anything suitable."

I gasped with dismay. Certainly I agreed that we did not want a graveyard memorial for Kingsley, the broken pillar of granite, the casket covered with a bit of napery, or the simpering angel whom stone masons always seem to dress in heavy folds of drapery quite unsuitable for flying.

But this wonderful scheme of ours in Bow had been scheduled for some far distant date. I was untrained, unbusiness-like, altogether unready for such an undertaking. To my father's vast amusement, I refused his offer.

He looked me up and down, eyes bright with mockery. Of course I had to reverse my reply immediately. Otherwise life wouldn't have been worth living. He had enjoyed hearing from me the Adult School men's recent animadversions on the subject of religion, their emphasis on action rather than talk, on Christian practice rather than on theological theory. And now like the hypocrites of all time I was repudiating my principles when my chance came to construct. ...

So the next time I went to Bow I gave the men his message. It wasn't likely that suitable premises would be quickly available. I was comforted by this thought. But a day or two later two of the men hurried in with the local postman. He had found the place, a disused hall, an old strict and particular Baptist chapel that had come on the market recently, known as Zion Chapel, situated in a back street which was little more than a blind alley.

What a job, to turn a Strict and Particular Baptist Chapel into a pub! When we got the keys and examined it, we found its creed had been left behind in a neat pile in the vestry. Of the first three beliefs required in this church, two were denials. "I deny that salvation is free" and "I deny that Jesus Christ died for all men." I expect those who worshipped here were infinitely near to God than those printed words implied, but we had no compunction in installing a heating system and burning the creed in its furnace, taking out the pews, bartering them for chairs, putting in a bar counter.

To our great comfort, Mary Hughes of Whitechapel offered to come and help us. That lifted the load considerably. Any one who knows *Tom Brown's School Days* can make a guess as to the way the author, Judge Hughes, would have brought up his children. "He was always telling us that we were in God's lowest class because we had so much and so many people waited on us and served us. In service lies greatness." Mary Hughes often repeated these words when one took some new friend to call on her in the tiny bedroom over the kitchen at Kingsley Hall. "There's no need for a fire," she often assures me. "I'm always burning with indignation at the wrongs inflicted on the dispossessed. Feel me." She stretches out her hand. It is hot in the coldest weather. I have never known her to get a new dress. The ten-year-old one can be turned again. That will enable a neighbour's child to have a holiday. She cuts a chunk off a brown loaf and drinks cocoa made with no milk. She tramps the street, a diminutive figure weighed down by a big canvas bag in which leaflets containing clinching arguments and the latest statistics on every imaginable human problem are stored ready to give away to any one who tries to evade objective truths by "airy, fairy" sentiment.

In the other little room lived Rosa Waugh, whose father, Benjamin Waugh, was the founder of the National Society for the Prevention of Cruelty to Children and whose brother-in-law was Sir William Clarke Hall, known by the lovely title, "The Children's Magistrate." After a few months, Rosa married Stephen Hobhouse, a brilliant scholar who for years had been living in a workman's dwelling in Hoxton.

The night before Kingsley Hall was opened, it was difficult to imagine how the public meeting could take place. The drainage had only just been finished. Piles of gravel remained on the floor. As a dozen of us anxiously surveyed the scene, some one seized a shovel. The rest of us found implements of various sorts, and before midnight the place was cleaned, scrubbed, and orderly, ready for the crowded audience that always collects hopefully when a new venture starts. The opening and the Sunday evening meeting were satisfactory.

It was immediately before opening the doors for the first night of the pub that my nerve failed me. I set out from No. 60, remembered I'd forgotten pen, ink-pots, paper, and envelopes, which surely any self-respecting communal parlour would provide, dispatched some one to purchase them. Then, as I threaded my way through the ill-lit streets, the whole complicated venture suddenly rose up like a black suffocating fog in front of my eyes; and I, who scarcely ever enjoyed the luxury of a tear even at the most poignant moment of a play, began to weep in the dark. But one cannot open a teetotal pub in the teeth of strong disapproval and widespread prophecy of failure with a damp handkerchief and a blotchy face. I had to stop.

Throughout the evening, billiards, cards, draughts, and chess kept the people occupied and happy. The refreshment bar did much business. There was the requisite buzz of conversation to banish self-consciousness. Ben Platten and George Bowtle, who had come up from Loughton, there and then gave the whole of themselves to the work. The Committee of the General Workers' Union had provided eight of their most trusted members to do the stewarding and look after the thousand and one details to be considered in a place where any human being over eighteen may enter. The last quarter of an hour was reserved for dancing. At 10 p.m. the public house chant was raised. "Time, gentlemen, please. Time!" The place quickly cleared and the group of us who had started this lusty infant on its life stared at one another, a little amazed, very thankful, determined never to worry again.

So started Kingsley Hall twenty-two years ago. It was a great idea, the people's own. Trying to clothe an idea in bricks and mortar may disillusion many. Creative ardent spirits prove to be mere creatures of flesh and blood. We worked very hard and we were sincere, but we have nothing to boast of. It is not too good a show. Yet, the creative fire that founded the Hall has never been extinguished. We have the great adventures in failure, joy, love, and danger.

Kingsley Hall was not the outcome of any streak of sentimentalism, of pitying charity. It was an overdue act of justice, recognized as such by all connected with it. Everybody must have a decent place wherein to spend the evenings. A one- or two-roomed home does not supply that need. Kingsley Hall came into existence to do so. In that it has succeeded. But an evening meeting-place is not a sufficient end in itself. We knew that all the time. We hoped the other good things — serenity, health, fellowship, service, tolerance, appreciation, self-respect, regard for others, a social conscience, courage, a sense of public duty, and reliability — would follow. But they don't come because one wants them to. They don't spring into existence as a result of seeing the lack of these qualities in other institutions and in other people whom we dislike or of whom we are jealous. None of these necessary things is forthcoming except by self-discipline, by refusing the second best (sometimes called self-sacrifice), by becoming the devotee of a Cause or a Lord.

So Kingsley Hall has its numerous friends, its adequate supply of normal, cheery, jolly members, its compact blessed and devoted little group of local volunteer helpers, past and present. But its seers, its saints and prophets, are a long time appearing.

*   *   *

In 1916 air raids began. Every glimmer of light had to be carefully kept within doors or else one was a proven spy, practising collusion with the Kaiser. Arriving at No. 60 alone after dark presented some difficulty. Curtain rods were amateurish affairs, and one had to grope about in the dark for some time before all the peepholes were draped and gas might be lit. ...

One night Kingsley Hall was shattered by a bomb. This fact counteracted some of our unpopularity. "Ain't it just like the old Kaiser?" inquired one of the crowd who were allowed by the police to come in one at a time to survey the havoc wrought. "Shocking to bomb a religious place like this!" It enlarged our sorely shrunken self-respect to find that the public deemed us religious.

*   *   *

Once we saw a raider hit. Watching its flaming descent, who could help feeling glad it could do no harm? Yet what horror for its occupants! One of our neighbours expressed the deep down reliable goodness of the human race as I saw by her kitchen fire one morning. We enjoying a talk over a cup of tea. She said in a meditative voice: "When you come to think of it, Miss, those Germans in the zepps, you carn't blame 'em. They're only made to do it, same as our men are, pore devils!" I heard another woman give voice to the same objective sort of sentiment. She was enjoying a confidential mood, rarely encouraged in the mother of a big family. "You know," she started, diffidently, "about those Germans, they're killing our men, I know; but our men are doing the same to them. And every German we kill is only some pore mother's son."

*   *   *

Doris and I made a slogan, "The best is not too good for the children of Poplar." We dragged unwilling people, who were ashamed to refuse, into the Nursery School at Kingsley Hall, pointing out the complete unsuitableness of the building, devoid as it was of a south window, the east ones letting in little light because of the high shops adjacent, the western ones inadequate by reason of wire netting, frosted glass, and soot. The visitors were always charmed by the twenty-six boys and girls at the most attractive age of two, three, and four, admired their brightly coloured pinafores, exclaimed approvingly over the rows of small wash-basins. We tried to lead them away from such easy sentiment, demanding that they consider the points of the compass and the total lack of outdoor space. ... [Yet] no visitors rose to our expectations. None felt the compelling force of the proposition that we must have an open-air school, or at any rate access to some garden. So we took our slogan into direct action. We started telling the comfortably-placed, middle-class respected inhabitants of West Bow, where gardens still existed, that our children needed them. We tried to convince one or two denizens of Wellington Road that their homes would be improved by have twenty-six children playing, eating, and taking afternoon naps within their garden walls. Two ex-mayors, a Liberal and a Socialist, considered the idea. One foresaw technical difficulties, valid ones. Another won my everlasting admiration by confessing he wasn't noble enough to do his duty. Scheme after scheme fell through. ...

Eventually Father announced, "I'll put a place up for the children. Arrange it as you like." Eighty-six is just the right age, apparently, to discover the best way of spending money.

At the far end of the road from Kingsley Hall a row of four rat-ridden houses stood. They had been condemned years previously as unfit for human habitation and acquired, with seven adjoining inhabited houses, by the London County Council, who planned demolition and the erection of flats or a school. They were not definitely for sale. Of course that was good labour policy. We had learned only too thoroughly the difficulties put in the way of social improvement by private ownership. Now I, a Socialist Alderman, had to start convincing London County Council members that our principle would be in this case more honoured in the breach than in the observance, a humorous situation. They kindly sold us the site.

Mr. C. Cowles Voysey was our architect. He seemed as keen about the idea as we were. London's first Children's House was to be very modern, without a single unnecessary line or curve, all its decorations being part of its structure. Every detail was talked over with the people of Bow. The row of basins in the nursery-school bathrooms must not only be low enough for a two-year-old to turn on the tap, but the constant flow of hot water, an almost unbelievable possession to Bow people, must be regulated so that from these particular taps it should never run hot enough to scald. The middle floor where the grown-ups were to live demanded as little expenditure as possible. We were only there as servants of the children. Our dining-room, study, six bedrooms and office had no rounded edges where wall and floor met, as had the children's rooms. This was rather fanatical, possibly, but we were afraid lest our sudden acquisition of a well-plumbed house might make us forget the rock whence we were hewn. It had been the work of so many plodding unadvertised years, this slow gaining of confidence, this mutual helpfulness, this friendship untainted by domination. And now our new plans for Children's House looked so imposing, so solid. The architect's drawing hung on the line at the Royal Academy. Supposing we found ourselves turning into an institution. The fear of it kept us awake at nights.

We decided to take on some regular menial task, each of us, sweeping, cleaning, floor-polishing, etc. The subtle power-bug had captured better people than we. We exchanged solemn promises to deflate each other's pride, should the Children's House ever go to our heads.

The flat roof proved a good place to sleep on, winter and summer alike. From it one could dimly see Saint Paul's Cathedral. The immediate environment was chimney-pots and squalid roofs. This was our parish. As long as we slept up there and said our prayers by the parapet, we could not forget how the will of God was being frustrated by an economic system.

We asked Mr. H. G. Wells to perform the ceremony at the opening of the House in September, 1923. He agreed and came to high tea at No. 60 to see the place. We were eager to see if he would fit into our regime, help clear up the tea table, lend a hand with the washing up as other celebrities had done. Long before tea was over, however, Joan Waterlow had introduced, somehow, the subject of Tolstoi's regular four-hours-a day manual work. Mr. Wells disagreed with the idea in a lively manner. I suppose we all waxed lively, for though I can't remember by what remarks the conversation developed, I do know that it ended in our suggesting to him he might write ever better if he didn't concentrate on saving time and energy by letting other people perform those many necessary jobs by which life is sustained. He was very nice to us all. At the opening ceremony he declared there was only one person really fitted to open a Children's Home in East London and that was Mr. Charles Chaplin.

[As it grew] the Children's House program [came to] consist of a graded school, play hour, classes, a health club, a parent's association, camps, Camp Fire Girls and holidays. The nursery school is its most attractive section.

*   *   *

After I had been leading the Sunday-evening worship at Kingsley Hall for some years, I gradually realized I was turning into a parson. I had not intended this to happen. I was ill-trained and unsuitable. But it happened as so many things happened in Bow, by the force of circumstances. At first our Sunday-night meetings were held at a quarter past eight, very obviously after the church and chapel services of the vicinity. We considered ours as strictly complementary to theirs . We had the best music we could get, silent prayer, and a hymn-book new to nearly all of us, the Fellowship Hymn-book, wherein poems of profound worship prepared us for the factual program of Christ's teaching. It contained music and verse from all ages and many countries.

The addresses were given by different people each week. When the benediction was over, we behaved like a large family reunited on a holiday at home. We ate buns, drank tea and

32

coffee, argued, discussed, and contradicted the speaker. It was always a hard job to get the people to leave at ten o'clock.

It was difficult building up something without any traditions to guide one, a fellowship based on the attempt to practise the presence of God, based on the unwary human spirit, so easily deceived. We had to go on, however, deepening our furrow,

> Our eyes for ever on some sign
> To help us plough the perfect line.

It had to be worked out somehow in bricks and mortar, in flesh and blood, in worship and devotion. But how abysmally poor was the quality of the leader's own character! John Masefield's *Everlasting Mercy* provided many a phrase a fit Kingsley Hall. Part of Saul Kane's naive remark is my own. Running Kingsley Hall

> ...made me see
> The harm I done by being me.

In 1924 a deputation of helpers forced upon me the need of considering our relationship to the church. Was I not deceiving myself in continuing to imagine that Kingsley Hall was only complementing the work of local ministers? Was it not true that most of our people never dreamed of going to church, had not attended since they were children?

*　　*　　*

As I pondered for weeks on the situation, I saw how little of all that had occurred at Kingsley Hall had been originally intended. It was to have been a teetotal public house, a straightforward affair which almost any friendly person could set up and run. And from even that I had tried to excuse myself. Now it comprised eleven whole-time workers, two buildings, a lecture series, men's and women's clubs, a football club, a penny bank, an adult school, a Sunday service, and a nursery school drawing a government grant and regularly inspected officially and unofficially by people from all over the world.

God had had other purposes than mine. I remembered how prayers had been instituted at closing time every night after club, how somehow or other we had set up the habit of standing in a big circle and keeping quiet, of having a sentence spoken to bring to a head our scattered and varied desires. And I remembered how atheists would attend this prayer and on occasion would voice our aspirations for us. Certainly there must be a definite spiritual unity if a group of us could meet as Brethren of the Common Table once a month and wrestle with the anomalies of our economic situation, in study, prayer, and redistribution.

I came to the conclusion that we already were a church. The deputation was right. It was romantic and egotistic not to face the fact that I had performed the duties of a parson for some time and had better bestir myself to fill up the gaps in my ministry. The communion service was instituted, a church roll formed, church meetings started, a church secretary and treasurer elected, a weekly prayer group set up, a week's mission held.

During the first mission, five or six came to the conclusion that they could no longer be interested spectators enjoying the game. They must throw in their lot with the little company of the followers of Christ, take up their position in the long and often straggling procession of the faithful that has stretched across the centuries, and assume their share of responsibility for the witness of the universal Church in every country. In the most remote areas of the earth's surface are to be found groups who are trying to substitute the will of God for their own, as Christ teaches us to do, individuals who have learnt to think eternally and to live courageously. The old declaration, *Je suis Chrétien, c'est ma gloire,* implies much. It is no partisan boast. There had to be some opportunity for its public expression in Kingsley Hall. We decided to mark it by holding a service for the "giving of the right hand of fellowship." The candidates for membership stood up facing me and four experienced older members, while each of us in turn made short statements as to what it meant to follow Christ. One spoke of the necessity to develop the health of the body by clean living, self-control, love of nature, and conquest of disease; another of the need to work for economic and social justice; another stressed the refusal to kill, because one can't overcome evil with evil. The way of the Cross is the way of forgiveness and creative peace. A fourth demanded personal service, as specific, as definite and as menial as that of Christ washing the feet of a traitor. Finally I explained that these high aims and requirements were all far beyond our reach unless we practised the presence of God by regular and constant prayer.

Then each candidate came forward and gripped our hands. After a rousing song of triumph, the whole congregation resumed their seats. It was extraordinarily difficult to be the first person to go through this rather exhilarating ceremony. "Can't I just come in quietly without standing in front of everyone?" The question was put to me over and over again in different words. I am glad I remained adamant. So were the candidates afterwards. The harder a thing is, the greater the sense of strength and satisfaction that follows.

*   *   *

We often had to take action in matters we would rather have left alone. For instance, how could we sit still without a murmur, complacently allowing God's gift of fresh air and blue sky, the unspoiled inheritance of the human race for a quarter of a million years, to become subject to the base usage of the Royal Air Force. Were we not in the direct line of succession from Telemachus the hermit? He learned in solitary prayer not only God's way of looking at things, but how to act in a hostile crowd. He walked into the Coliseum, took his seat quietly, and at the height of the gladiatorial games called upon the crowd to stop the murderous circus. Was it not an insult to God and man? He was killed. But so were the games. The lines about the crucified apply to him too.

> And so the lonely greatness of the world
> In silence dies.

> And death is shattered by the light from out
> Those darkened eyes.

We were working to save the world from militarism through our own political parties, by our parliamentary votes, by lobbying, deputations, public meetings. But there was our personal witness. June was approaching when the Royal Air Force always gave a magnificent display at Hendon. After much preparation, a group of some twenty Christians set out, men and women, ex-soldier and ex-teacher, factory girl, and unemployed. Twenty isn't many among two hundred thousand spectators. But holding up our carefully worded placards we marched up and down the narrow thronged street which leads from the station to the Airdome. Then we went into the Airdome. In varied ways we gave our witness. One working-woman called out, "Ain't you ashamed of yerselves, coming 'ere to watch this show? It's only practice for killing other people's children."

"Wot are you here for, then, if you think it's so wicked?"

"I'm 'ere because my church sent me. I'm trying to make all of yous wake up and think."

After the display the road was solid with people making for the station. Here progress was that of the proverbial snail. Although trains were continually being filled and dispatched Londonwards, our speakers had a grand time, perched on a chair behind the wooden fence, appealing to an audience that could not escape. Once a drunken man in the crowd ridiculed one of them, aping his queer hoarse voice. The young inter- rupter was still within earshot when the speech ended. He suddenly sobered and wilted when I started my address by explaining that the hoarse voice just referred to was the result of the speaker, an unemployed workman, having been gassed in the war.

The business of the Church of Christ touches life at every point, and it is perhaps better not to join it than to come in imagining that one can have a day off whenever one likes. Peter used the right word when he described a Christian as the "slave" of Christ. His dictatorship passes all others. Yet it is never imposed from without.

*   *   *

After Father's death in 1928, as soon as the executors of his will began to function, I called together a group of Bow friends and asked them to help me work out some scheme whereby my annuity of four hundred pounds might be di- verted into other channels. I pointed out that I was strong, well able to earn my own living, and certainly did not need over a pound a day for the rest of my life. As many of us were Socialists we did not believe in the cumbersome, outworn notion that a small class of people should have luxuries while the majority lack necessities. As some of us were Christians, we knew it was better not to be rich. Our Lord was a poor workman. He talked the language of working-people. The poor of every age and every race seem to understand Him as soon as they hear of Him. They never forget His apprenticeship at a joiner's bench. Even in the repressive wretchedness of a casual ward [a flop house], I've seen His words illegally written on the wall of the yard by disgruntled inmates. "Foxes have holes, birds of the air have nests, but the Son of Man has nowhere to lay his head." I have seen them chalked on the Embankment pavement by the hard benches where the homeless sleep.

The annual four hundred pounds was mine according to the law of the land, but God's law was better, saner, more up to date, more practical. I proposed we should act by it, now that we had a moment of brief power. I would return the check to the executors on the ground that it was not mine, but belonged to my neighbors in East London. At this point some of the Bow people objected to my reasoning. Of course I was to hold on to the money, they argued. I'd know better how to spend it than any of them. "Anyhow, your good old Dad left it to you and you ought to keep it," they said, trying to clinch the argument. I agreed that he was good and dear, but pointed out that he knew I was going to take up some such position as this. He knew all about our chapter of the Brethren of the Common Table. Nothing could induce me to keep his money for myself and they must work out a technique for getting rid of it sensibly.

[Eventually a representative committee of people was set up who, after careful consideration, set up a panel of "Home Helps."]

These were to be sensible middle-aged women who would take half-time employment in this capacity. They should be called in by any woman at any time of need to look after the home if one of the children had suddenly to be taken to the hospital, cook the dinner if the mother were ill, clean the house or do the laundry in any emergency, or mind the children if the mother wanted to go out for recreation or pleasure.

Mr. Poole, the committee chairman, led the way in a first-class piece of social service. He has enough letters of gratitude to fill a volume sent by the women of the district who found the very quality of life changed by having a Home Help to rely on in times of sudden anxiety.

*   *   *

Blazing a new trail is intimidating, and it was downright frightening to contemplate what might result if one forgot for a single day to consult the compass. So I was liable to be a bit doctrinaire. Day and night my mind was set on this job of getting a little community in East London to function as servants and lovers of their neighbours, cooperating with God by restoring their birthright to His dispossessed children, the birthright of music, art, poetry, drama, camps, open-air life, self-confidence, the honour of building up a new social order, the Kingdom of Heaven, here and now in Bow.

Pacifism

"No Moratorium on the Sermon on the Mount"

From the time young Muriel Lester read Leo Tolstoy's The Kingdom of God is Within You, *pacifism was central to her religious faith. Jesus, in his Sermon on the Mount, proclaimed a loving God who created one human family to inhabit the earth and who calls on his followers to show love to everyone, without exception, even to the point of loving the hated and feared enemy. This means "God is not a nationalist," reasoned Lester, nor is war an excuse to call a "moratorium on the Sermon on the Mount."*

But while she became a firm and outspoken opponent to war, that refusal was "only a by-product of the passionate desire to re-order the common life by basing it on what Jesus Christ taught us about God, in short, to set up the Kingdom of God here on earth." (Dare You Face Facts, *p. 118) Hence, she dedicated her life to working for an end to injustice and an end to oppression, of all those things that obscure the sacred worth of every human being. She worked tirelessly to build positive and hopeful expressions of the Reign of God. This shines through in all her writings and was seen throughout her life.*

From *It Occurred to Me*

The first casualty of every war is truth. Those who are aware of this remain obstinately sceptical about news, prophecy of speedy victory, propaganda lectures, atrocity stories and glamorous magazine articles which describe the suddenly acquired saintliness of the nation's defenders. The obstinately sceptical person is unpopular, and knows it. That makes him worse. I remember the politely silent, almost tangible exasperation I evoked from a long tableful of guests at a Devonshire Hydro one day when a bit of good news from the Flanders front had just been announced. There was little enough to announce, goodness knows, and on holiday people are surely entitled to their little pleasures. The brightness of their countenances suddenly faded when I croaked out warningly, "Is that official?" "Oh, Muriel, really!" ejaculated the friend who had brought the news. She was a remarkably sweet-tempered person. Those words perhaps marked her greatest lapse from serenity during the season.

At Kingsley Hall we refused to pray for victory, knowing that a victor's peace is usually vindictive and stirs up a passion for revenge a generation or so later. Such a stand meant that for the duration of war we could not sing "God save the King." The fourth line, "Send him victorious!" sung in peace-time can be interpreted to mean the conquest of slums, disease, ignorance. In war-time it implies killing, wounding, gassing, starving, lying, spying, drinking, and venereal disease.

Many of the factory girls who regularly ate at the Kingsley Hall Dinner Club were munition workers. "Don't you get tired?" one was asked. Her answer stayed with me. "Tired? Oh, sometimes. But when we do we say to ourselves: 'Think about your work. What are you making? Shells to kill Germans with. They've killed our men, now these will kill them.'"

The East End has for so long given harbour to unpopular causes that tolerance is the fashion there. But to see a new place opened where people talked of Germans as their brothers was too great a strain on some of the neighbours. I received an anonymous letter informing me that I went about with other women's husbands, that I'd got a German face, that if I showed it down A Street they'd "do me in." A Street proved duller than its word. When I perambulated up and down it, nothing happened.

On Sunday mornings we used to hold open-air meetings at the Dock Gates, pointing out that war was an unscientific way of trying to settle anything; that as cannibalism, chattel slavery, blood-feuds and duelling have one by one been recognized as foolish, old-fashioned, an insult to God and man, so war was an outmoded custom and a daily crucifixion of Christ. We could not suddenly look upon our brother man as an enemy just because he chanced to have been born on the other side of a river or a strip of sea.

But if East London tolerated such sentiments, Loughton was a neighbourhood of a different temper. As one saw acquaintances approaching, one had to decide whether to greet them and risk the cut direct, or whether to turn down a side street and avoid all chance of mutual embarrassment. I wish I could apologize to some Loughton folk now for the tactless, awkward things I'm sure I said. To be outside an almost universally accepted emotion of enthusiasm, forcing oneself to witness to an unpopular truth for four and a half years nourishes the growth of an extra-hardened skin. One cultivates a certain grim ruthlessness. I'm sure some of us pacifists must have appeared maddeningly superior in our refusal to accept the comfort, the cheer, and the national self-justification provided by an ever-watchful government. Even a skeleton sermon with carefully chosen hymns to match was issued to clergy and ministers. I wish I'd kept a copy. The hymn was "Once to every man and nation comes to moment to decide," and the sermon was intended to produce increased investment in war loan bonds. I forget the text.

In December, 1914, a hundred or so Christians of all sects met in Cambridge, drawn together by the immovable conviction that a nation cannot wage war to the glory of God. The doctrine of the Cross, self-giving, self-suffering, forgiveness, is the exact opposite of the doctrine of armies and navies. One must choose between the sword and the Cross. Thus the Fellowship of Reconciliation was formed, providing us with anchorage as well as with a chart for all adventuring.

From *It So Happened*

[One of the founders of the Fellowship of Reconciliation on the continent was the German clergyman, Friedrich Siegmund Schultze.] I must tell his story. In 1910 and 1911 he was the pastor of the church in Potsdam where the Kaiser worshipped. A brilliant young man of twenty-five, he was a convinced pacifist. In July, 1914, he attended an international conference of Christians where he and Dr. Henry Hodgkin resolved to take the same action if war came. Each in his own country would send out a letter calling on all ministers and clergy to realize the vast cleavage between the way of the Cross and the way of war, and to ask themselves whether the Church was not bound to become weak, almost negligible, if she blessed the arms of her nationals. Siegmund sent a copy of his letter to the Kaiser. Next morning he received an answer. The Kaiser agreed with him, but unfortunately it wasn't in anyone's power to do anything about it. Ten minutes later there was a peremptory knock on the door. Soldiers filed in to arrest him. He was marched away and strictly questioned about copies of his letter which had been intercepted. After an hour's gruelling examination the curtains which he thought were hiding windows were drawn aisde, disclosing seven military judges seated behind the table. He had been court-martialled and was prounounced guilty of high treason, and condemned to death. Had he anyone to speak on his behalf? He did not like to drag the Kaiser's name into the court, so he produced a couple of other letters from state officials. But these failed to impress the judges. Then Siegmund produced the imperial letter. There followed a psychological storm. He was passionately and hysterically upbraided for having put the officers into such a terrible position. Then they realized that their fury was making things worse. They became obsequious, clicked their heels, and begged him to return home. The soldier who was still standing guard over him, with fixed bayonet, enquired "Whither?" — and was hastily ordered to lead him ceremoniously to the outer gate.

Throughout the war and after, Siegmund's life bore witness to peacemaking. He struggled to break down horizontal as well as vertical barriers. He founded an orphanage in East Berlin and was there when Hitler came to power. After a while he was betrayed by one of the teachers from the orphanage. The S.A. [from the German *Strum Abteilung*, commonly known as the Brown Shirts, were the street thugs who carried out violent against civilians, especially Jews, in Germany and Austria] arrested him. After a trial with the Gestapo he was coerced to leave the country and became an exile in Zurich.

From *It Occurred to Me*

The day came when the *Lusitania* was sunk. It's a devastating spectacle, the sudden disappearance of any ship. At one moment, where the blue of sea and sky seem to touch, a vessel proudly cuts the waves. At the next, it isn't there. The sea is calm, untroubled as ever. After an hour or so some half-drowned people are dragged up on to the pier.

A certain newspaper incited the populace to passion point. That afternoon riots broke out in various parts of London. In Bow a gang of roughs led by a stranger attacked one shop after another belonging to people of German or Austrian extraction, leaving behind smashed windows, empty storerooms, and in some cases gutted houses. Suddenly our friendly streets became sinister, horrible, a welter of mad-dened people. From the upper-storey window of one shop, pieces of furniture slid down the stout canvas blind until they reached the wooden frame at the bottom and ricocheted into the crowded street below. So mad was the scene that a heavy sofa and a wardrobe were shot down by the same method into the crowd. People ran off with fifty-pound bags of flour on their backs. The police did nothing. A frightened German woman came out into the street, eager to get away unnoticed. Her nervousness attracted attention. Harpies jeered at her, tweaked her hat, grabbed at her purse. While I remonstrated with the women for being cowardly enough to attack three against one, my young companion slipped off with the German unnoticed. In the excitement and heat of argument, the women dragged my hat off, too, though, according to the custom of those days, it was fastened on with a long and serviceable pin. Rather clever of them! At this the policeman who had been serenely eating an orange as he walked up and down, carefully taking no notice of what was occurring, precipitately crossed the road and with a great show of determination laid a hand on my shoulder. "Come along now! We can't have none of this," he exclaimed, and piloted me homewards. That night my hat was returned to me anony-mously, wrapped up decently in white tissue paper.

I asked a parson who was conducting an open-air service one Sunday if he could include the Germans in our prayers. He explained confidentially that it would be dangerous. I made the obvious retort. He replied that the crowd might tear us limb from limb. I asked if Paul modified his good news out of a forethoughtful estimation of what the crowd at Ephesus might do to him. The parson was very angry and lectured me at length. I deserved it. Though it was always terribly difficult for me to start talking to people like him, once I'd started I'm sure I was unpleasantly logical, no doubt thoroughly perky, too.

* * *

In 1916 conscription was instituted. A good many of my friends refused to become part of the military machine. This meant stating the grounds of their objection before a public tribunal and possibly being given exemption on the grounds of religion. There was always an army officer in attendance to try to prove that following Christ and killing people were compatible. He generally quoted from the Bible and sometimes got rather tied up in his theology. After all, a good disciplinarian is not supposed to be particularly nimble witted, and he often embarked on his cross-questioning without realizing the intellectual calibre of the man who stood before him.

My days were now diversified by accompanying friends to tribunals, attending the subsequent proceedings, and visiting them in jail. Sometimes there were wives and families to see to and money to be collected for their maintenance. ...

Because so many alert, socially-minded citizens were serving time in various jails, a good deal of valuable information about prison life and its effect on the ordinary criminal became public property. Was it sensible to keep them so short of water that their plate, knife, fork and spoon had to be washed in the water they used for personal ablutions? Why forbid photographs of mother, father, wife and children? What was wrong with flowers that they should be so strictly forbidden? During his half-hour's exercise, a man I knew espied a tiny plant growing in a cranny of the high-walled prison yard. He delighted in its growth, unperceived by officialdom. Each day he looked out for it. One morning, its buds were just beginning to blossom. The next day it was gone, torn out. In official eyes it was an irregularity.

The worst time of all in prison is when an execution is being prepared. I do not think any one who has not experienced it can imagine the sense of strain that grips everyone alike—visitor, porter, warden, and inmates. Repressed horror or assumed nonchalance, which is worse? I only know that for days afterwards I did not feel normal. I can never forget

44

the young man who was lying in his cell, trying to read a comic paper and pretending he wasn't thinking about the other youth of twenty-two who was to be shuffled out of life the following day.

*   *   *

The Armistice suddenly burst upon the world. On November 11th, our newspaper carried a border round the columns of each page, a decoration of a single sentence repeated again and again, "Killing has stopped. Killing has stopped." As I had caught Mary Jane's mumps and was convalescing in the garden at Loughton, I missed all the celebrations. No longer to hear distant gunfire, no longer imaginatively to feel the stinging rip of a bullet, the thrust of steel through flesh and nerves, the suffocation of gas, to see the shops becoming normal and displaying unlimited chocolate cream, this was bliss.

Short lived, of course, for news soon came of the hunger across Europe. We found our boys were being used to keep up the naval blockade. As a result, our defeated enemies were threatened with starvation. We listened to the reports of eye-witnesses, journalists, and others who had gone to find out the facts of the situation.

[From Kingsley Hall we] called on newspaper editors who proved surprisingly loth [reluctant] to publish the facts or to make an appeal for ex-enemy children. "It would not be popular," confessed the representative of a great national weekly. We lobbied members of Parliament. We begged ministers and clergy to use their influence in making known documentary evidence with which we supplied them. We collected money from our members and neighbours. People gave a good deal. One old lady, a great nature-lover, withdrew the three shillings she had taken five months to pay in to a club for her annual day in the country, and put it into our collection-box without a word. No one would have known of her act if I had not chanced to meet her in the street after the excursion char-à-bancs [an excusion bus] had started off from Bow in all their glory, a cornet-player on the step behind, moaning out old-fashioned melodies en route.

Kingsley Hall folk adopted an Austrian child, Marie. Her presence in his house completely converted one of Horatio

Bottomley's devotees. Till then he had believed the leading articles in the *John Bull* of that day, even when they declared that "the just decrees of a righteous God would bring this Judas race before the bar of human justice." It is a little disconcerting to find that the only member of a "Judas race" one knows is small, gentle, affectionate, and unassuming and hasn't had enough food for a long time.

As our progress was too slow for the emergency, and the newspapers would not co-operate, we decided to turn our bodies into living newspapers and to walk the streets of London, from east to west, bearing posters high above our heads which should contain an epitome of the facts. We set out one day, a company of women in single file, dressed in mourning, accompanied by one or two of our own children, making for the House of Commons. Many thousands read the placards as we passed. We had kept them strictly factual, such as "In one maternity ward, 98 out of 100 babies born since the Armistice have died for want of milk." The last said, "It is not the will of your Father in Heaven that one of these little ones should perish."

The Sunday after the signing of the Peace Treaty in 1919 I went through an ordeal. An open-air meeting had been arranged by some King's Weigh House friends for 8 p.m. in Hyde Park. I was to be the speaker. As I stood there waiting to begin ... I remember gazing at the ground in front of me so desperately that it almost seemed I was boring a hole in it. Once the meeting started, all was well. I tried to tell the truth about war. Soldiers in khaki listened eagerly. I heard later one of them had turned to his mate at the conclusion and said, "That girl's talking sense."

The Khaki election was on us with the government's ridiculous slogan, "Hang the Kaiser!" I took a sort of vow with myself that in every speech I made for various socialist candidates, I would give publicity to what was happening in the Rhineland area occupied by French African troops. Here the future history of Europe was being prepared. Here the essential nature of war was being demonstrated. Here were little German towns, some of them without a brothel, being forced to set one of their houses aside for that purpose and to provide sufficient women to satsify the sex hunger of the victorious soldiers. At first the burgomasters refused to obey these orders of the French high command. One of them tore the requisition form that had been presented for his signature from top to bottom and threw it on the ground. Unmoved and immovable, the Frenchman presented a duplicate copy to the mayor, coldly informing him that it would be better to sign lest something worse befell the city. When the mayor ascertained the implication of his threat, he signed the paper to the accompaniment of church bells tolling as for a dirge.

The physical violence of man versus man, however crude, proves bearable, thinkable. But to turn victory into violence against women, a physical and psychological mastery, and to call it peace, is to begin a process that must destroy human joy. ...

Visitors from other parts of Germany came to this unhappy district and discovered its shame with a horror that soon turned to hate, fury, and a passion for revenge. Among them, they say, was a young man called Hitler. Though our government said that nothing could be done for women in German regions over which they had no authority, they were finding plenty to do ostensibly for women in another country over which they had no control at all. Over fifty million pounds sterling was spent in undeclared warfare to further the plans of Koltchak, Deniken and Wrangel. To induce war-weary men to volunteer for campaigns in the frozen north, heart-rending stories were told about the plight of women in Russia and how they were being commercialized.

Throughout the war we clung to the conviction that there were people in Germany and Austria holding the same pacifist faith as our own. As soon as the frontiers were opened, we sent emissaries to find out if our faith were justified. It was, and soon the Fellowship of Reconciliation became established in most European countries. The Dutch group had already been founded during the war by Cornelis Boeke and his wife, *née* Eleanor Cadbury. Since the formation of the Fellowship at Cambridge in 1914, these two had contributed to the movement humour, music, and the flame of the spirit, until a jingo press campaign in 1917 succeeded in getting them banished as undesirable aliens. It was sad to be deprived of Cornelis' fiddle; it had beguiled long hours in our Bow dugout during an air raid. He had the gift of getting at one's spirit. But probably Holland needed him more than we did and God let the wrath even of the *Daily Mail* serve the cause of the Fellowship of Reconciliation.

47

Cornelis sought out a convenient site, found a lovely stretch of pine woods near Utrecht, and settled there with his family of little girls. When he had earned his right to be trusted by the people of the city, they formed their pacifist movement, calling it The Brotherhood of Christ. The workmen employed to build its chapter house in the pine woods soon realized they were working on no ordinary job. They were helping clothe a great idea in form, in well-laid bricks, in good plumbing, and in woodwork painted bright blue, purple, red, and yellow. Cornelis soon lost his liberty. Accustomed to free speech in Britain, he determined to work for it in his own country. He was arrested in the middle of the open-air meeting he had called. As soon as his prison sentence was completed, he went back to the same place to start another meeting. The authorities were the first to grow tired of this often-repeated process.

I went to this Brotherhood Chapter House in 1920, along with a hundred or two other people from fourteen countries, for the second annual conference of the International Fellowship of Reconciliation. The very elements were in our favour; the warm summer afternoons, the pine's aroma, the shining silver sand, the spacious stretch of forest.

This was my first contact with the enemy. As I sat down and gazed round me at these unknown people, a bearded old Austrian professor in a black velvet coat brought me a cup of tea. Pain, witnessed or endured, had stamped his every feature. Had he too watched hunger patients? It was hard to swallow that tea.

Afterwards, while exploring the garden, I found great big Pierre Ceresol, secretary of the International. He introduced me to one of his fellow countrymen, a village schoolmaster, saying, "This is the man who showed the way to all of us in Switzerland." The schoolmaster and I walked through the woods till the pine shadows grew very long. After doing conscript service for years, he suddenly realized that it was no longer possible for him to stay in the army and at the same time read his Bible and say his prayers. When he told his commanding officer so, he was sent to a lunatic asylum for a month or two. How could any one but a lunatic refuse conscript service in Switzerland where it is an honour rather than a danger to be a soldier? Palpably sane, he had then been court-martialled in Lausanne. The Town Hall was crowded for the strange trial. He was imprisoned, but right across Switzerland the pacifist idea flashed like lightning. ...

A Roman Catholic priest in his early thirties, an Austrian, chanced to find an empty room with a piano. Here he would sing and play the perfect music of a Bach Chorale while people gathered silently about him, sitting on the floor or outside the windows, or by the garden door. As I listened I found myself wondering what extra thing God could provide even in Heaven. The priest could speak no English. Yet later on when he came to stay with us in Bow, a curious thing happened. We had been holding our regular open-air meeting in Hyde Park his first night in London. All at once he was missing from our bench. Peering below the trees and among the crowd, I spied him at length, standing on the last platform of the long row, talking to a crowd of Londoners in Esperanto. Where his strange words failed to register on their minds, the illumined serenity of his face held their spirit.

*   *   *

We began to hear about a man called Gandhi; a casual mention of his name in the press, at first; then more regular references to his movements. Soon an admixture of scorn, bitterness, admiration and disapproval proclaimed his growing power. We were lucky enough to get hold of a fat volume containing fifty-two weekly issues of his paper, *Young India.* We eagerly devoured it. Here was a great man, acting out on a world stage the same principles that we nobodies had been trying to live out in various towns and villages in England. In India, millions of people were conditioned to non-violence by religion, society, and tradition throughout the centuries. We, an adolescent race, had inherited the fighting tradition and been nurtured in it by school, literature, drama, art, sport, and church. In India the power of non-violence was being mobilized for a great patriotic and national purpose, obvious to everybody, for freedom. We in England were inevitably accused of lack of patriotism, and our actions construed as harmful to the body politic. In India newspapers were given a new lease of life by the upthrust of this message of Gandhi, his call to the people of every province to bestir themselves and to claim the blessing of freedom, God's gift to every people. Our movement was naturally ignored by the press.

From *It So Happened*

By the 1930s, Muriel Lester had turned the work of Kingsley Hall over to her sister Doris, and as traveling secretary of the International Fellowship of Reconciliation, Lester traversed the globe continually in the work of peace. The dark clouds of World War II were beginning to gather ominously on the continent. In 1938 many desperately hoped that Prime Minister Neville Chamberlain had brought peace out of his meetings with Adolph Hitler, but Lester did not hold to such optimism. By chance, members of the Versöhnungsbund, the German FOR, had scheduled Muriel Lester to visit Germany just after Chamberlain had met with Hitler. She writes about that visit in this second volume of her autobiography.

It had seemed impossible, but I arrived in Cologne, one of the first English people to enter the country after the dreadful days of tension. I had been warned to bring no names or addresses. I would be met and passed on from one hostess to another, staying a night in each city, town, or village, holding meetings in private houses for the interchange of experiences of the power of non-violence and for our mutual upbuilding in confidence and prayer. ...

I was properly welcomed and began, by watching and listening, to learn a little more about Hitler's Germany. What varied attitudes toward him there were! What bitter hate, what impassioned devotion! What strong support, given after carefully weighed consideration of possible alternatives to his leadership! What courageous disobedience, open, quiet, philosophically offered, day in, day out! Many of my friends had consistently refused to make the salute, calmly ignoring his obvious power to fulfil his threats of prison and torture, tolerantly explaining that such a man was inevitable, given the conditions of the postwar world.

Nearly all my ... hostesses were in danger, many of them in poverty because no Gestapo threats could induce them to say Heil Hitler. They'd lost jobs, home, and health, but this experience had added to their spiritual stature: something I gloried in, longed to acquire, but could not: a certain sense of power and a wisdom that glowed. Yet when I think of them it's the pallor of their skin that glows. One of these gave me her services as guide and interpreter. She was always serene, quite uninterested in herself. From others I heard of the very responsible public position she had filled for years before Hitler's advent. Now she was keeping body and soul together by giving English lessons to those few folk who dared to talk with a *persona non grata* for an hour a week. Their houses were scattered in suburbs of a big city; bus rides hither and thither were long; meals had to be eaten from a paper bag, in a waiting room. They seemed to be mostly crusts.

When one day I had to go to the woman Führer's head-quarters for a talk with her deputy who understands English, I expected this friend to wait outside for me, but in she came, among dozens of clerks, porters, and officials, responding to their ubiquitous salutings with a mere inclination of her head. To my dismay she accompanied me to the reception room, then sat down to wait.

"Why on earth did you risk all that?" I enquired when we were safely outside. "Why put your head into the lion's mouth?"

Her answering look was memorable, so much did it reveal of surprise at my ingenuousness. Then, soothingly, as to a nervous child she replied, "We mustn't let ourselves ever get afraid of Hitler, you know. That would only give him more power." While safely walking in a park where no trees were fitted with recording eyes or microphonic ears, I tried to get a further insight into her philosophy. "So many of you Germans have suffered through Hitler, yet I never hear you blame him. We British and Americans vie with each other in thinking out epithets suitable to his cruel deeds."

"How can we blame the thing we've created?" she replied.

"But we created him. Did not Sir Nevile Henderson lay it down that Versailles made him inevitable?"

"Of course you all helped. But we Germans mustn't try to load the blame on to you. Ours is a heavy share of responsibility and we must shoulder it."

"How did you create him?"

By merely being negative. After the 1918 Armistice we were glad to cast off the Prussian yoke. One by one we freed ourselves of various restraints: Kaiserdom, militarism, tradition, convention, every sort of discipline. We hugged our freedom, worshipped it. Any sort of control seemed a relic of our old slavery. But freedom

51

itself is negative. It supplies no aim in life. I began to see that unless we had something positive to work for, we'd get some new tyranny foisting itself upon us. The only adequate aim was to work out in actual life, in daily situations, in home, school, factory, and politics, the creed of Christ, the Lord's Prayer, the Beatitudes. That would need a discipline more constant and complete than anything we had struggled out from. As I wasn't willing personally to undertake it, I kept silent. As the years passed it became clear that we were deteriorating. Young folk who had inherited this freedom without having struggled for it found it savourless. Their elders were finding it sterile.

When utter boredom and purposelessness were widespread, folk began to repeat the slogans of a highly vitalized young man. Hitler publicized a programme, every line of it crisp, definite, positive. He demanded the whole of us, every second of our time, every ounce of our energy. Not a fibre of our body was to be held back. Not a word on our tongue was to be undisciplined. Our mind and our spirit must be put at his disposal, our power of choice sacrificed, our will handed over to him. Youth by the thousand hurried to get behind his banner and there found release from the bondage of their self-will. As I watched all this I knew that as a Christian I was responsible for not having trained myself perfectly to follow Christ's programme, not even in my own life. But now I am keeping alert, and as one by one his devotees become disillusioned, I try to show them this other way, the completely satisfying way of serving God and one's fellows.

Sometimes the meetings with my German friends were held in a big house, sometimes in a cottage, once in a one-man shop locked up for the night, once in a zoo. In the tiny sitting room of the man who looked after the bears I met a gentle-faced old friend of his, a gardener. As he wouldn't say "Heil Hitler," he had lost his job and all prospect of another. But he had his own half acre and on it he could produce enough vegetables to keep his adopted child and himself alive. Better a diet of herbs and peace than prosperity and hate.

At the same meeting I heard how one of their group, a young Christian pacifist, was walking down his street on the morning that scarlet paper insults were first ordered to be stuck on all Jewish shop windows. He stopped to read the label, and without a thought of consequences, tore it off, crumpled it up in his hand, threw it in the gutter, and walked on. Before he reached the corner the police had got him. In the exhaustive examination that followed he answered every question put to him by the Gestapo quietly and frankly, adding that he had always refused to learn to kill and always would. After two weeks in prison he was called before authority and given his freedom with the warning, "We've investigated your case. We find you hid nothing, and that you were unafraid. If we had discovered one instance of lying or of suppression of the truth, you would be on your way to Dachau by now."

From *It Occurred to Me*

In the terrible war years that followed, Lester continued her steadfast witness not only against war but also in working out plans to help the victims of war whether among the Allies or among the Axis nations. Reflecting on how to rid the world of the scourge of war, she wrote after a visit to the Far East in 1939:

Unless God meant the human race to be actually one family, we have no right to the phrase "Our Father."

Unless Jesus was misinterpreting God, we cannot overcome evil with evil, or gain security by armies and navies, or defend ourselves by preparing to kill potential enemies.

*   *   *

God's word is strictly practical. Its common sense is devastating. If you don't like the fruits of war, destroy its roots. Refuse to kill or to let your sons learn to kill, or prepare for killing by navies, armies or air forces. Don't produce the tolls of death. Don't help others to produce them by paying them to do so. Let us examine the sources of our comfort, our dividends, the investments of the banks where our securities lie. Only by being ready for economic readjustment ourselves, by taking the Cross ourselves, do we gain the courage and the authority to ask the rich to do the same thing.

It was American and British money that helped to build the fine colleges where sixty per cent of China's leaders were educated. It is American and British money that helped Japan to destroy them.

Who paid for the last meal you ate? Was its cost met from dividends you draw from steel, from oil, from army cars?

Can you eat the next meal unless you have begun to cause enquiry to be made into the holding companies, the invested funds, which were the source?

Perhaps you will have to put off eating for a few hours, for a day even. If you would vow not to eat until you had begun to act, you would act today. If it were your own child who was in danger of being raped, you would dare anything to stop supplies from going to the soldiers.

*　　*　　*

It is "five minutes to twelve." [Similar to the U.S. idea of the approach of the final reckoning at midnight, such as the Bulletin of the Atomic Scientists' Doomsday Clock in the nuclear era.] Is there a way out, an alternative? The vast mass of the world's people are sound at heart. Every normally developed man and woman wants peace. Besides, it happens to be God's will. We can achieve it as soon as we are willing to pay the price. "The things on which peace depend" are both economic and psychological. Our raw materials must be made of easier access. Tariff walls must be brought down. Imperial territorial possessions must be put under super-national control. It is no more wicked to covet empire than to cleave to empire. "What I want I grab" is no more vulgar an attitude than "What I have I hold." The things we have were "grabbed" by our fathers...We must abandon our irritating attitude of conscious rectitude. To give up our pride and prejudice will be painful to some of us, but it is the only alternative to poison gas, liquid fire and the hell of war.

The nations are rushing down the Gadarene slope towards destruction. We may call it doom, we may call it retribution, but we are choosing our route. We could still pull up, call a halt, turn around although it is a painful thing to stop suddenly in the midst of so swift a descent.

The Cross was a peculiarly painful thing, too. But its pain became the means of healing, sanity, salvation, triumph. It performs that function still.

On the road to Jerusalem, Jesus at last succeeded in making His disciples understand that He was not going to a Roman triumph but to the gallows. Peter seems to have leapt forward and confronted His Master, passionately calling on him to abandon the idea.

Jesus' very brusque reply translated into contemporary English applies to us all. "Get out of my sight, Peter, you're acting the part of Satan, tempting me. You're not thinking like God. You're thinking like men."

Is that what is wrong with the world? It is thinking arduously, hopelessly, deeply, fearfully, but it is not thinking like God.

Hadn't we better begin?

Women

"The Most Practical Half of the Human Race"

From her earliest years in the slums of London to her globe-circling work as an ambassador of reconciliation, Muriel Lester demonstrated an unerring and dauntless concern for the rights of women and for a recognition of their unique role in solving practical problems, from those of the workplace and neighborhood to the massive affairs of nation-states. She eloquently defended, by word and by example, the need for women clergy, the place of women in challenging imperialism, and the role of women in overcoming destitution and war among the world's peoples. Her prophetic vision left its mark on a generation and even now is pointing to goals that are far beyond what has yet been achieved.

In her work at Kingsley Hall, Muriel Lester little by little began to assume the role of a minister to the people of Bow. Many then—even as now, over half a century later!—thought the ministry was no place for a woman. She answered these objections in an essay she wrote in 1930 entitled "Why Forbid Us?"

From *Why Forbid Us?*

It seems a trifle ludicrous to write a pamphlet to prove that women should be accepted as ministers of the Church. Rather the onus of proof is on the other side. Those who oppose it must show rational grounds for the sex bar in matters of the spirit.

The creative spirit has been pushing, urging, thrusting men and women forward and upward from the day we discovered the erect posture. There must have been individuals even then who were sincerely shocked at the indecency of standing upright. One can only guess as to what was the equivalent of pamphlet writing in those days. But in the transition period those whose weaker spines predisposed them to favour the old style of walking probably tried to lay the responsibility of justifying the new custom on the still somewhat unsteady shoulders of the pioneers.

How interesting would be those arguments could we recover them today!

Ages later the same creative spirit urged a certain human being to turn away, slightly sickened, from the communal meal of broiled human flesh. The question as to whether that individual was man or woman is unanswerable, but it is certain that the first dissidents scarcely understood their own shrinking. Why this feeling of distaste? Could it be a queasy stomach in those vigorous days? It would pass. It would pass.

But it did not, and the squeamishness—incomprehensible even to the one who felt it—persisted. Then others were infected with the same malaise. As the numbers grew they were dubbed innovators, lawless, irreligious, betrayers of the customs handed down by their ancestors, enemies to God and the tribe.

How precious would be a gramophone record of the speech made by the old man of the tribe at the Spring Ceremonial dinner in which he pointed out that sterner measures must be taken against these daring non-comformists.

This energising Spirit of God is ever thrusting us out into situations where a wider view is suddenly displayed before our vision. Thenceforward we cannot help seeing—and the cautious arguments of the so-called practical person who cannot see are unanswerable since they are not pertinent.

This creative spirit persistently and steadily involved me in a situation where I had to do all the work of a minister, prophetic, pastoral, and priestly. It was wholly alien from my intention. It just happened. And I was not even conscious of the significance of the occurrence until several years later.

Women

*   *   *

As a woman tenant in a back street in East London my theorising was constantly corrected by the gross facts of everyday life. Living in a neighbourhood where thirty-three public houses are each within a three minutes' walk brings one to a solution of quite a number of interesting problems in personality that might have engrossed one's attention for years in an academic sphere. A neighbour comes in to say that Mrs. Leslie has just been fished out of the canal.

> Poor devil! She tried to do 'erself in; deep in debt she was, and the money-lender turned nasty and told 'er she must pay. Mrs. Leslie got scared. 'Er husband's a good livin' man and doesn't 'old with runnin' into debt. She was frightened he'd get an 'ear of it.

Mrs. Leslie is now in hospital recovering from the shock and the policeman is waiting near the bed, for she has broken the law. Scarcely an alluring or reassuring prospect for a person who already dislikes the world enough to try her best to leave it! When will our social habits catch up with our mental concepts, let alone our sympathies? Some of our customs seem a little idiotic. A debatable point, do we get only the government we deserve? Are our local institutions on the whole a reliable index of the common ideas of the population?

Speculations are cut short for the neighbour is waiting, evidently expecting me to do something. "Go and see 'er, Miss. It'd make all the difference." My heart sinks. Surely this is a priest's work, not mine. The situation is rich in human interest. I can see that. A woman is afraid to live any longer, decides not to, starts to kill herself, is prevented. Then she's dragged back to face life again, more afraid now, afraid of the debt and the husband and the policeman and the prison. Good gracious! What misery! Her life needs rebuilding from the bottom up! But I can't analyse it further while my neighbour waits at the door, surprised by my hesitation.

"Don't you want to go?" she asks.

I look the other way and try to assume a nonchalant air, as I equivocate.

"What about getting a minister?"

"Oh! She doesn't go to church, you know. She only lives in the next street." Tactful implication of the duty of neighbourliness. Who is my neighbour? Should not all the

Lord's servants be prophets? I pull myself together and get up to go.

Perfect satisfaction is portrayed on my visitor's face. She has no theory about it, she knows it is my job; she is utterly reassured as to the future well-being of Mrs. Leslie. What a terrible responsibility she has thrust on me, the unready!

But strangely enough the thing happens as she expected. The poor lady lies there with strained face and haunted, apprehensive eyes, until I sit beside her bed. Then things start happening—the break-up of strain, the tears, the returning confidence, the new hope, life reconciliation, peace. Meanwhile one has found oneself speaking strong words of comfort and release, relying on God, going to the husband and putting him wise to the situation, cleaning up the house and making it pleasant to welcome her on her return, for the policeman, as usual, has been recalled.

*   *   *

Another neighbour has a new baby. I am taken in to see him by the proud nurse. She puts him in my arms for the usual bedside prayer. Because I am happy and feel at home here, as in fact I do in most of my neighbours' houses, I prolong my stay. The mother in this unwonted period of quietness and leisure feels emboldened to talk of many things, things she cannot manage to express ordinarily, when she is acting the hostess or busy in the kitchen, surrounded by a score of petty jobs that are waiting to be done. She puts into words her fugitive hopes and longings, she displays a spiritual understanding so deep and so rare that I feel ashamed of the crude, limited, conventional, puerile sort of teaching that we in the churches have provided for these fiery sensitve souls who sit row upon row on hard benches at mothers' meetings all over the country. It is easier to treat them as a mass, instead of as personalities to be approached with reverence. ...

Years passed and the neighbourliness of the four or five adjoining streets had become so real a thing that when an empty building was put at our disposal there was no hesitation in accepting the gift and taking on the responsilbity of caretaking, heating, cleaning and lighting it. Men and women offered a night, a week's labour, or a half-day's scrubbing, taxed themselves for every meeting they attended, undertook the provision of refreshments and kept open house there every day in the name of fellowship. Everyone was equally honoured, equally welcome, rich or poor, Christian or atheist, British or alien, drunk or sober. ...

As soon as this habit becomes established, the neighbourhood came to rely on it. People who never entered our little community centre regulated their doings by ours. Our ten o'clock prayer bell warned the bar-keeper of the Redpion that it was "Time, gentlemen, please." Mothers found it a useful thing to order their children to bed by the prayer bell. Others would send messages round, carefully timed to arrive just before ten o'clock. "Please remember our Johnny tonight. He ain't arf bad, and the doctor can't make out properly wot's wrong. He's tossing and turning and screaming something shocking."

Little by little the neighbourhood house became useful to groups of all sorts that wanted to get up meetings for better housing, for temperance, for prevention of cruelty to animals, for saving, for child welfare, for sex education. I generally gave the visitors the welcome and took the chair for them. It was my privilege always to keep alive the interest after they had gone, for the price of freedom is eternal vigilance and the group of men and women even if they are drawn only from a few back steeets have great power if only they care to use it. Is there some crying evil, some local scandal, some long-tolerated cruelty? It can be removed and overcome to make room for a healthier growth, just so soon as the neighbours become conscious of it and of their own power and of God.

Soon we were having crowded and enthusiastic meetings on behalf of this or in protest against that, and open-air meetings held by propagandist groups throughout the locality wanted our support.

It is a wonderful thing to prophesy in a church, to speak out the truth, to show how Christ's way alone can bring joy and order and plenty a to war-tortured world, but to do this at the dock-gates, or in a London park week after week to an audience of two or three hundred, gives one an even greater joy. Inside the hall each Sunday I led our Christian worship and afterwards the whole congregation would stay on past ten o'clock, asking questions, arguing and discussing in the friendly atmosphere induced by smoke, sandwiches and coffee. One wakes up at length to realise that one has assumed all the priestly functions, except the sacramental duties. And what of them?

Very soon I found I had to christen my neighbours' babies, for it was irrefutably true that they and I were wholly at one in our interest and reverence for child life. We had been running nursery schools and graded schools, story-telling groups and play hours for the whole neighbourhood for years. We had so often helped each other to get nearer to God through our dealings with children, that I could not withstand the simple logic of their appeal, "Can you christen the baby next Sunday?" I could not refuse. And once I began to do it, I realised the tremendous force that can be released in such a service. It was a perfect opportunity to point out to a whole congregation that praying for a young child is a mockery unless we mean to live in such a way that, imitative as a child is, he shall never go astray through copying us. Standing during the ceremony we solemnly consecrated ourselves afresh to the tremendous task of making the world a fitter place for children to live in.

Many a time I have been to a funeral, conducted by an official cemetery chaplain who knew no single detail of the lives of the people huddled round the coffin. He just read the service. It was impossible for him to understand the immense importance of the fact that Johnny Leeder was managing for the first time in his life not to cry because now he must be like Daddy; that Mrs. Fairfoot had not tasted a drop of liquor that day meant nothing to him; he did not realise that now was the appointed time when Mrs. Fairfoot's destiny was to be settled. He just continued to read the burial service.

I soon found it necessary to take on that duty, too, because it was much easier for me to make the service a vital, a personal thing to each member of the family in their various reactions to loss; a source of strength and comfort to some, a challenge to the careless lives of others, a new conception of peace and triumph to all; particuarly, to see that the children instead of being led, forlorn, cold and trembling up to the big hole in the ground which may haunt them ever afterwards, should be taken away after the service to some neighbour's home, an innovation at which conventional funeral-attending relatives would be unutterably shocked, were it not intro- duced by someone in authority.

* * *

God forbid that I should suggest that all these duties and privileges of Christian ministry are not being fulfilled by men throughout the length and breadth of the land, every day of the year. They are. But who will dispute the strengthened authority of the recognised minister? We do not seek any added importance that recognition may bring us, but if such is going to make in any way our ministry more efficient, if it is going to strengthen our position as God's servants to our fellows, are we not justified in asking, nay, demanding authoritative recognition, not only for the added strength that it would give to us personally, but for the confidence with which it would inspire those institutional centres to which we are attached?

To manifest God to the world is the highest function anyone can perform and this is generally considered to be the specific function of those set apart as priest or minister. Can there be too many people doing it today?

Then why forbid women?

From *It Occurred to Me*

Muriel Lester spoke with enthusiasm about the powerful impact the independence movement in India was having on women in that vast subcontinent.

Mary Campbell arrived at Kingsley Hall. We had last met in India when she took me round the licensed drink and opium shops in Delhi, explaining the Government excise policy which seemed to both of us lamentable. Stirring events had been taking place since then, she said. The women of the country had risen, left their sheltered homes, torn down the veil and played a brave part in the national drama. Gandhiji had called to them from his prison cell. After her thirty years' work in India, she had seen the transformation of its womanhood with amazement and pride. She watched scores of Delhi women methodically station themselves in couples outside each licensed house and request every intending customer not to enter. She saw the crowds gather to watch this strange sight. Women who had covered their faces from men for forty years were now standing in the public streets, quiet and self-possessed, defying imperialism. She saw the police come up and warn them that they were causing congestion in the traffic and must, therefore, go home. But was it likely, having decided to disobey their own conventions, traditions, sacred rules, that they would be intimidated now by a policeman's order? Once more they were asked to move; otherwise arrest would follow. The women ignored the order. Still more people thronged the streets, Miss Campbell among them, to see the police wagon arrive and great burly policemen pick up the little purdah women and drive off with them to jail. Sales of opium and drink fell to zero. Even people who wanted to buy were ashamed to do so. At first the shops were shut up. Then the owners made the salesmen open them. How they hated staying there all day alone! They too were ashamed. All over India the same sort of thing was happening. Thousands of high-born women were in prison.

From *Kill or Cure?*

In country after country, women were shaking off the shackles of the past and taking their rightful place in society. Reflecting on the movement for women's suffrage, of which she had been a part, Muriel Lester wrote in 1937:

Women united in the suffrage campaign and emancipated themselves with tremendous energy and courage. This was a new phenomenon, bursting upon a surprised world which has not even yet realized that, because of it, things will never be the same again. They boldly questioned the right of certain ancient institutions to continue to exist. They directed their attention to hidden evils, to the White Slave Traffic, to the economic basis of prostitution. They made friends with the prostitutes and several even championed the rights of their own husband's illegitimate child or deserted mistress. With their zest, their realism, and their common sense, they invaded every territory of social life, prisons, asylums, workhouses, reformatories, and orphanages.

They looked at war, stripped it of its glamour, its age-long prestige, its specious glory, and saw it as a maelstrom of conflicting passions—greed, pride, lust, hate, lies, spying, ignorance, misunderstanding, fear, fortune-hunting, profiteering, prejudice, and ambition.

England had been involved in wars throughout her whole history, many of them now recognized as palpably unjust; but always there was so much courage and devotion evoked by military conflict that its inherent evil had been easily glossed over. But now, in the twentieth century, this scientific age, were we to continue to employ this worn-out and suicidal method of national defense?

"Whoever may be the enemy, our sons are bidden to fight in the next war," said the women;

> we know their lives will be sacrificed in vain. War settles nothing. Every victory has within its womb the seeds of future war. No country is ever wholly in the right or wholly in the wrong. In every nation there are good and bad. You cannot punish the pride of an Emperor by killing numbers of his peasants. We are not willing to go through the long months of pregnancy and labor merely to produce more cannon fodder.

The period during which Frau Wagner held the copyright of "Parsifal" at Bayreuth terminated. The play was performed all over Europe and helped the new movement. It demonstrated to huge audiences, through ear and eye, that the hero-deliverers of mankind must be pure from self-seeking, courageous, the servants of the people, men of God.

A play was published portraying the idea of a perfect Christian. In it a Viking, Kiartan by name, was grossly betrayed by friend, brother, and lover, yet he refused to defend himself by killing them and fell at their hands saying,

> Brother, by thy hand liefer were I slain
> Than bid thee die by mine.

(from "Kiartan the Icelander," by Newman Howard)

With these words, which have been handed down through the centuries in one of the Icelandic Sagas, Kiartan is said to have introduced Christianity into the island.

It was realized that Constantine had done almost irreparable injury to Christianity when he stopped the persecutions and proclaimed it as the State religon.

People began to scrutinize the hymns and prayers used in worship and to refuse to sing or repeat sentences they did not really mean. Could they continue to sing that verse of the time-honored "O God, our help in ages past," which includes the lines,

> Sufficient is Thine arm alone
> And our defense is sure?

Did they really mean that? If the answer was "Yes," they must give up Army, Navy, and Air Force. If "No," we must stop singing it, for a creed that sounds beautiful and has noble phraseology, but does not work, is an offense to God and man.

*   *   *

Muriel Lester and the women of Bow were espe-cially moved by the plight of children starving in Eu-rope because of the Allied blockade that was keeping food away from former enemies, even though the end of the war had come. British soldiers, stationed in Germany, wrote home about the suffering.

> ...technically it was the Navy, and not themselves, who were actually keeping out the food. "Still you couldn't exactly go blaming it on the men of the Navy. Wotever would young Len Blackmore, 'oo was stoker on the *Invincible*, say, 'im wot teaches a class of kids in Sunday school at 'ome, if 'e wos to see the state these young nippers were in? And if 'e came to see that it was 'is own ship wot 'ad kept up the blockade. Well!....The only thing was to give them a taste of proper Christian food once a day anyhow."...

As I was going down Botolph Road one day, I passed Mrs. Smith with a letter from her boy in Cologne in her hand. "Look, Miss, wot my boy says," she called out and began to read to me: 'Dear Mum, things are something shocking art 'ere. The kids are 'ungry. We feed them up a bit, but it's not enough. Can't some of you at 'ome get busy?'

Mrs. Smith got busy. Food was just beginning to appear in plenty in London shops. Even bars of Fry's chocolate cream were procurable. It was quite a thrilling sight. One could buy butter now, without having a coupon, if the cash was avail-able. Rich people could get as much cream as they liked. To Bow people, it seemed a shame, when all this was happening, that the blockade was kept on month after month. More news kept coming through about the hunger diseases rife in Central Europe. ...

But hardly any news of this got into the British daily press. We started on a campaign to call on London editors and beg them to publish the indubitable facts. We called on clergy and town councilors too. Strange were some of the answers we received. "It wouldn't be popular." "We must wait until the Government gives the lead." "It can't be true or we should have heard about it before." "They deserve it."

This was of babies born since the Armistice.

When we passed on the suggestion that people should adopt for six months or a year a child from the distressed areas, one man answered that it would not be fair to one's own children to introduce a devil into the home. To such a pitch had four and a half years of news falsification brought kindly fathers of families.

The Bow people wrote a letter to the Prime Minister saying that "they knew what it was to be hungry and because of that they and their children didn't want anyone in any part of the world to be hungry." They pointed out that it would be kinder to bomb these ex-enemy children outright than to let them suffer the pangs of slow starvation, and they asked in God's name that the blockade should be raised.

They decided to take their letter by hand. They felt that if the newspapers would not enlighten the public as to the state of their fellow human beings in Germany, they must try to do so themselves. They would turn themselves into a living newspaper. They would walk in single file dressed in mourning, carrying high enough for all passers-by to see, homemade posters mounted on wooded frames. They got the news compressed into short neat sentences.

A little set of nobodies, we set out. One mother had to bring her two little girls with her, so we hung on each side of their perambulator the message of the children of Bow, "We don't want any children anywhere to go hungry." The last poster bore the words, "It is not the will of your Father in heaven that one of these little ones should perish." The cavalcade aroused a good deal of attention. Though Parliament was in session and it was therefore illegal for a procession to approach within a mile of it, no policeman seemed to have the heart or the mind to turn back these quiet, experienced, hard-working mothers. When they reached St. Stephens they put down their posters with a sigh of relief, put them up in two neat piles against the friendly, solid wall of Westminster Hall, and trooped into the lobby to look round and rest their feet. One of the girls stayed outside with the two babies in the pram, and shared a bag of toffee with the policeman on duty.

This took place four months before the peace treaty was signed. Very soon after the "Save the Children Fund" was founded by Miss Eglantyne Jebb. The International Children's Charter, put forward by the committee of this world-wide society, may prove to be of great moment to the setting up of real peace, turning men's minds, as it does, from every other consideration to the one universally important criterion by which every new measure should be judged: "Will it help or hinder the well-being of the world's children?"

Decades passed, another world war came and, with it, the same ensuing barbarity, including another blockade of the continent of Europe. Muriel Lester again cried out for human decency and compassion. This time she addressed the women of America with a widely read essay, "Speed the Food Ships."

From *It So Happened*

A common sense sort of war work awaits all women. It needs no training, only imagination. It can be done in one's spare time or can fill sixteen hours of one's day.

This work is nothing less than the feeding of Europe. Numerous difficulties and obstacles immediately leap to one's mind. But we are accustomed to difficulties and obstacles. We have learned throughout the ages how to circumvent them, by passion and by pity.

Send ship-load after ship-load of your surplus food to Europe. Distribute it yourselves.

Grow even more food to load up this sort of Armada — American 1940 style. It will be a new sort of invasion, an entering wedge into the old-fashioned unscientific surgery of Europe. Perhaps it will prove to be a new page of history written in gold letters for all the world to read, America's impact on Europe's body politic.

Let us examine the obvious snags. First: Perhaps Britain won't let the ships get past its blockade of continental Europe. Second: Perhaps Hitler won't let the ships get past his submarine blockade of Britain.

Only in so far as the leaders of both countries depend on starving out women and children can they object to this action of the U.S.A. The vast mass of the common people of Europe, British and continent, will hail it as sublime common sense. After all, it will be supplementing the resolution put forward a few months ago at Westminster by the Bishop of Birmingham before the House of Convocation, that "We should feed our enemies." None of the high ecclesiastics present could support his plea. Sorrowfully, though sincerely, they pointed out that Britain's national policy made it impossible. Then they waited for the bishop's reply to their regretful speeches. But he had nothing to say, except that it wasn't he who originated the idea.

Numerous Britons agree with the bishop rather than with the starvation method. They remember the last blockade in 1918 and 1919; long after the Armistice and long after the Peace Treaty was signed, children were to be seen in the parks and streets of German cities, children whose bones bent if you put even a little pressure upon them, children whose bodies were described as "flimsy."

If Hitler refuses to call off his U-boats from the food ships which convey their precious caroges to the rest of Europe, what's to happen? Must the will of God be ignored if the War Office objects to its fulfilment?

It may be that the British government would welcome the whole conception as an honourable way out of a situation which may ruin both protagonists. But even in that case they would have to take a firm stand against the project at first. They would probably complain that the U.S.A. was interfering in European affairs, that you were being naive, sentimental, idealistic, meddling with mercy instead of munitions.

It may be, on the other hand, that the War Office would consider the plan tragically misconceived. They might implore you to desist, point out that it would be a stab in the back, actually as mortal as Mussolini's. They may use all the psychological methods known to government to rebuff you, to impugn your motives, your good faith.

To the military mind, both British and American, it may look like treachery. But most human beings don't possess the military mind. Ordinary people look at things differently. This often creates awkward situations for the ordinary person. It may also create awkward situations for the militarists. In this situation the War Office may feel so sincere a dread of the scheme that they have to inform the U.S.A. that they must keep the food ships outside Europe, by force if necessary; that they must sink any ship that defies the blockade. They would be within their rights if they did this. In which case the U.S.A. would send ships regardless, for they would be manned by Americans, millions of whom would gladly risk death in the effort to save life. This would introduce a new technique for the settling of international problems.

Seeing that it is the common instinct to feed the hungry, no political or military situation is likely to be able to hold back for long the great stream of generosity once it has burst its way through the obstructions that have so long impeded its life-bringing flow.

*   *   *

This appeal had grown out of a ten-day period of intense prayer at the Isle of Shoals, with Glenn Clark and others over the conflagration spreading world-wide. She wrote,

I received a warning from friends in England to be careful. But I had been. I didn't want to write the thing. It wrote itself. I had tried to keep my name off it. But my American friends were convinced that it should be published as it stood. We were in deadly earnest. It was actually a race with death. We hoped we'd win, but we didn't. Behind the scenes opposition was gathering momentum.

*   *   *

Something deeply damaging to the human race was happening. From time immemorial we women have tended the bodies of mankind, washed them, clothed them, fed them, cherished them. Now we were being asked by leaders we trusted and admired to abdicate from our age-old position, evade our destiny, do violence to our very nature—and let children starve.

In an open letter to women, Lester wrote:

In 1937 in the John Finleys' New York City home, some friends were discussing the probability of war in Europe. Some thought it inevitable, as in 1914. "But there's one new element

70

in the situation, don't you think?" said our hostess. "Women have power now. Might not that avert the catastrophe?" All of us looked at the editor of the *New York Times*. He thought a moment or two, and then said, "Yes, it might."

But it didn't. Why not? What has happened to us women of the West in the last twenty years? During this period Indian, Chinese and Japanese women have made a colossal advance. What's the matter with us women of the Christian tradition?

In these twenty years women have gained victory after victory and grown more defeatist. We've won entry into professions, into businesses, into politics, into the diplomatic service. So proud have we been of our precious achievements in these narrow spheres that we have ignored, and at last almost forgotten, our destiny. For a million years our job has been to preserve, cherish, and protect the human race. Every fibre of our being urges us to feed the hungry, comfort the crying child, practise the antithesis of violence.

But this is the generation of women who have abdicated instead of trusting to our intuition. We have forced ourselves to think along the lines laid down by men throughout the centuries. "Follow your head, not your heart" was the slogan of the almost passionate appeal issued by publicity and newspaper editors as soon as news of the hunger of the little democracies reached the United States. A careful campaign was carried on to "denaturize" us. For women might so easily have risen up in all their might and demanded that food should be sent over and the belligerent governments would have had to listen, as occurred in 1915.

The campaign was successful. Women didn't want to be thought sentimental, unworthy of the places they so proudly held side by side with men folk. They wanted to show they were realist. They could match the men in hardheadedness. They abdicated. Henceforward they preferred to praise Jane Addams, instead of following her. She took a very different stand as regards feeding Europe, and she made men listen to her. It's always more pleasant to adorn the tombs of the prophets than to follow their leadership. Soon women became almost as adept as men at declaring, "I know this course of action is against the teaching of Christ, but we must take it. ..."

A woman who was driving me to one of the evening meetings ... remarked, "I try to look at the world situation from every point of view and I only grow more bewildered and confused." It seemed that from that instant God took charge of things. I asked if I might have those words of hers; if I might use them as a text; copyright them, for they mark an epoch which is nearing its end. Permission was granted. For several days I pondered on the terrible strength of will of women in all countries who repress their own nature, forcing themselves to embrace programs laid down by men, to follow the zigzag course of diplomacy, to support their leader, or prime minister, or president even when he bargains over the bodies of babies with offers of shiploads of milk. I tried to consider what happens to us when we force our wills to go against God's will. I recognized the inevitable disintegration of personality which occurs when we no longer keep in touch with the creative and untrammelled Spirit of God, the Breath of our life, apart from whom we cannot exist for the next hour.

I remember the woman who happened to sit opposite me in the Pullman dining car a month or so previously. Her face looked haggard above her pearls as she started a conversation. "I think it terrible, what's happening in Europe. I can't sleep at night for thinking of those children." "Do you think of them during the day?" I enquired. "No, I try to forget during the day." There's the trouble; we try to forget the facts. Prayer makes us face them and see our own share in them and do something about it.

The following Thursday morning in Washington, D.C., I suggested that it was up to us women to follow our own line in the future; to reject even the most respectable plea or the best church-supported current if it clashed with our true nature, if it did violence to our common sense, for we are the most practical half of the human race. I quoted the remark of my chauffeuse and her willingness for us to use it as a text. I appreciated the value of learning to look at things from various points of view. It is an obviously useful exercise, part of the training of a well-equipped mind. But the vital and indispensable thing is to have a point of view of one's own which is utterly stable, durable, basic.

Without it life doesn't make sense. Only from God's point of view can one see straight without flinching, without gloom, wihout fear. I suggested we should spend an hour that day in silence, facing the world situation no longer from the British or the German, the exporter's, the banker's or the administrator's point of view, but wholly and solely from God's.

I said I knew some were probably already objecting and saying to themselves, "How bold, perhaps even arrogant, to imagine we can! Isn't this a presumptuous sin, perhaps even a little blasphemous?" Especially would those demur in some way or other who did not want to take the trouble of devoting an hour to such quietness. But this way of looking at things was not my invention. Our Lord suggested it in what He said to Peter on the memorable occasion when He likened that very dear friend of His to Satan. In one of the modern translations the words are, "Get out of my sight, Peter. You are playing the part of Satan, tempting me. You're not thinking like God. You're thinking like a man." Evidently we are rather disappointing to our Lord when we are content to think in the human way. Keeping to the old categories of convention, morality and expediency. We're obviously supposed to think like God. We had better begin.

*   *   *

Muriel Lester practiced this plain speaking wherever she went. We see it evidenced, for example, when she went to Japan with news of what the Japanese troops were doing in China. What she said was sharply at odds with the government propaganda that is the staple of wartime news:

From *It Occurred to Me*

The people seemed to know very little about what was happening in China. The sight of wounded soldiers returning from Shanghai caused spectators wonderingly to enquire what they had been doing. They were told, "These are our noble men who have been over in China helping the people there get rid of their bandits."

"Tell us if it's true that people all round the world hate us?" was the final question put to me at the end of a dinner party given by some public-spirited women intellectuals.

There was tenseness in the silence that followed the request. I put up a prayer. Trying to tell the truth is difficult. Then I said: "Yes, I think it is true. You see, when we British were seizing our Empire, radio wasn't invented; communications were embryonic. We could gobble up some huge area and no intimate details of the transaction would be known to the general public. But nowadays at every breakfast table round the world there is a report of every new bit you take out of the living body of China."

There was an anguished silence. Very gently I continued, "Did you know there was a gramophone record in Geneva, made in Shanghai, recording the cries and screams and groans of wounded and dying civilians?"

"It's propaganda!" exclaimed one of the women.

"No," I answered, "it's the desire to know what is happening. We British women can speak to you honestly like this, only because we know what it's like, ourselves, to be hated all round the world. D'you think we can't feel it as we travel about? We've borne it for many years and it's a terrible burden. Now you are beginning to share the same experience. It may be, in the providence of God, that you are the women destined successfully to combat imperialism, to show the world how inevitably the ruthlessness of militarism destroys the value of what it tries to save. We women are guardians of life. Some of us in England are working pretty hard against our own imperialism. Aren't you being called upon now to take up your share of responsibility?"

Politics

Socialist Alderman
of the Poplar Borough Council

After World War I, Muriel Lester had a short, four-and-one-half year foray into politics that grew naturally out of her involvement in the life of the people of Bow, as well as out of her religious vision of the meaning of life. Believing that all of life should be seen through the prism of the Kingdom of God, she began to identify herself with the growing socialist movement in Britain, especially as espoused by Christian Socialists like George Lansbury. For the rest of her life, even after her brief stint as an alderman on the Poplar Borough Council, she was a strong critic of both capitalism and communism and was an advocate of a democratic socialist alternative to the extremes of individualism and collectivism. Always the pragmatist, she was a harsh critic of ideals divorced from the real life of the people.

From *It Occurred to Me*

I began to think about homes. The churches expended much time and some sentiment upon the subject of the Christian home, but seemed definitely averse to considering its material prerequisite, the house. Though the sport of church-baiting is beneath the dignity of a thinking person, being not only too easy but also too obviously a bunk-hole for those who are trying to escape from their vague sense of guilt, one had to acknowledge that young people's societies were encouraged to discuss the evils of drink, of gambling, of atheism, and of foreign sins such as untouchability, child marriage and purdah, while propaganda for better housing was dubbed political and side-tracked. Young converts and incipient church leaders mainly followed the safe course marked out by the beneficiaries of the *status quo* ....

The street in which Kingsley Hall stood was rat-infested. The rats themselves were so diseased and poisonous that the professional rat-catcher forcibly dragged his dog away from their carcasses after the kill. Mothers were anxious about their babies. It wasn't only at night that the creatures came out from their holes. One of them scampered over a young neighbour's bed in broad daylight as she lay there after confinement. In one basement home their incursions were so regular that the children were kept up each evening till the father came in; their games and quarrels and cries kept the creatures away until he could cope with them. ....

Vermin are notoriously adaptable. Their will to live defies each of the successive invincible specifics for clearing them out of their haunts in the walls. You may tear down the homely cosy-looking wall paper and austerely colour-wash the plaster; you may bung up the cracks and holes and half-suffocate yourself with sulphur fumes in one of the two rooms which constitute your home; after two days you unseal the doors, sweep up the corpses, open the window, create a thorough draught, and start again with high hope of self-respect. Before the week is out the creatures appear again. You accept the inevitable and put aside fourpence each week, the price of a loaf of bread, to buy insecticide.

In Doris' absence, I was once asked to broadcast for Children's House. I stressed the need of such a place, citing among other things the rat-ridden homes of many of our children. Called early next morning to the telephone, I was confronted with a furious voice. Disembodied anger is always upsetting. It's difficult to see the funny side of a mere voice. Ours was a wall telephone, and I remember how hard it was to continue standing when my knees wobbled so violently. The speaker, a Poplar gentleman, was annoyed at my factual remarks about rats. If I had talked sentiment and "sob stuff" he probably would have sent me a check. Telling ordinary facts elicits sparkling, crackling anger.

I have never regretted the radio rat speech. Soon after, a ten-foot trench was cut into our road stretching from Kingsley

Hall to Children's House and new drainage pipes were laid. Rats were effectually expelled for the next ten years or so.

* * *

In the maternity ward of one of our East End hospitals six of the mothers lying there were homeless. They were not vagrants in the accepted sense, but respected citizens whose husbands were in full-time work. They had been evicted because the landlord's son wanted their house or because the adjacent multiple firm was expanding and had bought up the row of dwelling-houses for conversion purposes. These women had spent their time of pregnancy sleeping in licensed lodging-houses, where there is no privacy and a different bed is occupied each night, where diseased, drunken, and dissolute companions are their accepted lot.

One of the difficulties of making half a house into a whole home is that the upstairs people often have to pass through the downstairs people's kitchen in order to get to the lavatory in the yard.

The weekly "wash" is a problem in a one-room home. After the linen is clean, the drying process has to be undertaken in the kitchen. It is a chancy business, stringing cords just below the ceiling to and fro across the room. People have to dodge the wet garments as best they can. A clammy shirt sleeve suddenly cleaving to the nape of one's neck does not improve the disposition. Throughout the next day, a pile of rough-dried garments accumulate on the arm-chair, table, and dresser. Such a demoralized-looking bundle!

* * *

When some specially flagrant unfairness occurred, causing me to protest to the first hard-headed business man I met, whether he were relative or friend, the advice nearly always given was: "Write to the press. Such things ought to be widely known." They always took it for granted that editors wanted such news, that I had time to write, rewrite, edit, type, and post off articles on top of a sixteen-hour schedule. This business of telling the truth about conditions presents a continual problem to me. Publicity is the only thing some people fear. An aroused public opinion has been the cause of most reforms. Telling the truth is perhaps the pacifist's only weapon. Over and over again, even the suggestion that one may publish the facts has changed a scornful, bullying opponent into an almost subservient helper.

*　　*　　*

At the end of the war came the municipal elections in which Labour swept the polls in many boroughs. George Lansbury, our beloved Member of Parliament, now also became our first Socialist mayor, with thirty-five Labour supporters and a Conservative opposition of only six. We began to plan for setting up the kingdom of heaven! The Maternity and Child Welfare Act had just been put upon the statute Book at Westminster. This law made possible far-reaching improvements if energetically administered. Some local authorities in various parts of the country were not prepared to work it to its fullest capacity, but we East Enders had some thirty years of civic education behind us. A set of reliable people were appointed on the Maternity and Child Welfare Committee of the Borough Council, most of them women, nearly all working-people, determined to safeguard the lives of the children committed to their care.

Unemployment, unknown for five years, was becoming rife once more. Our Borough Council after long and careful consideration decided on a policy which evoked obloquy and fear from the unimaginative rich. The councillors decided that the standard of living should not be allowed to drop to the unhealthy low level which we had known in the past, that destitution and disease should not be thus encouraged, anyhow in Poplar. Our total expenditure on the poor assumed formidable proportions. Our Borough Council argued that unemployment was not a local but a national problem, precipitated by war, and aggravated by the terms of the Versailles Treaty and other Government acts. Because we let France take several trainloads of coal free every day out of the Ruhr, not only would German labour approximate to slave conditions, but our own colliers in Wales would be unable to buy our London industrial products. Because the Indian nationalist leaders were antagonized, irritated, snubbed, and spied on by the servants of our imperialists, they refused to buy our products, preferring those of any country to Britain's.

So Poplar's rates soared to 25 shilling in the pound. The landlords passed on the burden to us tenants and we paid, gritting our teeth and knowing that something must soon be going to happen.

Since pre-war days, there had been a steady pressure of enlightened public opinion upon Government to equalize the rates of London. The Poor Rate, so solid Liberals had argued, should not bear with such heavy incidence on the East End boroughs. As Westminster, Kensington, the City and other rich boroughs were served by the denizens of the poor boroughs who drove their trains, kept their drains in order, unloaded their fruit at the docks, and manufactured their household goods, they should pay more towards their welfare.

For years deputations urging this had been gravely received, and their requests docketed. A measure of relief had been granted in 1894 when every borough was obliged to contribute something to an equalization fund, about sixpence in the pound. Such a sum was obviously insufficient. When another rise in the rates appeared imminent, our Poplar Borough Councillors publicly declared that they would not sanction it. As the Government refused to take action to enlarge our receipts from the Common Poor Fund, we must take action ourselves. We would not risk lowering our people's health. We determined that our expenditure on the poor should continue, but as a result we would be unable to pay our annual share of the Expenses of the Metropolitan Police Force, nor could we meet our bill for water due to the Metropolitan Water Board, nor could we afford to pay the London County Council for the luxury of education. We were proud of our schools and of our children's aptitude for learning, but physical health came first and it depended on food, housing, and fuel, which we had to provide. We could not meet our liabilities incurred in fever hosptials and mental asylums conducted by the Metropolitan Asylums' Board.

To refuse to pay the precepts legally due from us was an exciting gesture. The population was proud of its Borough Council's courage. They knew that the processes of law immediately set in motion would eventually land them in jail for contempt of court. Enthusiasm was widespread.

So the mayor and several members of Parliament, some twenty-six men and women in all, went to Brixton or Holloway Prison. They were arrested at various hours and on different days, but as each Councillor was apprehended, the citizens' pride and approval grew greater—cheering crowds filled the streets. It was all great fun. It also meant something very real and solid.

For the most part, working-people are inarticulate. They can rarely explain their hopes, aspirations, and principles, but this time there was a clear issue to present to the world. Those twenty-six men and women accepted incarceration to symbolize the principle that persons are more valuable than property, the community more important than private gain. This is not to suggest that those twenty-six were saints, but we were conscious that our rate battle of 1921 was a high-water mark of citizenship.

Those in authority apparently expected the prisoners to give way after a few weeks, but they wouldn't. On only one condition would they give up their intransigence and sign the checks for the unpaid precepts, and that was that the Common Poor Fund be substantially enlarged by contributions from the rich boroughs.

An impasse occurred. Neither side would give way. The poor Prime Minister, Mr. Lloyd George, taking his holiday in the highlands of Scotland, was pursued from loch to loch, from hotel to hotel, by a deputation of London mayors, all Labour men, who were trying to make him face the issue. We voting citizens of Poplar likened our imprisoned mayor to St. Paul, who embarrassed another Imperialist government by refusing to come out of jail until he had gained his point.

After about nine weeks it was decided to push a bill through Parliament, called the Metropolitan Borough (financial provisions) Act which permitted the charging on the Metropolitan Common Poor Fund of all the expenditure on outdoor relief and increased the allowance for indoor poor from fivepence per day per head to one shilling and threepence. The expenditure on outdoor relief was thus equalized throughout London. In addition the local authorities were to be allowed to borrow money in anticipation of the expected receipt from the Fund and to charge the interest of such borrowings on the Fund. This brought over £450,000 annually into our coffers, and relieved Poplar's rates by more than ten shillings in the pound, and every other poor Borough benefited proportionately.

There was one casualty. Alderman Minnie Lansbury, George Lansbury's daughter-in-law, Edgar's wife, contracted some throat trouble during her incarceration and died soon after her release. It was to take her place that I was nominated to the alderman's seat. But I never took her place. I hadn't her grasp of affairs, her whole-time devotion, her vivacious and wonderful knack of getting things done. I was a passable stop-gap for four and a half years' service, nothing more. I think my splendid and experienced fellow Councillors recognized that my chief contribution would be to "stand up to" the army of critics who spoke and wrote as though we were anarchists, to reply in their own language to the superior Oxford-voiced, almost supercilious, arguments put forward from time to time by permanent Government officials.

I was made chairman of the Maternity and Child Welfare Committee. Of course we were proud of our numerous clinics. We were the first local authority to set up dental clinics for mothers. These and the new artificial-sunlight clinic improved the health of our babies. We distributed free milk wherever the total family income was below a certain scale approved by the Ministry of Health, and it cost us £5,000 to do it. Our infant-mortality rate dropped from the highest to the lowest in all London. Then, one afternoon in committee, a Government order was received requiring us to cut down our expenditure on these services. We stoutly refused. As chairman I proposed a resolution, stating that as it was against our conscience to reduce the milk supply by a single half-pint, we refused to obey the new regulation. One official, the only man present, profoundly objected to our action and his efforts to talk down the resolution extended for several minutes. Of course we women enjoyed the struggle. When at last he paused for breath, the resolution was put, seconded, and passed unanimously. The Ministry of Health sent for us and we went up to Whitehall, reinforced by most of the Councillors, including our four M. P.'s. The Ministry also had marshalled its forces in battle array. I felt sorry for the doctor who had been roped in by them, surely involuntarily. But a Government official has to obey. An awkward thing to have to back up arguments to prove that milk for children was not so important, after all.

They began by reminding us that it was no wish of theirs to curtail our expenditure, but when the Treasury orders economy, there is nothing to do but obey. We countered by reminding them that whenever an economy policy is ordered, the War Office and the Admiralty always find some reason for not obeying and we hoped our action would furnish the Ministry of Health with an excuse for taking the same line.

To and fro the polite arguments sped. It was good fun, for we knew that in no circumstances would we give way. The last question fell to my lot as chairman of the committee to answer. One could not have chosen a more apt finale. "Can you tell us why," inquired the suave voice, "when every other local authority throughout the country has accepted the unfortunate necessity of curtailing expenditure on maternity and child welfare, you alone have refused?" "I think I can," I answered in mild tones. "It's because ours is the only Maternity and Child Welfare Committee composed wholly of people who themselves live down the same streets and alleys as the children. We can see them every day. We should have to watch them growing pale and thin and weak if the milk grant were to be lowered."

Three weeks later we heard that we had won. The five thousand pounds expenditure was to continue. It is a dangerous thing, however, to rest on one's laurels. At the next committee we staked a further claim. We sent a requisition for a further grant to permit us to provide Grade A Tuberculin Tested milk, instead of the ordinary brand, for our delicate children. Although this was expensive enough to be debarred from the average middle-class table, our claim was allowed.

*　　*　　*

Bernard Shaw's *Saint Joan* appeared in London. The heat of the summer I shall always remember because I spent so many evenings in close contact with the theatre roof. Many parties were made up at Kingsley Hall. We would travel west together, stand an hour or more outside the gallery door, pay our one and threepence, climb up to the heights, and take our places on the benches. Such narrow benches! And so ill constructed that even those with short legs couldn't sit straight! Our knees had to point all the same way, to the right or to the left. When one of us shifted his position, the rest had to follow suit. I saw the play seven times that summer. Finally I wrote to Sybil Thorndike, feeling she would want to know

82

what *Saint Joan* meant to working-people. I told her how, at the end of the first court scene, a girl thrust her elbow into Mary Jane's ribs and the midst of all the applause exclaimed, "Coo, Miss, when she says 'Who is for God and for Joan?' don't it make yer feel yer want to jump down on to the stage and stand beside her and shout out, 'I'm with yer?'"

* * *

Six or seven members of the General Workers' Union had been giving their services every week to Kingsley Hall. As they did their jobs of stewarding, stoking, clearing, keeping order, looking after the billiard table, I began to understand something of the selfless devotion that lay behind the history of that great trade union. The banner of the local branch was a noticeable bit of work. It portrayed various symbols of brotherhood, painted or appliqued onto a rich blue-and-silver satin background. Rolling and unrolling its thirty square feet of colour was almost a ritual. Whenever it was loaned to us for some special occasion, the hands of the old workman who was responsible for its safe-keeping were manifestly tender towards it. I was proud to be allowed to join the union.

Soon a struggle for better hours and more adequate pay drew the railway men out on strike. They asked me to address their open-air meeting in Reeves Road. Although they knew the entire situation better than I, some of the ablest workmen were still inarticulate, and our family has too obviously the gift of the gab. It was real joy to be accepted and trusted by this valiant, anxious crowd. As I finished my speech and steadying hands were helping me descend from the rickety platform, one of the older men gripped my hand and muttered in a gruff voice, with a look of serene satisfaction, "Come and 'ave a wet, mate." Inside his kitchen, the kettle was already singing on the hob and his wife had everything set out for tea.

* * *

We set to work on the Borough Council and put up communal laundries in little back streets where a big copperful can be washed by machinery, dried and pressed in an hour or so for a shilling and two pence. At first there was difficulty about getting the machinery. An association of laundry-owners told the engineering firm which produced laundry machinery that if they sold any of it to the Poplar Borough Council they would withdraw their custom. The threat was ignored and carried out.

*   *   *

Variously to divide mankind into two parts according to temperament, character, cast, or creed has been a favourite pastime with amateur philosophers. I wonder if there exists a more positive line of demarcation than that dividing the man who has and the man who has not an extra half-crown that he can lay his hand on at any moment. The person who is always in sight of his last shilling develops a different outlook on life. The missing of a train may spell disaster. He cannot take the next. He only holds a workman's ticket. Or suppose he meets a person in distress. He is a good Samaritan by nature but he stifles his impulse to help. It is bad form to make a fuss at the loss of a coin, but he must, because there isn't another to take its place. A feeling of inferiority grips him at last. There are so many inhibitions for a man without an extra shilling.

Apart from special occasions there is a constant long-drawn-out anxiety as to what will occur when his coat won't hold together any longer. One of the bravest things I remember took place at a public meeting when a boy of seventeen, already burdened with stage fright, gave his club's report in the momentary expectation of splitting his trousers. But for his admiring mother I should not have known why he made so many excuses when he was chosen for this bit of service.

A carpenter consistently refused to do his share of speaking. As he was an able and popular person, I asked him eventually what rights he had to hold back from giving service. It was his upper dentures that were unreliable, not himself. They habitually descended. He could only camouflage the fact by affecting a silent manner.

Herein is the bitterness of poverty. Material shortage creates a feeling of inferiority not directly, but by devious routes, shaking confidence in oneself, leading inevitably to a loss of confidence in others, in God and, at last, in life itself.

*   *   *

These four and a half years have been compressed fairly stringently to confine them within the limits of a few pages. It was at the beginning of this period that I was induced by Paul Gliddon, of the Fellowship of Reconciliation, to speak every week at open-air meetings in Hyde Park. For two and a half years I pursued this great and exhilarating game. What agony I suffered during the hours immediately preceding each meeting! What elation once I'd got going! One starts talking to a dog, a lamp-post, and one's companion who makes a valiant attempt to appear a stranger arrested in the act of passing by. Park habitues stroll up, stare, listen critically, and then either drift off to the next platform, twelve feet away, to test the oratory there, or, scenting the chance of some good brisk heckling at the end of the address, they settle down to listen intelligently. Sightseers and strangers join the group, diffidently, poised as though ready for flight at the first intimation of either atheism or evangelistic appeal. A drunk interrupts some important statistical information. The good-humoured crowd knows how to deal with the situation. At first they ignore him and advise the speaker to do so. If he proves persistent they growl at him, or make some humorous remark at his expense calculated to drive him either to silence or to quit. If he is too far gone to react in the proper way to these tactics, some self-sacrificing person will edge up to him, engage him in conversation, showering such flattering personal attention upon him that he is led step by step out of the circle, to where his animadversions upon the universe lead to no antisocial effects. At the end of the forty-minute speech comes question time. That is where a sort of intoxication threatens the speaker and definite steps have to be taken to moderate it. My subject was always the same, something that had occurred during the week, published in the news columns devoted to foreign affairs, argued out in Parliament or seen down our street in Bow. We examined the happening critically instead of accepting it as part of the natural order of things. We would analyse it, considering how it might appear in the sight of God, and draw our conclusions as to its significance according to its eventual effect on the coming generation.

All the usual anti-religious traps were prepared for me, ingenuously introduced. The misquotation of the words of

Jesus about the poor and about the coming of another world war were generally in evidence. We rarely missed the amusingly naive justification of military preparedness by reference to to the bit of plaited cord with which Jesus shepherded the gentle sacrificial beasts out of the temple courts where they surely never wished to be penned. Very often too, the question was asked: "Which should one concentrate on first, the conversion of the individual sinner so that he may change his manner of living, or the improvement of social conditions so that the individual shall have the opportunity to improve?" One became accustomed to the expression of childish triumph on the faces of such academic hecklers. It seemed almost heartless to evade their little dilemma and ask them why not do both things at once? They looked quite nonplussed, almost hurt, by such vulgar realism. When the superficial questions were well over, we would get down to fundamentals. Then quite often the human spirit, diverse, sincere, and steadfast in its longing for God would stand revealed. We would separate long after dark—unknown as to names, dwelling-place, or politics, but trusting each other. After a time the meeting took on some of the features of an open-air church. During the week, this sense of loyalty and solidarity would gradually evaporate, and by the time I climbed on the bus the following Tuesday for an hour's jolt to the West End I had lost all feeling about the meeting except a vague sense of wretchedness. Carrying the platform the half-mile to the Park did not tend to improve matters. It was a collapsible wooden affair. Its legs were supposed to fold up and remain tautly fastened to its sides, but they always came adrift and flapped against my own and my companions' and, alas! sometimes against passers-by. When the contraption was safely erected in our pitch, I knew the horrid hour had arrived. I remember once setting myself on the lowest step of the platform, facing the green of the Park, with my back to where the crowd would be. I gazed into the foliage of the Park's fine trees, not with an eye to inspiration or delight, but caught in a miserable mist of spiritual bankruptcy. What have I to give to these people? Plenty, if we could sit and talk quietly together, one at a time or in groups; but facing a crowd, where one must be as alert as a winged dandelion seed in the spring breeze? The silly questions need one sort of treatment, the sincere questions another. The high calling of a speaker is to justify the ways of

God to man, and I'm certainly not properly prepared. I have a wealth of illustrations from my neighbours' daily lives and my own as to the unchristian nature of the social and economic system under which we all live. But I know that we need a lot more self-discipline, all of us, rich and poor, before we can create anything strong and sound enough to take the place of what we are trying to get rid of. We need to practise the presence of God, voluntary poverty, and offering the other cheek. Shall I be able to get that across to a crowd? Oh, why did I come! I can't even think of an introduction, and the introduction is of the greatest importance at an open-air meeting. The main argument must not be allowed to begin for eight or nine minutes in order to give the crowd time to collect. And suppose the crowd doesn't collect, after all! At last in sheer desperation I jerked myself to my feet and turned round to climb up the rickety couple of steps. There in the twilight stood some two hundred people, quietly assembled, awaiting me, kind-eyed and with a little anxiety in their look, as though they had sensed my hesitations and self-distrust.

It was a very lovely time we had together that night.

Training
Preparation for the Disarmed Life

Muriel Lester believed that the universe has phys-ical, moral, and spiritual laws that express the har-mony and purpose of God. Abiding by these laws requires that we lead disciplined lives, which will prepare us to live life to the fullest and which will further the Reign of God in the world.

In her speeches and writings, Muriel Lester fre-quently referred to the need for training. Good inten-tions and sentiments are woefully lacking in building the strength of character and courage necessary in a world where war and injustice are rife, a conviction that grew in her in the 1930s as totalitarianism grew to alarming proportions. In 1940, with war breaking out across Europe and Asia, the future looked very ominous. In response to this situation, Lester wrote a booklet entitled Training, *which did not contain theo-retical reflections. She had traveled in countries mo-bilizing for war and in places where war had already broken out. She agonized in the face of tyranny, death, and destruction. She sought a response that would speak to the present moment in the light of the Reign of God rather than by the claims of nation-states and the popular passions of patriotism.*

From *The Prayer School*

Gerald Heard (in *The Code of Christ*) declares that the word "meek" in the Beatitudes means *trained.* It is naive to want peace or justice or happiness or any other fine thing unless we train ourselves to get them and study how to hold them when once possessed. "License they mean when they

cry Liberty! for who loves that must first be wise and good."
Milton's splendid cry is pungent with meaning for us in these
days. There will be no New World Order unless we are "wise
and good.": until we become "meek": if we are not
trained. ... Canon Pym translates the words of Jesus when He
explains to the disappointed disciples why they had failed to
cure the epileptic, "You can't expect to drive out evil like that
unless you equip yourselves by prayer." ... What you sow you
reap; the moral universe is as orderly as the physical. Professor Henry Drummond asks why we are so foolish as to accept
the fact that grain grows in orderly fashion according to the
seasons, according to conditions of soil and climate, according
to the hard work put into its cultivation by each individual
farmer, and then to imagine that character grows by caprice.
It does seem a little mad to keep saying one is seeking truth;
wanting to be religious; wishing one weren't so weak-willed
and so on, when day follows day and finds one still aimlessly
wishing, still ineffectually talking, and doing nothing.

Gerald Heard also tells us of the Indian who wanted
enlightenment. At least he said he did. He kept coming do
Buddha with much talk but did not find what he said he was
looking for. One day while they were bathing, Buddha held
the man's head firmly under the water for a long time. When
he let go and the poor fellow had got over his choking and
spluttering, Buddha asked what he had wanted more than
anything else when he was submerged. With no hesitation the
man answered, "Air." "Well," said Buddha, "when you want
enlightenment as much as you wanted air just now you'll get
it."

Our world has been called "a school for saints." This
conception seems to fit the facts. Those who refuse to learn
the lesson set [in front of] them get into horrible muddles later.
The pupil who is so baffled by a complicated sum that he gives
up the attempt to work it out and copies the answers from his
neighbour's book is going to find the next problem far harder,
and the next after that actually unsolvable. If you try to take
easy short cuts like that, you won't arrive.

You never learn wisdom so long as you have to look on
the world as a place where you can do what you like, a domain
in which you have a right to happiness: if you go on being
surprised at injustice, regarding it as a sort of aberration or
a personal affront for which you must exact redress or apol-

ogy, you become narrow-minded, however much you pride yourself on being an intellectual; sometimes this attitude leads to a sort of psychological apoplexy; one gets stiffened up, rigid with censoriousness. ...

We have to train ourselves to strip off the hard crust which we have allowed to grow around our sensitiveness: to get rid of the demanding side of our characters: to learn to look on the whole universe as God's and ourselves as part of it, subject to His laws. We have to work unceasingly at learning the tempo, the rhythm, the orderliness of which God has made us part.

If, in the middle of a paragraph or even of a sentence in the thriller we happen to be reading, we remember something God wants us to do, we must be ready to break off. "Is there a thought within my heart that strives with Thee, Thy throne to share? Ah! tear it hence and rule alone, the Lord of every motive there."

"But that's beyond me," says someone. Of course. So was Differential Calculus when you were at the beginner's stage. So, for that matter, was your multiplication table before you had begun to get the hang of it, but sticking to it and practice brought ease and confidence. Let us therefore work out a very simple discipline that touches the three sides of our personality—body, mind and spirit.

The Body. Stilling the tongue for a certain period each day. Walking alone. Giving up a meal or two every week. Relaxing one's muscles. Physical exercises. Learning to look *through* one's eyes instead of *with* one's eyes. Seeing in every quarter we are wont to spend on ourselves a clear, unexaggerated picture of a Chinese person provided with nourishing food, who otherwise would die. Approaching Socrates' state of freedom spontaneously expressed one day when in his wanderings he found himself in a big and popular market place glutted with food. "Good Heavens!" he said, "who would have thought there were so many things I don't want?"

The Mind. Spending the minimum of time on newspapers and radio news. Eschewing most magazines. Reading something solid at least half an hour every day. Those who think they can't spare this time should explain to friends or family and read at one of their three meals. Reminding ourselves that what we read must not be absorbed as necessarily true; it only sometimes is. Guarding against the common tendency to imagine that the superior tone of many of the post-war critics, essayists and poets means that they know the truth about life: it is interesting in this connection to discover the writer's personal outlook on the world, how he's running his own life, developing the various sides of his own nature; whether he knows even how to be happy. Never dodging a difficulty; always facing it steadily even if you can't see the way through: if we face it, we'll see a little further every year. Never grumbling, speaking out the truth boldly, any time, anywhere: for to grumble is to fritter away precious energy; cynicism partially paralyzes one; it is effective only as a poison for suicides. Remember that the possession of a healthy, free and unoppressed mind can be ours if we are willing to observe the necessary discipline. And in this, what applies to the body applies equally to the mind. The golden rule to keep unswervingly, unflinchingly, is never to grow slack. Whatever the form of discipline you adopt as your own, let it be as beautifully balanced, as poised, as the supple body of a ballerina.

The Spirit. Ignatius' *Spiritual Exercises.* The Indian saint's habit of letting the food remain on his plate until he had fully recollected that it had come to him from the Hand of God. Brother Lawrence's *Practice of the Presence of God,* which turns every moment into a joy. Thomas Trahearne's dictum:

> Your enjoyment of the world is never right till every morning you awake in heaven: see yourself in your Father's palace, and look upon the skies, the earth and the air as celestial joys. ... You never enjoy the world aright till the sea itself floweth into your veins, till you are clothed with the heavens and crowned with the stars." The mediaeval mystic's habit of stilling the senses one by one, then trying to break down in imagination the bounds of time until one tastes eternity, then recognizing that the bounds of place also are not real, not binding upon one, "that God can spin one backwards or forwards, to the right hand or to the left hand, for behold! we are in His hands, ready for all. We desire nothing other than the doing of His will. Oh! that we may do it willingly and perfectly.

From *Training*

In Germany and Russia they specialize in the disciplined life. Our lives have to be even more disciplined. We must out-train the totalitarians, out-match their "intrepidity, contempt for comfort, surrender of private interest, obedience to command" with a superior courage, frugality, loyalty and selflessness.

Our job is bigger than theirs. It is to spread the Kingdom of Heaven, the Rule of God. Our business is to stop war, to purify the world, to get it saved from poverty *and* riches, to make people like each other, to heal the sick, and comfort the sad, to wake up those who have not yet found God, to create joy and beauty wherever we go, to find God in everything and in everyone.

Without confidence the body politic tends to disintegrate. Without confidence business is impossible. Without confidence we can do nothing. There is power, unseen, indefinable, inherent in the stuff of life which always responds to confidence. How can we link all of ourselves to this power? What must we do to acquire the strength of spirit, the carefree joy without which life is a lame and rather smirched affair? Are there any rules?

During the past few years groups of people, young mostly—in America, in Berlin, in Vienna, in Fano and in England—have met together at odd and awkward hours to work out a set of techniques for living the disciplined life. Here are some:

To disarm—not only our bodies by refusing to kill, or to make killing instruments in munitions factories—but to disarm our minds of anger, pride, envy, hate and malice. We should stop praying the Lord's Prayer until we can see that "Our Father" means we are "tied to the same living tether" not only with fellow countrymen but with everybody on this planet. In this perspective, righteous indignation is soon found to be a noxious growth, fostered by the pleasure we feel unconsciously in comparing our imagined rectitude with the obvious evil of other nations. Owning up to our own share of blame in any awkward situation that arises in international as well as home or church or social life, is a pre-condition of getting a new start made. Usually it is the most sensible and perhaps least blameworthy person who makes the first move. He may not be conscious of any particular guilt of his own, but he takes it for granted that, being in general a sinner, he had some hand in it, and he sets the healing process going by not excusing himself, and by shouldering his share of the general blame. No matter how morally superior we feel, this fact remains: no one can suddenly become our enemy because he happens to have been born the other side of a river, or a strip of sea, and two governments have signed a bit of paper called an ultimatum. Violence creates violence. This applies to our mental moods. Our anger, pride, envy, hate, malice and "righteous indignation" are murderous. However deep they have twined into our personality, we must pluck them out, though such drastic uprooting may entail agony. Self-pity also has to go. Self-pity is a perfect preparation for dictatorship.

What we call non-violence is not enough. It may still be camouflaged cowardice. Non-violence to be effective must be allied with the vow of truth. To pretend that the aggressor is not aggressing, as was done by certain great powers during the rape of Manchuria and the destruction of Spain, is to stultify personality; it is to destroy morale and imperil the future by destroying the ability to think straight. Gandhi's followers train themselves to speak the truth without fear and without exaggeration; to tell it to people who do not want to hear it, or in the quarters where the telling of it may lose them their jobs or land them in jail. Gandhi was obeying the vow of truth when he declared that the British *government* was "Satanic" but that the British *people* must be loved and on occasion copied, for they have certain virtues which the Indian lacks, just as the Indian has virtues which the British lack.

But even non-violence plus truth is not enough. There is a third necessity—non-co-operation. This takes sublime courage; the courage not to raise one's hand and say "Heil Hitler;" the courage of Japanese soldiers who have refused to kill Chinese. War-resistance implies non-co-operation.

If our country were suddenly Hitlerized, or Stalinized, we should have to refuse to keep the imposed laws at whatever cost. This implies that we must make ourselves spiritually and physically fit to endure torture.

We must keep at the top of our form, ready for anything. It is rather an insult to God to make it appear that He is such a bad engineer as to be continually turning out machines that don't work. Poise, endurance, strength, the serenity that comes from the open-air life—all these things characterised Jesus. To walk three or four miles a day is one step in this direction. (Mr. Ford will somehow survive.) The body is the temple of something far more holy than we may suspect. Holiness means health, wholeness and completeness. To let the spirit of God thus rule our lives eventually brings real fulfilment. On that basis problems such as sex solve themselves. And voluntary simplicity becomes exhilarating just as going without pie sharpens the alertness and staying power of a long distance runner.

We must face the fact that the present economic order is not God's. Why do we wait for revolutions or elections? Why not begin now to readjust our personal economic life? "If you possess superfluities, while your brethren lack necessities, you are possessing the goods of others and are therefore stealing." A growing number of people realize that they have a right to the satisfaction of their needs, physical and cultural, but beyond that their property is not really theirs at all. According to the law of the land it belongs to them. According to the law of God it belongs to the people who need it – God's other children. It's rather a lark working out all these common sense ideas, even in the midst of a distraught and distressing world. We might meet with like-minded people, a group of three is enough to begin with, and state how much money each of us received during the previous month by earnings, income or gift, and exactly how we spent it; confessing thus the measure of our greed and our need with equal frankness. The persistence of the worship of the golden calf is due in part to a secrecy and pride and false sanctity with which we treat money matters.

We discuss with our friends our thoughts, our religious ideas, our love affairs, but we rarely let them know our income.

We might leave out one meal a week, not only to provide a little fund for the propagation of our ideas, but to recall our errant thoughts to the hunger of many friends, and raise other people's standard of living by lowering our own. Ours, even in peacetime, not to promulgate vegetarianism, to despise the delight of chocolates, to fear the effects of nicotine, but it seems a bit vulgar to consume in a few seconds the price of a week's food for a Chinese family. The more we like candy, smokes and cakes, the more potent reminders they become, when we refuse to take them, of our unemployed friends and of the undernourished millions in the Orient. To do without dessert so that a Chinese child may be kept alive for a whole day (it only costs three cents to do that!) does not rob one of energy. It enhances one's sense of solidarity. It makes ones more alive.

There is a plentitude in the world of all good things; enough raw materials for food, fuel and clothing to satisfy the needs of every inhabitant of the globe. But we cannot enjoy too much cake while others have no bread.

If you and I love God with all our hearts and all our wills and all our wits, we will not leave the job of breaking down barriers of class, nation or race to isolated efforts here and there. We will work together with other people in organized social pressures to distribute goods according to a sound economic plan so that the "haves" and "have-nots" shall gain equitable access to the abundance of this earth. Ought not all the Lord's people to be ready to speak out the truth, to face officials, magistrates, editors, archbishops and dictators, and give them a message of common sense in the name of God and the common people? "I claim no privileges that others cannot have the counterpart of on the same terms," said Eugene V. Debs. [A labor organizer and co-founder of the Socialist Party.] Can't we who are relatively over-privileged go a little way toward his position?

The idea of being stripped of superfluities is so that others may enjoy what otherwise we should be stealing from them. It is also so that we ourselves may be more athletic, more alert to expect "that of God" in every man we meet. Let us remember that it is far easier to love enemies whom we have never seen, who live hundreds of miles away, than our next-door neighbour whose dog or radio irritates us. The vertical barriers that separate country from country are easier to break through than the horizontal barriers that separate man from man in the same city; barriers between those of different races, class and character. When one has learned to recognize a spark of God's spirit in the least reputable of one's neighbours, one has more power to drop all labels and to work for that justice which must underlie the making of peace.

The only way to get strong enough to keep at it is to practice the presence of God. We have to force ourselves to return many times in a morning from worry and self-pity, from fear and defeatism, from conceit and callousness, to the Unseen Reality of the Eternal.

When we are overtaken in a fault, in sin, in a new realization of our own pitiful weakness, and hypocrisy we do not grieve overmuch. We lift up our hearts to God immediately as Brother Lawrence advises, not delaying a second, and we say: "Lord, I shall always go on doing such and such, unless I keep closer to Thee." Those who are not rooted deeply enough in God, who are not disciplined by prayer to face facts and repent of sins and gain power to make a fresh start, tend to project their self-disgust on to others. They lose confidence in the future, in life itself.

We keep silent, solitary, if possible, for half an hour a day. During this period we enjoy completely relaxed muscles and nerves. We walk or sit or lie and we let our breathing become slow, and deep and regular. The surprising restfulness that ensues at the end of fifteen minutes or so makes one understand that the rhythm of the Universe of God's, and is keeping our own bodies and minds sane and sound. God's spirit breathed into man's nostrils the breath of life and he became a living soul. His Creative Spirit is also the Recreative Spirit. Our nights and our awakening are no longer haunted by apprehensions of things undone, by self-disgust, by dread of some coming ordeal, for each of these fears and shames is faced in the presence of God. How is it possible to dread an interview with anyone, when we know God will be the third Person present at that conversation? The world is God's, though one has to rally all one's forces to keep aware of the fact. The world is God's, though our breakfast coffee is spoilt by its proximity to a newspaper full of horrors.

We can no longer make the affirmation lightheartedly. Yet to confess that the world is not God's, to say He has failed, abdicated, that another method, not God's must be adopted, is to court disintegration, to commit the ultimate blasphemy. It would blacken the skies with bombing aeroplanes and with despair. And by no stretch of the imagination could it be called a noble despair. For if we forcibly detach ourselves from our particular fears and hates, recriminations and regrets, if we submit ourselves to the cleansing power of events, we see that our narrow vision, our callous self-indulgence, our lazy, purposeless living, our profit-seeking, our tenacious hold on national, racial and personal privileges, *have materially helped to create the present agony.*

In quietness and confidence is our strength. From now on, we're committed to the exciting, dangerous but never dull task of using all our available powers. It is because we have used only a fraction of our available powers that our bodies have been poisoned with silly, bitter, angry thoughts, or the sense that we have no place in the world.

We accept the fact that most of God's work is done slowly, remembering how long it takes Him to make a tree. Lots of His work is done in the dark, in secret, underground. Isn't it an honor for us to be given work like that, quiet and low and regular rather than the showy kind? We may face the firing squad. Again, nothing externally dramatic like that may ever happen to us. What difference?

Ours is to keep sensitive enough to be in contact with God daily, to practice life as an art. Many times a day we are to sharpen our hunger for that perfection which is the goal of all art by putting ourselves through certain necessary scales and exercises just as a good pianist does.

* * *

Under such a discipline the pride of the whole world, regimented, mechanized, apparently almighty, may be arrayed against us. Even so, we will not "bow our heads to insolent might." We cannot say why God has revealed it to us, but having once seen we cannot un-see it. It is the will of the Eternal that we should refuse any longer to hate and lie and kill. And we can discover our individual lives merging themselves ever more completely into the life of the world.

Most of us need the reinforcement of a small intimate group of friends plugging away shoulder to shoulder toward the same objective—if we are to persist rigorously. Over the world are many vital experiments in such team work.

One group has had some success following this procedure:

(1) Each meeting begins with a reminder that during the discussion the aim is not to exert power "over" others but to gain power "with" others, not to beat somebody over the head with a dogma but share experience and find the truth.

(2) Then a moment or two of silent meditation in which each person present thinks of every other person present with a special effort to understand and appreciate. That moment should also be one in which each person seeks to open himself as a channel for the best.

(3) After social and personal issues are discussed and action planned, the lights are turned out. Each one in turn

states in a sentence what comes to him as most significant at the time. He may even ask the group to pray every morning for a few days about this matter. For example, he may be facing a very difficult situation with his boss or he may have on his mind the problem as to how to get churches to undertake the penny-a-meal Chinese rice-bowl project.

Finally, with or without words, each one briefly prays. Either during these prayers or in the silence that follows, absent friends are remembered and contact is renewed with persons like Kagawa [a radical Japanese Christian who lived a life of voluntary poverty in the infamous Shinkawa slum of Kobe. A poet and mystic, peace advocate, preacher and evangelist, he was also a prolific author and a recognized leader of Japan's labor, peasant, and cooperative movements.] and with causes like the peace movement.

(4) Members of the group are at some appointed time during the day, preferably in the morning, brought into consciousness. One after another is thought of as living up to his best during the whole day, being surrounded by the light of God's purpose.

(5) Sometimes daily questions such as these are undertaken for a period of a week or more: Morning, "What shall I do today to help make war impossible?" Evening, "What, today, have I done?"

(6) At various times this motivation is recalled: To embody in action the insight discovered in the group.

The more faithfully the members practice the individual discipline described previously, the better for the spirit of the group, since what happens during a meeting mostly depends upon the preparation that each individual as a result of daily practice brings to the group. Every group, of course, should work out and agree upon its own conditions to be fulfilled, no matter how at variance with other groups their procedure may be.

One indispensable feature of this group and indivdual discipline is the atmosphere of frankness and mutual trust. There must be the willingness sincerely to share insight in an objective manner, whether the realism punctures anybody's egocentricity or not.

There must also be regularity, faithfulness in attendance. Three or four are enough; more than a dozen, probably too many. There should perhaps be a check-up once a week to see who is careless about following through. Those that don't should understand that they are doing definite harm whenever slack. It should be made easy to drop out. High pressure methods and the kind of comradeship we desperately need just don't go together.

It was through the fellowship of the catacombs that early Christians achieved "the courage of the coliseum."

It is through the confidence of a small intimate group that we may find new energy, reverence and joy.

Why not you yourself—after reading this and thinking over the difficulties and the possibilities—start a group of two or three, right away?

From *A Way of Life*

...our job is to set up God's kingdom, God's reign, God's law on earth, in our own club and street and home. There's no end to the surprises that crop up once you start in on this job. It may take you to all sorts of places: it may take you half around the world or to the workhouse; it has taken quite a lot of people to the workhouse; some to the gallows.

It's exciting and surprising; it may be dangerous, but it's never dull.

Some people can manage to follow beautifully this way of life while they are attempting difficult things to do for God. They are splendidly courageous. Then, when the danger is past and the thrill over, there comes the call for a spell of quiet, unexciting spade work; at that point they go all to bits and give it up. That's because they've never understood God's way of work. Most of God's work is done slowly. ...

If we are to keep sensitive enough to be in contact with God daily, we must practise life as an art, just like any other art, through the humdrum discipline of scales and exercises, thus sharpening our hunger for that perfection which is the goal of all art. ...

The more one practices the scales of the devotional life, the more aware one becomes of both potential harmonies and disharmonies. Sometimes in the cold light before dawn, in an unexpected moment of solitude, we suddenly find ourselves facing stark reality—our future, the world's future, war, pain, hunger. We feel almost intimidated as we consider the condition of men and things.

One half the world is sick, fat with excess. The other half, like that poor beggar past us even now, who thanked us for a crust with tears.

The issue becomes clear and urgent: Are we going to spend our lives struggling and fighting for a place in the fat half? Or shall we tilt against the old spectres of war and inequality, unmasking them, stripping them of their glamour, revealing them as old fashioneed imposters whose tyranny we can no longer tolerate in a world that might be full of common sense, plenty and goodwill?

From *Dare You Face Facts?*

It's God's business after all, this business of saving the world; ours is only to go or come, to speak or be silent, to live or die. Some are already in prison in France, in Germany, in Japan and many other countries; some already are seeing more clearly because they have been freed from the body. More and more will be shot as war resisters. Some will outlast the war even if it drags on for many years. In that event Europeans will have learned to live in the dark, underground, or in caves. When fighting peters out through sheer exhaustion, when people dare at last to emerge into the open air, dazed, uncertain in their movements, suspicious, the barbarism of the Dark Ages may last many years. We can now start training ourselves for it. In God's mind is the perfect solution of every problem that torments mankind today. How can He communicate that to the world except through people who will attend to Him, forget for a time their puny selves, and expose their minds and souls to His wisdom? The question Isaiah heard in the court of Heaven is still ringing through the universe: "Whom shall we send and who will go for us?"

We must become the sort of person who can conserve the best values of civilization, who can hand them on to others who have become savages, who can spread again the sense of confidence between man and man, who can bring cooperation into being once more. Numbers of such disciplined people may be needed to cover the whole of Europe, each of them rooted deep in the Eternal and Unchanging, each of them focal points toward whom all people will gravitate, suspiciously at first, but with increasing confidence, until at length little communities will evolve and gradually unite into a commonwealth.

Worship

"Seeing Deep Down
Into the Heart of Things"

Worship, both public and private, was for Muriel Lester a necessary and central ingredient of life lived to its fullest. Unyielding in her criticism of dull, pedantic services and private devotions gone through out of unthinking habit, she nonetheless believed that a person of faith needed to consult her "compass" regularly for grounding, direction, inspiration, and meaning. To worship the God of all truth, beauty, and goodness is to bring those manifestations of divinity into one's life and to prepare one for extending the Reign of God into every aspect of personal and social existence.

From *Why Worship?*

There is nothing more illumining, more ennobling, than to be one of a company of people who have come together in order to free their spirit from entangling personal bonds, quiet their soul by silence, release their aspiration by music and poetry, concentrate their mind on spoken wisdom, open their heart to all that is good, true and beautiful, thus to tune themselves to God and to come into touch with Jesus Christ.

The practical effect of corporate worship is to weld varying individuals into a unity that can stand against the evil, disruptive forces of the world, its quarreling, its envying, and its war.

You cannot concentrate your mind and spirit in the worship of anything, good or bad, without acquiring something of the nature of the thing worshipped. To worship truth is to assimilate a part of truth. To worship beauty is to become in some measure beautiful. To worship courage is to begin to be brave.

Wherever worship becomes stereotyped and loses its spontaneity, a great calamity has occurred, for to worship by rote is to corrupt a holy thing to base usage.

What is the real meaning of this good old Anglo-Saxon word, "weorthscipe"? Weorth—worth, scipe—ship. It is the practice of seeing deep down into the heart of things and finding their real worth, looking out for essentials, discovering the worth of people, discerning God in them.

This may mean that you suddenly see an old friend actually for the first time, because never before have you noticed the real person, never before have you seen him in his relationship to God. It may mean that you recognize in a thorough-paced scoundrel, liar and shirker, a patch of goodness, native or acquired, so radiant that the memory of it inspires you ever afterwards.

There is a simple statement in the Hebrew Scriptures:

"Jacob worshipped, leaning upon the top of his staff" (Hebrews 11:21). As he stood at his tent-door in the twilight, gazing out into the trackless wild, as the great silver stars illumined the growing darkness, that lonely figure was the forerunner of our socialized and over-complicated programs of Divine Service in our multitudinous places of worship. Ruskin says we ask God for things as a child would ask his father for cake; we sing songs of praise as a happy child might sing songs about his father, "and yet we are impudent enough to call our beggings and chauntings 'Divine Service.'" Are we content to leave it at that?

One August, in Cornwall, long ago, I set out with a dear companion for a thirty-three-mile tramp. The sun was not yet up, but the birds were pouring out their song, heralding its coming, in what seemed to be a passion of ecstasy. Thus welcomed, it suddenly appeared between the thick branches of friendly trees and flooded the deep, narrow, winding lane along which we were tramping; everything was very quiet.

> Still, still with Thee, when purple morning breaketh,
> When the bird waketh, and the shadows flee;
> Fairer than morning, lovelier than daylight,
> Dawns the glad consciousness, I am with Thee.

As the lines came to my mind they were no longer merely part of a hymn from under a section labeled "Worship"; they interpreted reality; there was now beginning for me that which Watts-Dunton called "The Renascence of Wonder." To use the words attributed to Jesus Christ, "He that wonders shall reign and he that reigns shall rest. Look with wonder at that which is before thee" (Clement of Alexandria, *Stromateis* 2, 9, 45.)

We know the look in a child's face, when slowly awakening from sleep he begins to fix his slow, wondering gaze upon objects that surround him, the look that the great Florentine masters were able to perpetuate with their brush illumining the face of their Divine Bambino. It is to be found, as Wordsworth knew, in the eyes of every normal child. But we grown-ups have to win back for ourselves, after adolescence, that which was our birthright as children, when wonder was natural, worship instinctive, and the world new and fresh.

Milton tries to describe in words the jocund air of the earth in its first innocence; Handel uses music for the same purpose; Michelangelo color—but not even a genius can communicate it to us until we are ready for the revelation. Our childish experiences harden into the adolescent's pride, his jealous independence of spirit, his craving for consistency, his cruel logic. This self-sufficiency lasts long enough and blinds us very effectively. But throughout the whole of this egoistic phase, if we are honest with ourselves, if we keep what Jesus Christ calls "the single eye" (Matt. 6:22) which is a certain quality of steadfastness and alertness, a necessary condition of clear vision, then, when the time is ripe, we shall get our illumination, we shall suddenly find ourselves endowed with new powers of discernment; we shall rediscover the world and our neighbor.

Our childhood's wonder had its roots in ignorant innocence and was lost in the storms of self-development. But now we have won our way through to something infinitely more precious, a childlike acceptance of the whole universe of God, as our very own.

*   *   *

Worship Releases Us From the Domination of the Self. Just as a prisoner who is suddenly set free has no sort of doubt about his release, because it is a fact that has altered the very quality of life for him, so there is no doubt at all when we find ourselves definitely released from the prison-house of self. This release comes just so soon as we see our true worth, just so soon as we recognize ourselves as part of a worshipful whole, united to Him who is the source of all lovely things.

There is no greater tyrant than oneself. The most skilled tortures of the Inquisition were slight and transitory in comparison with exquisite agony inflicted by people on themselves. Until you can get release from self you are only half alive. You are the victim of your own good or bad moods, "or wailful or divine;" you are unstable, cramped, dissatisfied, rudderless.

That is why people of real capability and enthusiasm, endowed with a sincere desire to serve, sometimes remain failures for so long. At first they get on well in their job and are highly appreciated by those whom they are helping; but after a month or two they cannot help beginning to pull up their roots to see whether they are growing; they start taking their spiritual temperatures, analyzing their feelings inquiring into their own motives, suggesting that someone else might do their job better, wondering if they might not be, just as usefully, somewhere else.

They become impatient for results; they desire "to see of the travail of their soul, and to be satisfied," (Isa. 53:11) and, of course, they cannot. Only God can be satisfied. They fancy they are being slighted, or taken advantage of, or put upon. They convince themselves that they work harder than others do, but are less appreciated. They start estimating how much they have done. They remind themselves how tired they are. They ask why they shouldn't be "having a good time." They start pitying themselves; and to get sucked down into the slough of self-pity is a most perilous experience. Once immersed it is so easy to wallow there, without knowing that this particular mire, if it cling to one, can damn. Soon their own personality has come to loom so large upon their horizon that they cannot see anything straight. They are blinded. They feel everyone is against them, but actually they are their own worst enemy. Their little opinionated self is compact of the very stuff of tyranny and lords it over them unmercifully. "Who is this that follows me in the silent dark? I move aside to avoid his presence, but I escape him not. He makes the dust rise from the earth with his swagger; he adds his loud voice to

every word that I utter. He is my own little self, my lord."
(Tagore, *Gitanjali* p. 30)

The victims of self grow daily more wretched. They try to extract some consolation from the fact that they are free, independent, that they rely on no one but themselves. This cold comfort cannot satisfy any human soul, which, by its very nature, needs to be mastered by something stronger and better than itself before it can fulfill its destiny. Isolation, sleeplessness, thoughts of suicide, fear of madness, these dread visitants are thrust away time after time, yet they return. There is only one thing that is more potent, more constant, more overwhelming than these; that is God's love.

When the soul accepts that, then indeed comes immediate release from self.

> Make me a captive, Lord,
> And then I shall be free;
> Force me to render up my sword,
> And I shall conqueror be.
> My heart is weak and poor
> Until it master find;
> It has no spring of action sure—
> It varies with the wind.
> It cannot freely move,
> Till Thou has wrought its chain;
> Enslave it with Thy matchless love,
> And deathless it shall reign.

> —George Matheson

The forces within that were becoming muddy, turbulent, and dangerous, through having no outlet, are now set free. The ardors pent-up, hitherto reserved for a sterile thing like independence, now have free access to all created things. They find themselves suddenly endowed with the freedom of the Universe. Even death has no power over them. They begin their eternal life now, for "this is life eternal, that they might know thee the only true God, and Jesus Christ, whom thou has sent." (John 17:3)

Their job now—and it takes a whole lifetime to accomplish it—is to learn how to fit all the facts and theories that interest them, all the people and all the happenings of which they are cognizant, into their proper place against the large framework of meaning that they are beginning to discern throughout the fabric of the Universe.

*   *   *

Worship Releases Us From the Domination of Others. The extent to which most of us allow ourselves to be ruled by the opinion of others constitutes a virtual slavery. The summing up of a situation with the words, "It's not done," has put an end to many an instinctive act of generosity. Phrases such as…"Don't let the neighbors know," reveal the same fear of other people and consequent enslavement.

The denizens of Suburbia worrying about each other's opinions is a perennially amusing subject for satire from which much literary capital has been made. The people of a certain new housing estate to which enterprising and hard-working East Enders move out imagine that to work in one's garden is vulgar; only after dark, therefore, and even then rather furtively, the tenants sally forth from their back doors to cultivate the strip of land that they have longed for so many years to possess.

"What nonsense!" laugh the emancipated, forgetting that in their own degree they are sticklers for an etiquette that is often just as amusing and possibly more hurtful than this pathetic convention.

"They say. What do they say? Let them say!" The old pronouncement rings out as true as ever today, but it takes a terrific amount of grit as well as a strong dose of stoic philosophy to act up to the challenge. Even if you do not allow yourself, as a concession to others, to swerve an inch away from the course your own free choice has marked out, there is a good deal of nerve strain involved in taking such an independent line.

Yet all this fearfulness about our neighbors disappears like ice before the sun, so soon as we become conscious of God. When our roots go deep enough down into reality, the little surface happenings seem of small importance. When our anchorage is sure, when we know ourselves inalienably bound to God, it is impossible to mind much what anyone says about us. God consciousness precludes selfconsciousness. What we seem to be, what we sound like, what we look like, are so many irrelevancies in view of the glorious fact that God knows everything about us, the good and the bad. He sees us more clearly than any neighbor does. He understands and appreciates us much better than our parents do. He sees in us something much finer than we have ever guessed was there. He is watching for this something to emerge and develop and He is waiting for us to take our rightful place in this universe of His, to add to its worth and its beauty by our sturdy independence of spirit.

The only thing that matters is this union with God.

> Speak to Him, thou, for He heareth, and
> spirit with Spirit shall meet—
> Closer is He than breathing, nearer than
> hands and feet.

*   *   *

Worship Brings Release From Fear of Death. A certain girl, ... full of vitality, carefree, loved by everyone, would never go down any road that passed a cemetery. If by some inadvertence she found herself near a graveyard she forthwith turned her head in the opposite direction until the unpleasant sight was passed. She could not bear to contemplate the fact of death; she dared not face it; she was trying to thrust from her one aspect of reality; she was blind to its worth, its value, its relation to God. The whole fabric of her desirable life was endangered by fear; only by shutting her eyes could she retain her joy; but on such terms it was impossible to retain it.

St. Francis sang, "Praised be my Lord for our little sister, the Death of the Body," and many of us have learnt, like him, to hail its coming as a friend.

"Mors janua vita." The words are carved on the wall of the crematorium. Death has often proved the gateway of life, even for those who are left behind after a most beloved one has passed through. Their going seems to have thrust a way through for us, made a rent somehow in the thick curtain that ordinarily separates us from the next phase of life. Sometimes these dear forerunners have seemed almost to pull us a step or two across the threshold with them; so close, so infinitely dear was their love that it was impossible to be wholly cut off from them.

The way of worship does not allow us to turn away from death in fear. It, too, is God's servant.

* * *

Worship Brings Relief From Anxiety.

Father, I know that all my life
Is portioned out for me;
The changes that are sure to come
I do not fear to see.

Those who can truthfully repeat the second of these couplets are the blessed ones of the earth, for the numberless people who are the prey to anxiety are utterly pitiable. It is no good saying to them, "Don't worry!" Quite often the victim does not even know what she is worrying about. It is nothing definite, but just a vague anxiety. Friends argue with her trying to take her out of herself. She was made that way, they say, and it's no good trying to alter her.

Diversions, change of scene, society, the theatre, all these specifics fail. They do not go deep enough. To cure such, you must go to the root of the matter, reveal to her the deep hidden springs of life, get her to face reality, to face every aspect of life, to lay open every corner of her mind to the all-pervading Spirit of God, so that she begins to feel something of that deep serenity which is the indisputable sign of His presence.

To many people the contemplation of change of any sort causes anxiety; in their eyes the conservative-minded individual is the right person to trust, to follow, and to obey.

"Do what was done last time is thy rule, eh?" jeered Joan to Courcelles when he declares before the Inquisition Court that she must be put to the torture because "It is the law. It is customary. It is always done." (*St. Joan,* by G. B. Shaw, Scene VI)

A continuous burden of anxiety is experienced by many parents as they watch their child developing along lines that are unfamiliar to them. The adolescent boy is just beginning to feel his own feet, examining life, trying out his own powers, testing his judgment, learning to be self-reliant. These are all good things, but in the course of these experiments he, perhaps, shows some unpleasant trait of character, breaks some hitherto accepted convention, or offends a family taboo. The parents are overwhelmed with grief. Their feeling is neither resentment nor anger, but a very deep sorrow. Their boy has begun to sin. Their agony of soul is terrible. Surely it is just for such a situation as this that Jesus Christ spoke his revealing and releasing words, "Judge not."

Just as surely as there is no worse grief than to watch a greatly loved one deteriorate, so surely, is there to be found in the way of worship, comfort, strength, and power sufficient to redeem him. You need not fear for him while God has him in hand. Wrap him round in your own love and in God's love, then leave him free; do not judge him, but trust him; let him win his own way through all his difficulties until he has found reality, until at last he has acquired the habit of relating everything, every person, and every circumstance to God.

*   *   *

Worship Brings Release From Prejudice. The scientific mind is open and receptive to truth from whatever source it comes. To have an open mind is not to be unable to make up your mind. The latter is a pitiable, if not a damnable state. For not to be able to make up your mind is not to be able to convince others, to comfort those who need comfort, to strengthen those in trouble, to act creatively; for you must think, and think accurately, before you can create.

The architect sees the vision of what he wants to construct; then he sets to work to make it come true. Beethoven thought, then created a symphony. Michelangelo saw the angel imprisoned in the marble and then set to work to release it. The poet thinks and feels, then writes. You can tell how a man thinks by looking at what he has made. God thought, then created.

Jesus Christ was evidently disappointed when impetuous Peter, in face of his Master's pronouncement about His future, flung out hasty, passionate words of dissuasion. Jesus reprimanded him severely and compared him with Satan the tempter, adding the rebuke, "You're not thinking like God. You're thinking like a man." (Matt. 16:23) Evidently Christ is disappointed with us if we are content with merely thinking like men. Something more is expected of us than to jog along in the ordinary way, "behaving like decent fellows." We are supposed to think like God.

To fulfill this great destiny it is necessary for us to preserve the open mind, open to truth from whatever angle it comes, for truth is God. We must never allow ourselves to get into a rut, for "all ruts are bad—even good ones." We must not do good out of mere habit; we must not pray by rote; we must keep ourselves sensitive to every breath of the spirit, to inspiration from whatever quarter it comes. It is possible to get inspiration from a sinner or a criminal; if love is shown to the loveless, they become lovely, and in their loveliness they give one a benediction.

To learn to think like God means to ignore barriers of class, race, and nation; it means the dropping of all labels. The spirit of discernment is the mark of the man of God. It cannot be commanded. It falls upon those who are willing to be the servants of humanity, who are humble in spirit, who are expectant. It fell on the little group who waited together in an upstairs room, day after day, week after week, until they should find themselves strong enough to tackle their lifework. They waited, ready, receptive, knowing that the way would be made clear. They waited seven weeks in that spirit. Then, one morning, they found that courage and serenity and joy came flooding into their hearts, and that morning's experience carried them through life and adventure and death, to God.

* * *

Worship and the Creative Instinct. While concentrating your mind and your spirit in worship, you automatically, as it were, begin to acquire some of the qualities and something of the nature of the object of your worship. This is an unconscious process, but it is inevitable. As we worship God we begin to become creative, thus partaking of His nature. The musician forgets himself in his work. The poet and the artist proverbially forget to take their meals. The doctor forgets his personal pleasures. The mother finds her joy in the hardest menial labor. It is true that the zest of creation inhibits for the time being the sway of the senses.

...Once you have found your relationship to God, you need never look around for work. From that moment every person is your friend and your brother. Your job is to build up the Kingdom of God, here, now, on earth. You find every circumstance and every moment rich in creative opportunity. Even sin, your own or other people's, is found to be a steppingstone to a deeper knowledge, a clearer understanding. Your task is to set up, here and now, wherever you happen to be, the reign of God, the Kingdom of Heaven on Earth. ...

St. Joan had to explain to the Dauphin how God could bring him out of his aimless, hopeless position into fullness of life.

"Minding your own business is like minding your own body: it's the shortest way to make yourself sick. What is my business? Helping mother at home. What is thine? Petting lap-dogs and sucking sugar-sticks. I call that muck! I tell thee it is God's business we are here to do: not our own." (*St. Joan*, by G. B. Shaw, Scene VI)

* * *

The Choice. Have you a favorite walk, perhaps through forest glades, or up a steep hillside, where young larches in early spring seem to be bursting into vivid green flame? You have taken that walk in many a varying mood. But was one day or one night specially memorable? You were alone, and God was real, and you seemed to be getting every ounce of joy out of everything ("Thou has pressed the signet of eternity on every fleeting moment." Tagore); colors had never before been so vivid, forms had never before seemed so richly endowed with grace, the latent beauty in every leaf seemed to manifest itself, every bush and blade seemed akin to you, part of you and part of God's great whole.

Now, think back to that same walk on another occasion, when everything was just the same outwardly. You were alone then, too; but really alone this time, without the sense of God; you were in a bad mood, jaded, nervy, anxious; perhaps you were "very angry, very small," like the solitary rider in V.L. Edwinson's *Temper in October*. Anyhow, the redolent perfection all around evoked no worship from you. You missed its significance. It only accentuated your feeling of wretchedness. You were a stranger to joy and beauty. For the time being you were one of those "without God in the world." (Eph. 2:12)

But it is the future that matters. What is your choice to be?

You can try to live without worship if you like! You can preserve your sturdy show of independence and self-reliance. You can go through life trying to face facts fairly, unaided, with no deceptive nonsense about spiritual values. You can bid your soul ally itself to Nature, not to God, like the fugitive in Thompson's *Hound of Heaven:*

> I triumphed and I saddened with all weather,
> Heaven and I wept together,
> And its sweet tears were salt with mortal mine;
> Against the red throb of its sunset heart
> I laid mine own to beat
> And share communing heat;
> But not by that, by that, was eased my human
> smart.

You can declare that the mind's the measure of man and there's nothing greater than man. You can stake your all on the proven worth of human nature, your own or other people's, however often you have found yourself let down by it, however perilously near barren self-worship this path has led you. You can go along Cornish lanes in a rapturous dawn, taste the salt air, hear the birds' aerial music, see the new sunlight, feel vigor in your every limb, rejoice in it all for the moment.

It is there—it is past—it is gone.

Alternately, by giving yourself to worship you can make every moment immortal. You can find your individual life merging itself ever more completely into the life of the world. You can forget your own soul because you are so engrossed in the great design that God's economy is weaving out of our short, broken, and tangled threads. By the way of worship you can come so close to this great Weaver that you find youself learning from Him not to waste a broken thread of time by impatience or resentment, not to throw away the most tangled skein of opportunity by self-pity or regret. Henceforth you need "let nothing you dismay." "Your ship is abroad on an uncharted sea, but having given up the hazards of self-direction, you can steer unhesitatingly on."

Prayer

The Practical Mystic

Muriel Lester — social worker, Hyde Park speaker, advocate of the poor, indefatigable traveler, peace activist — was also a woman of prayer. The supposed conflict between involvement in social issues and the life of the spirit was totally foreign to her understanding of religion. The Reign of God involves the whole of life, setting one upon an inward/outward journey that is demanding, joyous, dangerous and deeply fulfilling. The giving of oneself for others requires being deeply grounded in the Eternal Spirit, who gives life and who provides strength, renewal, perseverance, and hope for the journey.

Muriel Lester came upon this practical mysticism not long after the founding of Kingsley Hall. Overworked and tense, she developed symptoms that might have ended her chosen career — in fact, that is what her masseuse implied when she told Muriel that she had the wrong temperament for such work! In the agonizing inner struggle that ensued, she discovered what became for her the secret of abundant life.

From *It Occurred to Me*

The effort to respond to everyone's eager expectations overwhelmed me. My heart began to do all sorts of funny things. It seemed occasionally to jump about inside of me. Sometimes it missed a beat, sometimes raced like an engine, sometimes felt as though it were falling, a cold stone down a steep and narrow well. Then several doctors took matters in hand and I had to go home, stay there, get up at ten, go to bed at nine, walk for hours in the forest alone, go upstairs only three times a day. As soon as the doctor got me stronger and allowed me the narrowest latitude, a tea party or the mild excitement of a concert, I was as bad as ever. This lasted for eight months. At the end of that time I was told by my dear masseuse who sought me out twice a week and did her best for me, that I would never be any better. It was my temperament, she said. I enjoyed things too much.

This ruthless pronouncement was about the best thing that ever happened to me. It forced me to face facts. And I had to ask myself some searching questions. What sort of disorderly universe was this in which the person who most enjoyed things was incapacitated thereby? Or was it I that was disorderly? Immoderate? If my masseuse were right, it would prove God's craftsmanship to be very poor. What would one think of an engineer who produced machines that were liable to break down whenever they performed their proper function? I had blandly accepted the face of my heart having gone on strike. I had expected cure to arrive mechanically, as long as I obeyed orders and swallowed medicines. Now I realized that something much more fundamental was involved and I had got to face it at once.

As soon as the masseuse left and my rest period was over, I got up, dressed, threw on a cloak, and went out into the garden. It was a dank, misty November day, late afternoon. I roamed round and round the tennis-lawn, head bent, eyes on the ground, trying to see straight, trying to analyse the source of my weakness and of power. I remember gazing at the moist, dark green winter moss that had spread parasitically over the gravel paths. It seemd to match my mood. I don't know how long that perambulation lasted. As the darkness engulfed me, I knew only one thing, that there could be no respite from struggle until I had somehow discovered how to harness my own puny, unreliable spirit to the Eternal Spirit. The effort was so agonizing that it phrased itself memorably. I felt as though I were "crawling about on the floor of hell." To make any effort is distressing after eight months of being waited on. I supposed I'd become spiritually flabby too.

Eventually I knew what I must do. My masseuse's depressing philosophy could not be disproven by argument, only by accomplishment. I was not going to let my temperament become my downfall. I was very lucky to have been born with the knack of enjoying things. The point where it had become a source of weakness instead of health was the crux of the whole matter. I had inherited from God and my parents a thoroughly sound constitution. I had taken it for granted and used it to exhaustion point carrying out my Bow program of work, instead of realizing that work is not an end in itself. It is one's way of doing it that counts, one's way of life. An accomplishment may be technically quiet correct but its value is nil unless in the doing of it one keeps near the source of all beauty, truth and goodness.

The creative spirit of God, whose orderliness, rhythm, and reliability are at the very heart of the universe, upholds life in all creatures. It is the source of our delight, our physical strength, our imaginative powers, our energy and stability. My whole being was a part of God, and whatever effort or pleasure or struggle or bit of responsibility I undertook was His responsibility, not mine. My jerky breathing, my heart's fluttering, my unreliable career were all of a piece with the way my toes would curl up inside my shoes as I watched the crisis of a play or reached the climax of a novel. Each was an indication that I had got unhitched, somehow, from the source of strength and serenity.

Somewhere I had read that the power and life-giving qualities of the great Gulf Stream can flow through the channel of a single straw if the straw is set in the right direction. I must realize that with every breath I drew I was actually breathing in the spirit of God. His great creative spirit was also the re-creative spirit. I must consciously cooperate with "that unseen Power which is ever moulding men and things to higher uses." I mustn't strive to hold steadfast control over myself in a difficult situation. I must let go and imperturbably watch God dealing with it. That's an exciting and often a super-humourous situation. One's energy and joy must come direct from God. Then they are continually renewed. What a contrast between the old idea and the new practice! The firm, reliable, rhythmic flow of the Eternal Spirit and the tense, screwed-up, compartmentalized experience of a busy schedule!

So next day I began the new discipline, and in a month I was well and went back to work. But it wasn't quite so easy as it sounds. I think nothing but that preposterous challenge to one's whole philosophy of life would have kept me at the job. I wondered if my masseuse had administered the means of my cure with her wise eyes open. The technique I worked out dragged me away every afternoon from whatever conversation, book, or amusement I was absorbed in. I had to go upstairs alone into a locked room for one hour and practise relaxation. I lay on my back on the bed or on the floor, and emulated the limpness of a kitten by the fireside, or of a sleeping child. The tautened nerves must be made to loose their hold on the muscles. The muscles must be coped with specifically, one set at a time. The hand that so readily screwed up its fingers and clenched its fist must be made to lie on the bed, half open and inert. The foot muscles must be released, and the tightly held toe muscles; then the face muscles, specially those round the eyes and mouth. By this time the hands have screwed up again and the process must be repeated. Feebly at first, a feeling of intrinsic well-being began to assert itself, a sense of restfulness. Perhaps it would take some fifteen minutes before relaxation was acquired.

Then came leisure enough to notice one's breathing. I didn't try to regulate it. I merely made myself notice how it was becoming slower and slower, deeper and more regular, until the sense of well-being was complete.

Many similes can be used to describe the effect of the process. Imagine the surface of a garden bed in August; the earth is dry, pale, and prickly to the touch. A shower falls. The earth becomes dark brown, smooth, and beautiful. A delightful odour exudes from it. Imagine a piece of over-strained elastic or a bit of yesterday's ill-preserved lettuce that has no resilience. ... Imagine a shaky old bicycle with a punctured tire. One has no wherewithal to repair it. The journey must be accomplished. There is haste. One pedals on with a flat tire, riding on the rims. That is how one may live and fall ill.

But imagine the deep waters of a turbulent sea. Their depth does not destroy you. You are on a raft actually upheld by the salt waves. Imagine, too, a pond frozen over at its brink and children eagerly waiting to skate. Before they are allowed to start, men go all round the edge of the pond with axes, hacking at the ice to detach it from the earth. It is safer when the floating sheet relies only on the buoyant water, not cleaving at all to the encompassing land.

Strangely interesting that the expression on a face when its muscles are relaxed is a smile! Study the face of the dead when the nerves have ceased functioning and the muscles are no longer drawn into lines of pain.

After half an hour or more, when serenity and a sense of well-being are established, you can begin to utilize the new force. Quietly, rhythmically, to match your breathing, such words as these may repeat themselves in your mind.

> Breathe on me, breath of God,
> Fill me with life anew,
> That I may love what Thou dost love
> And do what Thou wouldst do.

Life certainly becomes new when you have made yourself love what God loves; sinners, drunks, traitors, enemies, members of an "inferior" race. But you can get the Spirit of God on no terms but His own. Jerky, irregular heart action is free to develop as soon as you get contorted with pride, scorn, or anger. One by one the people you fear, despise, love, or worry about come into your mind. Let them stay there until they are linked with God. "Breathe on them, breath of God." Repeat the prayer for each of them, leisurely, quietly, without making a sound. "God breathed into man's nostrils the breath of life, and he became a living soul." See each of these people waking into new life. At the end of the hour, you get up as from a bed of roses. You feel you could jump over a house. You proceed to join in the ordinary life belowstairs without apprehension.

Of course I lapsed often enough during the day. Sometimes I wrought myself up with fear or pride, but such things tend to lose their hold over one in proportion to one's practice of the presence of God. So it's just a common sense, mathematical affair each of us has to work out for himself. The only difficult effort in the whole technique is dragging oneself away from pleasant company or some engrossing job to take the hour's practice. One's extraordinary facility in thinking up new excuses as to why on this particular day of days one need not undergo the discipline, is soon recognized as humorous. Sometimes my excuse was that I felt so free from all taint of weakness or weariness, so very much alive and alert, that it seemed pure folly to go and lie down. On these occasions I would generally find myself physically aching with weariness after the first fifteen or twenty minutes of relaxation.

It was fun to go back to Bow quite well in a few weeks and find how useful this experience had been.

From *Ways of Praying*

As a result of this life-changing experience, Muriel Lester "practiced the presence of God" throughout the remainder of her life. She shared what she learned through her speaking and writing, as we see in this small book.

...Any one can live the life of prayer. It is not long periods of quiet and leisure that are the great necessity in prayer; it is a habit, a humble spirit; a disciplined mind, a sense of order, self-control, an intelligent associating of ideas. And all these you can acquire while you dress, bathe, brush your hair, walk or work or sit in the bus.

Spiritual gifts are useless, and may even become corrupt if not applied to the ordinary happenings of everyday life. Every one must win his own soul. It is not a job that can be done for you; yet, if it is not done, you will never be master of your own life. Unless you can evolve a working philosophy of some sort, unless you can fit the joys and pains, the hopes and struggles, the beauties and the failures of your daily life into some large framework of meaning; unless you can get a sense of unity, of completeness, you are at the mercy of whim and circumstance.

These notes, then, are intended as a guide to those who want to pray. Do not be discouraged by difficulties. Prayer, like any other art which aims at the attainment of perfection, persistently demands your best, and no province of your daily life can be outside it.

The art of praying can be learnt, for contact with God can be practised at all times, whatever one is doing. The exercises and problems of prayer are educed out of the very material of life itself.

The Necessity of Prayer. "I need no idea of a God to lean on, and I wonder that you do. I concede that such may be necessary to some rather weak-minded people, but not to me, personally."

Variations of this statement are constantly being made by people of fine character. People who hold this viewpoint seem to take it for granted that Christians have the unpleasant habit of needing to lean on something. ... On the contrary contact with God makes for independence of spirit; it lessens a person's timorous qualms, rids him of worry, and, giving him tolerance and courage, drives him into action, unconcerned as to what people say or think about him.

However, there may be fortunate individuals who in their nature possess all these good gifts that most of us only gain from prayer and the strenuous attempt to follow Christ. Probably they had excellent parents, their ancestors were of good stock, their home life was happy, they had a sensible upbringing, were neither rich nor poor, and were early made to consider the rights of others and the wrongs of the dispossessed. When adolescence, with its baffling conflicts, came upon them, they had wise older friends to guide them through its stormy period; when sex first got its powerful grip on them, there was no wreckage in their lives.

Such as they might easily feel no need of God. Actually they need God tremendously so that all their natural, inherited, and acquired gifts may be co-ordinated, and they may fulfil their destiny and become natural leaders, saviours of their generation.

Any person thus richly endowed is failing the rest of us if he is not fulfilling his function of setting up the way of salvation for the oppressed, the downtrodden, and the dispossessed.

"I will accept no privilege that others cannot have the counterpart of, on the same terms," asserted Eugene Debs, the American. Fortunately nurtured individuals inherit countless privileges of which others are dispossessed. Redress is needed.

John Wesley said, "The world is my parish." The parish priest of the world has no time to waste in arguing about religion; he is knitting up a brotherhood that shall confuse the war-mongers; he is abolishing poverty and riches; he is creating imperishable beauty wherever he goes; he is redeeming mankind from the curse; he is establishing the Kingdom of Heaven.

Come down from your pedestal. Join us of common clay, who are conscious of our need of help to keep from sin and crime. We look to God and our neighbour to provide it.

The First Waking Thought. Immediately you awake set your first thought on God. Keep your mind on Him for a few seconds.

Do not think of Him subjectively, as to your relation to Him, your failures, your sins, or your needs, but rather objectively. Let your whole self become conscious of Him. Think of Him as shining beauty, radiant joy, creative power, all-pervading love, perfect understanding, purity and serenity. This need only take a moment or two once the habit has been formed, but it is of inestimable importance. It sets the tone for the whole day.

One's waking mood tends to correspond to the state of mind in which one falls asleep. If, therefore, as a result of a disturbed night or simply because of lack of practice, this first thought of God should evade you, look out of the window for something obviously made by Him, trees, flowers, the sky, or a wind-shaped cloud, even a grey one, and ponder on the perfection of His handicraft.

Perhaps you are living in an overcrowded home, without fresh air, entirely divorced from nature, deprived of the natural means by which God manifests Himself to His people, so that from your narrow window you cannot even see the sky for smoke. If so, let your thoughts rest on a beautiful picture. But if all outside aids are denied you, a memory will suffice, a picture in your mind, or the recollection of a cool breeze you have once felt on your brow.

If unpleasant memories press in upon you so that you cannot fasten your mind on Him, do not worry about it. Laugh at yourself and think, "What a good thing God does not look at me as I look at myself! He sees something thoroughly lovable in me. He thinks of me as a potent sort of person, and is expecting something rather great and fine to work itself out through my life, and is waiting for it to show itself."

...who sees the deeper into the reality of that very ordinary-looking girl, the passer-by or the lover? It is the lover, of course, because he has discovered the hidden jewel that never sparkled nor shone, until he brought it to the light of his love.

...as God looks upon us He sees the inherent ability, the hidden beauty, the unused power of spirit in each of us.

Do not get out of bed, therefore, until you have set your thought on God. Then remind yourself that He knows you better than any one else does and sees more wonderful things in you, and is waiting to illumine your spirit each morning as you awake.

God's power set the stars in their courses, restful, reliable, and steadfast. His mind created the grace and symmetry of the larch, the silver birch, and the poplar; His joy set the birds singing; His serenity produced the night sky, and His love understands your better than you understand yourself. ...

The Morning Prayer. Consider yourself not ready to start the day, ill equipped, unprepared to mix with your fellows, until you have spent at least fifteen minutes in prayer. Count it as much a social necessity as washing. Some people spend this pre-breakfast prayer-time in a Church, others in a garden, some by their bedroom window, others walking abroad.

There is something about walking—something in the rhythm of it probably—that conduces to progress in prayer, and the pray-er must expect to make progress.

We may find ourselves suffering from spiritual growing pains and mistaking this unpleasant experience for deterioration, think we are losing ground. But it is growth, not retrogression, that is making us dissatisfied with ourselves, and while, because of our higher standard, we are more conscious of our shortcomings, yet we find ourselves seeing deeper, gaining a wider outlook on life, a clearer understanding of our fellows.

The cultivation of the spirit should be considered with at least as much intelligence as the cultivation of corn. If the field is of good soil and well ploughed, if good seed is sown in it, if each day it gets a normal amount of sunshine and rain, if the four winds of heaven blow upon it, good corn inevitably appears. So it is with ourselves. If our mind is prepared and disciplined, if the teaching of Christ is sown in it, if each day it is set towards God and without anxiety and fuss laid open to His influence, good character inevitably appears. "Is it likely," asks Henry Drummond, "that the growth of corn should be regulated by law and the growth of character by mere caprice?"

*   *   *

Self-consciousness—that bane of youth—disappears as we practice praying. During this pre-breakfast quarter of an hour we become more conscious of God than of our fellows and learn that achievement is worth more than anything else in life. Of course, half an hour is much better than a quarter, for during the morning prayer-time new aspirations form themselves in one's mind. A fresh attempt should be made to accomplish a much-desired and long-delayed aim; a new assault ought to be planned against the fastness of evil, allied as it is with hoary vested interests; a different approach by a hitherto untried route must be made to that poor young soul, sick in his own self-pity, secure in his scorn for others.

"Am I ready for such tasks?" Anyhow I am ready to be made ready, as I wait in quietness for God's help and cooperation.

The day will not be the jewel, the poem, the joy it might be unless one can come to the pitch when one can say the prayer: "Behold me, O Lord, in Thy hands ready for all; spin me backwards or spin me forwards, for I desire nothing other than the doing of Thy will, and oh! that I might do it worthily and perfectly!"

"Faith is the conscious co-operation with an unseen force which is ever moulding men and things to higher uses." If we want to play our part in this cosmic process we have to hold ourselves in readiness to do anything at any time and in any circumstance. "I would fain be to the Eternal Goodness what his own right hand is to a man." God needs one to be perpetually ready to serve, like the Knights of the Grail, even like Kundry [Kundry, part sorceress, part mortal woman, is one of the characters of Richard Wagner's opera Parsifal, based on Wolfram von Eschenbach's poem about the Knights of Grail.] in her sane interludes, ready to go half round the world for a healing herb to give to a sinner in pain.

The willingness to do this, even though we never get further than our own back street, turns grey and black into gold and purple for us. But do not be too sure that your call abroad may not come when you least expect it; when you are in the dullest of moods, beware. Be ready. Do not let yourself become immersed in the humdrum, work-a-day world. Prepare yourself, offering yourself afresh each day to God to serve at any sudden call, anyhow, anywhere—even on the Cross.

Acts of Recollection. Robert Browning worked out at some length, in his poem "Pippa Passes," how a single person walking down a street, past a garden, into the country for a day's holiday may affect the destiny of many whom she has never seen. The process of walking down a street, stepping into a crowded lift, strap-hanging in the Underground, and emerging once more into the upper air, can be either a boring routine or a new adventure, fraught every day with fresh significance.

It is a good habit on entering a room or a train or a bu'bus to practise conscious reverence for the personality of each of those already there. The mystics used to take time to untie themselves with their environment, so that, whatever it was and however unpleasant, it had no power to oppress them.

Our job is just as hard; it is to keep ourselves in harmony with our fellows, even in the crush of an overcrowded tube. We can do it by remembering the Presence of God, looking at our fellow passengers and reminding ourselves that each of them, though perhaps they have no idea of it, is near and dear to God.

As one looks round at the weary, jaded expression on the faces of some of them, one longs to introduce to them the thought of God. This thought is infectious; it can be spread in many a 'bus and train so that Tagore's words ring true, "Thou hast pressed the signet of eternity upon many a fleeting moment of my life."

The critics of grace-saying are right on one point. It is not only meal-times that should be associated with acts of prayer and recollection. Each one of us ought to make his own association. Some link up the striking of the hour with the thought of God. Some let the climbing of a staircase, or the washing of hands, be a reminder of Him. Like posts that mark a snow-hidden road these moments of contact with God become invaluable.

One woman, whose life was distinguished by her many friendships, made a practice, whenever she met a stranger or whenever a newcomer entered a room, of saying to herself, "Now I wonder what of God I am going to find in this person?" Another was able to meet many a crisis successfully by her habit of looking at people—prince or beggar alike—not as strangers, however aloof they might hold themselves, but as dear comrades by the silent use of the formula, "The spirit of God within me is going out to meet God's spirit in you."

Sometimes there comes an almost unbroken sense of joy, peace, and harmony with God and our fellows which lasts for several days; we begin to think it is going to last for ever; all our conflicts are in abeyance; we are at rest yet full of vigour; everything turns out right for us; there is no worry, no weariness, no hurry; everything happens to suit our needs, we feel that we have actually begun to enjoy eternal life here on earth.

Then comes a clash, a minor crisis, a disappointment, and the current seems insidiously to have changed without our knowing how. One false move, one outburst of ill temper, or one bitter word spoils the whole thing. We become so disgusted with ourselves at having lost control, that we feel everything is hopeless. Giving way to irritation has robbed us of our self-respect; we do not stop to reason it out, we do not pray, we just sink lower and lower in a slough of self-disgust until our very power to get free from the enveloping depression seems to have gone. What is the good of trying? Gloom and disillusion rule, and, but for the anchorage of the regular praying habit that holds us, the mood might hasten us, by geometrical progression, into spiritual bankruptcy.

As it is, there is no need hopelessly to throw up the sponge; by retracing our steps to the last point of harmony with God, we can make a fresh start.

Brother Lawrence had his own healthy way of meeting this emergency. When he had failed in his duty he simply confessed his fault, saying to God, "I shall never do otherwise, if You leave me to myself; 'tis You must hinder my falling, and mend what is amiss." After this he gave himself no further uneasiness about it. His way works, but only when one is living the prayer life, constantly and consciously turning one's thought to God, practising the Presence of God. ...

The acts of recollection we make during the day ensure a healthy habit of mind, a turning of our thoughts outward to God rather than inward to ourselves. Minute fragments of poison, such as a sudden jab of jealousy, a pang of selfpity, a gust of pride, cannot then accumulate to the enfeebling of the whole constitution.

R.H. Benson in his *Richard Raynal* describes how the young man, when assailed by the fiend with the fierce temptation and doubt, used to "cry upon Jesu in his heart and then set the puzzle by." This is the way of spiritual health.

The Prayer of Relaxation . [At this point Muriel Lester speaks of her personal experience recounted at the beginning of this chapter and the regenerative power that comes from prayerful relaxation .]

Grace Before Meat . ... [There are those] who refuse to have a grace said at all. "Why this crude and primitve emphasis on food?" they ask. "Is eating the only thing for which we are

126

grateful? Why single out meal times? Food is by no means the greatest blessing of the day."

Thus speak the assured recipients of regular income. This sentiment is alien from the standpoint of the vast majority of human-kind whose food-supply is not assured to them. It is the accident of birth or of economic conditions that has made some so lordly and superior in their attitude to food.

"In the sweat of thy brow shalt thou eat bread," was a statement of fact which still applies to most of us. We should never allow ourselves to forget how the procuring of our daily bread has bowed the back and used up the energy of numbers of men for whom Christ died. The long process starts with the ploughing up of the hard brown earth by some Russian peasant or by "old Callow at his task of God." It is finished by the boy with the delivery-van at the back door. Farmers, engineers, millers, railway-servants, steamship companies, wholesale dealers, retailers and a host of commission agents have each taken their toll from the grain, some of it legitimately, some of it wholly indefensibly. Bakers grow pale through lack of sleep and sunshine and miners also through providing the bakers with the necessary fuel for their ovens. And eventually the loaves are sold over the counter to my neighbour who has nine children and has to take fewer than she needs. The children learn self-control and go hungry, without being the least bit sorry for themselves, while the same hunger is being experienced at the other end of the process by the cultivator in Russia, India and England. Agricultural labourers often fail to feed their own families adequately. In India they have discovered the usefulness of water, not merely to quench their thirst, but to fill their stomach, thus ridding themselves temporarily of that empty, uncomfortable ache due to lack of food.

The whole question of an adequate food-supply for the world needs more thought and prayer, not less. Let us remind ourselves of the problem every time we sit down to eat. The economists assure us that there is enough raw material, enough power, enough sunshine, enough water to supply the needs of the whole human race. God has seen to that. Our trouble is not under-production but over-production, resulting in an artificially produced scarcity. It is the problem of distribution that is baffling us. ... And to solve that, goodwill is needed, knowledge is needed, a willingness for self-sacrifice is needed. To give up some of our privileges in order to procure necessities for others, is that hard? Yes, unless we have love like God's in our hearts. Grace draws our thoughts to God regularly three times a day, so that during those quiet moments we get something of His outlook, a generous desire that all shall have their wants supplied, a willingness to work for that end, a feeling of power enabling us to overcome petty thoughts and low aims in order to follow Christ in the way of service. ...

Intercessory Prayer. "Come," said St. Catherine, when she and her friends were faced with a grave crisis, "let us storm Heaven with our prayers."

... Most of our friends ... enter our mind when we are at prayer, for their problems elicit our acute interest and in some measure our own. Many of them definitely ask for prayer, but a long list of names can become a deadening, depressing affair even though each individual name brings lovely memories and comfortable friendly thoughts to our mind.

Then there are those whose need keep obtruding themselves on our minds just because they seem so unaware that they need anything. They have never seen the vision of perfection, and are in the suffocating throes of pleasurable comfort and an all-pervading sense of satisfaction which was Mr. A. C. Benson's [an English essayist, author and scholar] idea of Hell.

It may be necessary to keep several different periods during the day or during the week for different friends, unless, indeed, you have reached that stage which is the essence of prayer where even thinking about a person links them with God.

It is easy to become stale and bored in praying regularly for people, so let us consider a few specific methods.

There is the habit of Frank Laubach, a missionary who shares the life of the Moslem Moros of the Philippines. Alone and far from home and kindred he pins up on his study wall photographs of all the people for whom he wants to pray. Every night after supper he goes into the room alone, and leaving the place dark, he lets his electric torch illuminate one portrait among them all. To this person he talks aloud, putting into words his every wish for them. Then when his thoughts have gone as high and as far as they will, he writes to that friend telling what he has done. ... There is the habit of seeing in your mind's eye the person for whom you would pray and then letting various things happen to him. Is he bored and listless? You see him reinvigorated by salt breezes from the sea. "Breathe on him, breath of God; fill him with life anew," you pray.

Is he weak, suffering, lying in a hospital ward facing some death-dealing disease, or threatened by madness or suicide?...Take time to make a new picture of your friend radiantly happy, in perfect health, utterly self-possessed.

See him out in the open air on a balmy day of April, new life everywhere, in plant and tree. Life is the essence of God. ... Can He now renew, reshape our lives?...

Is he narrow, crabbed, congested in his ideas and prejudiced? You see him on the prow of a ship in mid-ocean, unmeasured space in every direction. Can he remain so unaware, so petty, when God is surrounding him with illimitable wisdom?. ...

Sometimes praying may make you physically weary. It may be a wrestling of spirit, a struggle for attainment, an agonizing spiritual contest so acute that you find yourself holding your breath; an assault upon the forces of cruelty, prejudice and callousness so energetic that it tires you out, or a passionate attack on evil in some form threatening a beloved friend or child that seems to reproduce the terrific elements of a cosmic struggle.

In going to the help of a drowning man, the rescuer may become so exhausted that all he can do is to hold up his subject's head until help arrives from some other source. So in the realm of prayer, one has sometimes to hold on to the soul of a friend and, in spite of utter weariness and exhaustion, to refuse to let go.

Wrestling for the life of a patient who was thought to be already half-way through the gates of death, a certain nurse set her teeth and refused to accept defeat. The patient recovered. Afterwards the nurse described the crisis.

> You know how on the river the passing of a big motor launch may sometimes so endanger your little boat fastened to the bank that you have to grapple with your boat-hook to avoid being shaken and bumped against the bank. The waves toss your boat violently up and down but you exert all your strength to keep your grip, while the hook fairly bites into the earth and your wrists ache with holding on. Well, I felt all through the crisis, as

if I'd got my hook into my patient. I did not let go for three days. I was tuned up to the struggle, and I won.

So in other crises, when the danger threatening one's friend may be due to spiritual causes, inertia, pride or despair, one wrestles for him. Duties, pleasures, daily routine continue to claim one's attention, but there in the background of one's mind is the friend "held still and serene" in one's love; that unchanging, unshockable, imperturbable love that will not let him go, that holds him in the presence of God.

Pray for your friends. Continue instant in prayer, in season and out of season. Pray them out of their moods, and their partial, unbalanced lives into the fullness of knowledge of God.

The Evening Prayer. Never get into bed with a burdened or a heavy mind; whether it be a vague oppression or a definite fear, shame or remorse, anger or hate, get rid of the evil thing before you lie down to sleep.

Night is a holy time, a healthy time, a time of renewing and refreshment. He giveth to His beloved while they sleep; our unconscious mind, that most faithful servant, is active during our slumber. Settle down restfully to let your mind get clear and your spirit unclogged. It would be better to sit up half the night, wrestling in spirit until you have won your way to peace and wholeness rather than embark upon hours of unconsciousness with an unresolved conflict, an unacknowledged fear, or an unforgiven friend in your mind.

Throughout the whole day your stream of consciousness has been flowing in many directions. You have been seeing, hearing, feeling, remembering, noticing things all day long and each experience has made its due impression on you. Most of the impressions have fitted themselves quite naturally into the general design of your everyday life. Some were new, but soon found their correct position in the general framework or background that each individual creates for himself in life.

But some impressions stood out, could not be placed, rebelled against order. That gust of unreasoning anger, for instance, that suddenly swept over you; that incomprehensible fear you first glimpsed; in the eyes of a friend and then experienced yourself; that new line of thought that threatened, if pursued, to upset one of your most cherished convictions; that bitter criticism of yourself that you heard in such a disconcerting manner form the lips of a neighbour; these all come crowding into your mind. They collect in an inextricable tangle, as soon as your work is over, as soon as your attention is freed from routine duties, as soon as you have leisure and are alone—and that is probably not until bed-time. Very well! Welcome them all, meet them cheerily. ... It is a folly ever to shirk the issue of a single, worrying, doubting thought. Face each one before you get into bed, face them in the presence of your Father who knows all your muddled feelings and understands your tempestuous passions.

It does not take long, this process, but it forms one of the most important parts of your evening prayer. Silent in God's presence, you can relax yourself completely. Rely on Him as on a Father. The restfulness of being alone at last, facing reality, may even make you laugh aloud for joy as you open your mind in perfect confidence and summon the whole bustling medley of burdensome thoughts before Him. One can almost stand back, as it were, and survey them bursting out of one's mind—these rampageous, weakening, strange and startling thoughts! Let them come, waiting quietly for each, without a shadow of dread. See how they shew up in the deep calm of God's presence. "That anger I felt this morning, it was like murder, it did real harm to the person it was vented upon, others are re-acting to it still; it was anti-social, a sin. God forgive me. It is not remission of penalty I am asking for, when I say 'forgive.' It is a longing to be made whole again, a passionate desire to save my victim from the consequences of my anger, a willingness to do anything to make amends. ... "

One may wait a few moments before the next impression comes to the fore. That new line of thought: it seemed dangerous, but there was no time to explore it. Now, you can welcome it, pursue it with far greater clarity because; of the presence of God, the Master-Mind. No thought can be alien to Him. He is always pushing His people out into further regions of thought. With every fresh discovery mankind discovers a little more of God. Patiently seek the truth. Certainly one of your most cherished convictions may be threatened if this line of thought is true, but why have you been cherishing this conviction? This new idea may lead to something nobler; it looks promising. You must continue to observe its course. You must talk it out with wise friends. You can go no further just now, alone.

As one waits quietly, other thoughts of fear or anxiety come to the forefront and are faced in the same way. Most of them disappear, vanish incontinently in the presence of God.

One is at peace now with the world, with oneself and with God. One is ready for bed. If bed means a mattress on a balcony, in a garden, or on a flat roof under the stars, so much the better. Then, as drowsiness increases, the words of committal can be used. "Father, into Thy hands I commit my spirit."

With Gandhi in India
and at Kingsley Hall

Muriel Lester's enduring friendship with Gandhi is one of the most interesting and significant aspects of her life and work. She first learned of Gandhi and the Home Rule for India movement prior to World War I and quickly recognized the justice of the cause as well as the parallel between that movement's nonviolence and the Christian pacifist movement in the West. Therefore, when she was invited to India in 1926, she accepted joyfully. Out of that and successive visits to India she became a strong ally of Gandhi in the struggle for India's independence and in the building up of a global nonviolent movement.

From *It So Happened*

It was during 1919 that I happened to get hold of a bound copy of Gandhi's weekly paper, Young India. I read it from cover to cover, revelling in the discovery that the principles for which a few thousand of us in the West had been standing between 1914 and 1919 were being put forward with power over an Eastern subcontinent. Soon Romain Rolland's *Mahatma Gandhi* was translated into English. Now it was becoming clear that the two movements — Non-violence and Christian Pacifism — had much to learn from each other. The one had a great leader whose word was accepted as final, while ours had local groups, encouraged to think for themselves and to act on their own initiative. Whereas news about the Indian movement was reported eagerly in India by dailies, monthlies, and weeklies, ours was deliberately ignored by the press. The Indian movement was popular and many nationalists supported it as a temporary policy. Ours ran counter to nationalist interests. Indian non-violence was part of the fabric of Hindu society in its refusal to kill. Ours ran counter to a two-thousand-year-old tradition which gave honour to the soldier and the fighter, dotted the streets and crowded the churches with monuments to them.

Meanwhile, Rabindranath Tagore's *Gitanjali* had begun its great work in England, bringing us a beauty and wisdom born of personal experience. ... One Sunday evening [in 1926] the poet's son-in-law, Dr. Gangulee, came to Kingsley Hall. He said he felt at home in its quiet, unhurried worship. He invited me to go to India, stay with Gandhi and Tagore for a month, and then travel round the country to study conditions and situations for myself. He would arrange it all, he said. And he did. Thus, in October 1926 my eighteen-year-old nephew, Daniel Hogg, and I arrived at Gandhi's ashram in Sabarmati. It was the leader's fifty-seventh birthday.

From *Entertaining Gandhi*

[There were two hundred men, women and children in the ashram,] "...all of them following a simple rule of life not at all strange to anyone accustomed to our life in East London. There was the same sharing of the housework, the same absence of class distinctions, the same ignoring of sectarian labels, the same sleeping out of doors, the same gaiety that voluntary poverty brings, the same joy that comes from breaking down all national barriers, the same sure hold on reality that comes from constant prayer.

The inmates were a strictly disciplined set of people, their lives regulated by the imposition of certain vows.

We got up at 3.50 a.m., bathed, met for forty minutes' prayer, fetched our water, did our house-cleaning, washed our clothes—though I hated the approved fashion of standing in the river to do this; the fishes seemed distinctly to prefer the taste of white calves to brown. We span, cooked, ate, studied, swam in the river and attended Mr. Gandhi's series of lectures on the Sermon on the Mount. Here gathered business men from Ahmedabad as well as all the college students, each of whom had a large Bible under his arm. Pictures of scenes from the New Testament adorned the walls. Flowers in brass pots stood on the floor, sweet-smelling tapers burned, Eastern music set our spirits in tune to listen to Mr. Gandhi's exposition of St. Matthew's fifth chapter.

In August 1914 a handful of men in various European chancelleries had issued ultimatums to each other. Was their action capable of reversing the whole process of nature and suddenly converting children of God, brothers, friends, into murderous enemies just because they happened to live on opposite sides of a river or a mountain or an artificially drawn boundary line?

Kingsley Hall people said, No. We refused to pronounce a moratorium on the Sermon on the Mount for the duration of war. We could not conceive of God as a nationalist; we knew that, strange as it might appear, the Germans were as dear and precious in His sight as the Allies.

Forthwith we became extraordinarily unpopular, among high and low. Anonymous letters threatening to "do us in" were received from local people. Police raids, threats of vitriol throwing, social boycott, virtual excommunication and organised hooliganism enlivened our days.

Now ten years later I found that the inmates of this Indian Ashram were amazed to hear of the adventures we had had in ours. In their naivete they thought English people had no struggles and ignominies to endure. They thought they alone believed in non-violence. We exchanged ideas. I told them of the numerous groups to be found in almost every European city, as well as in most parts of America, who hold this unshakable creed, who put into practice Christ's method of overcoming evil by good, choosing to suffer rather than to make others suffer. They told me how they had discovered that disarmament of the body was not enough, one's mind also must be disarmed, set free, all bitterness and malice rooted out, all self-pity, jealousy and hate destroyed.

From *It Occured To Me*

Seated one day on the verandah of Mrs. Gandhi's house, eating the excellent meal she regularly prepared for all visitors, I heard scraps of conversation issuing from Gandhiji's room. A young American was having a long talk with him and towards the close of it asked him what he thought of the troubled situation in China, whither a few regiments of British soldiers had been dispatched to assure the safety of our nationals, traders, teachers, missionaries, and others. The clear tone and precise words of Gandhiji's answer have stayed

135

in my mind ever since. "If you Christians rely on soldiers for your safety, you are denying your own doctrine of the Cross," he said.

*   *   *

Two residents of Ahmedabad became my special friends, Anasuya Sarabbai and Shankarlal Banker. We liked hearing about each other's similar experiences. Anasuya had broken away from the conventions of a rich mill-owner's home and organized the workmen of the city into a labour union. For years this had been increasing in influence. Now it ran twenty-two schools in the city, several of them for Untouchables, who were accepted gladly even on the governing committee of the union. Anasuya had led a strike for a thirty-three-and-a-half-per-cent increase in wages, for the lowering of the working-hours from twelve to ten and the raising of child-labour age from ten to twelve. After ten weeks' struggle they attained their objective, but only when Gandhiji took a vow to eat nothing until their just demands were granted.

Shankarlal Banker as a young man had been brought up in Western style, frankly scornful of Gandhiji and what he considered his eccentricity. On the occasion when he had to go to him to get support for internae, [internees] he refused to sit on the floor to talk with him. He waited for a chair to be brought him. After he had gone home, he could not rid his mind of the contrast between himself and the Mahatma, proud fatuity and humble service, assumed and inherent dignity, his own self-respect demanding artificial aid and Gandhiji's complete forgetfulness of self. It was not many weeks before he discarded his leather shoes and Western clothes, put on Indian dhoti and sandals, apprenticed himself to the Ashram discipline of ginning, carding, spinning, and weaving, and gave himself and his whole life to build up the All India Spinning Association.

We spent three hours together comparing notes.

"Why don't you talk to Gandhiji like this?" they repeatedly inquired. "He would be tremendously interested."

"I'd like to," I would answer. "But it doesn't come naturally to talk of such things when he is always surrounded by so many admirers hanging on his every word. How could I start?

Can you imagine any one saying, 'Gandhiji, I want to tell you lots of little things that have happened to me in East London. You must listen.'?"

"But the stories you tell us about your non-violence movement in war-time! And the spiritual giants of the Fellowship of Reconciliation in various countries of Europe and America! He would love to hear of them," they persisted.

"Of course he would," I answered. "But you can't push a story on to any one. We three evoke them from each other."

The weeks passed and nothing but polite and pleasant greetings as to the good morning or the fine evening passed between the great man and me, though a fellow Ashram-dweller said that he asked one day, "Who is this English-woman who sits reading in her room and doesn't come talk to me?"

Presently my two friends grew restive. "Will you come with us and talk to him?" they inquired.

"I'd love to," I replied, "if you'll start the talk."

It was a night or two before my month's visit ended that the moment came. I was shown into Gandhiji's room, bare of furniture. He asked me to sit by the wheel at which he was spinning, his eyes always intent on the yarn. My two friends were ensconced and silent in a corner. It seemed that nothing was going to happen. I felt it was a case of "now or never." I suddenly blurted out, "Mr. Gandhi, will you please come to England? I think it's very important that you should."

Rhythmically turning the handle and drawing out a fine, strong thread, he proceeded to spin out in a monotone the fitting rhythmic reply: "What would be the good? We have not yet attained enough success by our non-violence methods to justify my coming to England and teaching your good Fellowship of Reconciliation people anything."

Here was my clue. Dared I interrupt him? I'd got to.

"But Gandhiji, I don't want you to come to England in order to teach us. I want you to come and learn from us."

It is an achievement to surprise Gandhiji, and I'd done it. I'd got past his guard. Better still, I'd made him laugh, long and heartily, too. We had become friends.

I returned to the subject, "Will you please come to England, Gandhiji?"

"On conditions," he answered.

"What are they?" I inquired.

137

"I will come if you will go home and convince your people and your Government that they must give Home Rule to India. Or if you will go to the Lancashire cotton magnates and persuade them to stop sending their goods here."

"Is there any easier condition?" I inquired.

He paused a little. Then very deliberately he answered: "Yes, I will come if you will rouse public opinion, stir the churches, get hold of Members of Parliament, convince Cabinet Ministers that what you have seen here as regards your Government's drink and opium policy is thwarting our passion for the prohibition of these two evils."

I pondered a little. I had seen some horrible things. Then I said, "I rather think I will take that on."

Then I discovered what it meant to keep the "Vow of Truth" which was evidently considered by Gandhi to be part of the bargain. "You must see everything you can," he said. "You've already seen Anasuya's school of Untouchable children, themselves regular drinkers before she weaned them away from it. You must go to the opium shops licensed by the Government. You must see the English secretary of the Prohibition League and get information from him. You must go to excise officials, too, just in case they can prove to you that your opinions and mine are all wrong."

I accepted the wisdom of these tactics, but demurred when the further requirements of truth-telling followed.

"You must go to the Governors of Bengal and Bombay and tell them what you intend to do on your return home. It's not fair to leave their provinces intending to talk about conditions publicly without giving them notice. The Viceroy, too, should be seen."

Heavily burdened though I felt, it was obvious that this technique was only common fairness and common sense.

"On your arrival in London," the evenly pitched, inexorable voice continued, "you must go to the India Office and see the Secretary of State, Lord Birkenhead."

"No!" I exclaimed, "I really can't!"

He paused for a moment, then continued, "Nevertheless, it must be done. Why do you shrink? The worst they can do is to refuse to help you. In that case you will turn their refusal into your strength."

I started that afternoon. I collected from Indian Civil Service officials, from Excellencies and from people in the

India Office further proof of what I had seen and heard. This "Vow of Truth" stood me in good stead at the many big meetings which I addressed during the following twelve months in England. Every sort of critic seemed to be in my audiences; the hard-boiled person "who had spent as many years in India as the speaker had days"; the complacent patriot who cannot bear to think that Britain ever does anything wrong (a few regrettable incidents occurred in the past, perhaps, but things are different now); the brewer's agents who honoured me by devoting a a leading article to my discredit in their daily paper. All I had to do in rebuttal of their charges was to state that my quotations were furnished by Government officials.

I left the Ashram and started on a two months' tour. My hosts were Indians. It was amazing to see the surprise of the Hindus on finding I was a vegetarian and had been for many years. As for being a tee-totaller, they wouldn't believe it. They thought British people could not live without beef and beer. I used to notice the puzzled expression on the faces of visitors when they found me enjoying Indian customs. A whispered colloquy would ensue; amazement increased; soon, serenely smiling, the newcomer would approach me, make a formal speech of welcome, and invite me to stay in his home next time. Handed on from one delightful home to another, I have travelled across India, and up and down it three or four times.

*　　*　　*

The scene is five years after Lester's first visit to the subcontinent.

The thing we had been longing for happened. Lord Irwin, the Viceroy, responded to the urge of the spirit within him and, breaking through the cast-iron barriers set up by the imperialist machine, brought Mr. Gandhi out of his prison cell to confer and pray with him in Simla. That section of Simla society which is less aware of the things of the spirit experienced some chagrin when Mr. Gandhi arrived in the summer capital and began driving to and from Viceregal Lodge at will in his borrowed car. In the narrow steets of this super-select town, no car is allowed but the Viceroy's and the Commander-in-Chief's. Rickshaws are the only wheeled means of transit.

Perhaps the two men were closer in spirit to each other than either was to most of his fellow countrymen.

The pact was front-page news in London. It seemed certain that Mr. Gandhi would decide, after all, to come to London for the Round Table Conference. Then, of course, he must stay at Kingsley Hall. Where else could he get a bare-walled, stone-floored cell on a flat roof and live among the working-people as he was accustomed to do in India? I wrote him at once, and his reply was carefully worded. I took it straight up to Mr. Polak, an old friend of his South African days.

In his office stood C. F. Andrews. They had evidently been discussing arrangements for hospitality. There were plenty of good offers to consider, ranging from that provided by His Majesty King George to all delegates in the West End to the Hindu Arya Bawan in Hampstead, which was already being redecorated and made ready for his use. I produced the letter just arrived from India. There was no mistaking its purport. "Of course I would rather stay at Kingsley Hall than anywhere else in London, because there I shall be among the same sort of people as those to whom I have devoted my life."

C. F. Andrews immediately recognized and accepted Gandhi's intention. Mr. Polak argued steadily, politely, and convincingly. He was one against two.

"We must, in spite of his desires, consider first his health," he said.

"Bow air is good," I answered, "Sooty but definitely healthy."

"Ah, but it is altogether too far from St. James's Palace," he objected.

"The car drive there and back will be restful to him," I suggested.

"Others in the West End would also enjoy his company," he reminded me.

"They can get it all day long," I retorted. "Let him have the company he likes, at night, anyhow."

We were winning! We were winning! I shot my last bolt. "Isn't it time some one broke through the old custom of letting diplomats and ambassadors confer only with diplomats and ambassadors? The people of Bow can understand the sufferings of the people of India better than even the most sympathetic and sensitive diner-out. Will peace ever come until it's based on the will of ordinary people? Let Mr. Gandhi be the first plenipotentiary from a foreign land, summoned to an imperial city, who throws in his lot with the working-people."

So it was arranged. Kingsley Hall once more shuffled the furniture round and left a row of five cells suitably bare for Mr. Gandhi's party. Soon our post showed how many rumors were flying uncensored over the country. Scurrilous insults came from strangers, and letters of congratulation from people hitherto known to us only by fame. One subscriber vowed never to give Kingsley Hall another penny; others contributed a check or a loan of cups, saucers, and plates to ease our prospective burden; a picture paper showed me anxiously searching for a few goats with which to provide my guest with the only sort of milk he drinks; another reported we were going to keep the animals penned on the roof. The actual fact was too dull to print, merely an order to the local dairy to provide one pint of goat's milk each day until further notice. A talking-picture was made of us polishing the brasses and working on the roof garden, although cleaning and polishing are routine affairs at Kingsley Hall whether a conference delegate from India is expected or not. I had been on the screen once before when the Ovaltine firm had kindly made a film of the Children's House Nursery School. I was playing for the children's march and by error the piano got photographed. But to hear onself speak is an experience of a very different calibre. The mirror acquaints us from babyhood with our appearance, until our reflection becomes at last, I suppose, our oldest friend. But it's strange indeed to hear one's voice. A totally surprising voice mine was to me. I rather like it.

The Communists held a protest meeting close to Kingsley Hall, calling with customary thoroughness at every house, leaving a printed statement declaring Mr. Gandhi to be a traitor to the people, the ally of big business, and a camouflaged Imperialist. They wrote to me personally, explaining that I mustn't interpret this action as aimed at myself or at Kingsley Hall. It was only against Mr. Gandhi.

*   *   *

The people of Bow were massed in the street and inside Kingsley Hall, awaiting their guest. After a reception by the mayor, Gandhiji went on the veranda to greet the crowds

141

below. Finally he climbed the last flight of stone stairs and reached his quarters on the roof. Powis Road stretches at right angles to the row of cells in which he stayed. Householders found they could just see his head when he walked from one cell to another or to the roof bathroom. There'd be a sudden cry, "There 'e goes!," or "There's Gandy!" and mothers would rush out to join the men, gazing upwards. ...

The first Saturday evening stands out memorably in the minds of all who were at the hall. Joy Nights were something of an institution. They cost threepence, took place every Saturday, and were prepared for by a group of men whose serious and careful program-making filled their every Thursday evening. It was the mothers' and fathers' night. They could bring their small children. It consisted of competitive games, dancing, a stunt or two, refreshments, and finally "Auld Lang Syne," sung by the whole company making one huge circle, holding hands with their arms crossed. The younger fry, between eighteen and twenty-five, had a very different sort of program upstairs in the clubroom. The under-eighteens were probably entertaining themselves in most sophisticated style at the old Hall or in Children's House.

In the middle of this party the corner door leading to the staircase suddenly opened and there stood Gandhiji, gazing delightedly at the animated throng. They had been hoping against hope that he would come for a moment and they yearned to stop their activities and stare and cheer. But "manners is manners" in East London and will continue to be long after they're forgotten elsewhere. This man was their guest. They must not lionize him or make him feel as though he were still in public. He had walked into an evening's party in his own home. That was all.

He stood quietly until I remembered our blind member and began to pilot him among the crowds to the opposite side of the Hall, where she sat. As he passed through the throng, everything became immobilized. It was like a moment of suspended animation, as though everyone was holding his breath. As he shook hands with the blind woman and began talking to her, people gathered round in silence, leading their children by the hand or carrying them. As soon as he turned round, they pushed them forward and kept still. One put a child in his arms. I've never seen quite the same look on our people's faces before or since. Then the music struck up and a dance started. As he stood by the piano, up came one of the mothers and said, "Mr. Gandhi, come and have a dance with me." With a look of surprised pleasure at being treated with so little ceremony he thanked her, adding: "But I'm afraid I don't know how to dance. Will you see that I learn, please, Muriel?"

For nearly three months, his every week-day was full and long. Often he arrived home at two or two-thirty in the morning, was always up for his prayer at four o'clock, went to sleep again till five-thirty and then out for an hour's walk before breakfast. This consisted, like most other meals, of oranges, grapes, and goat's milk. He ate in the cell with window and door wide open to the freezing December air. When Charlie Andrews and Horace Alexander, his most regular visitors, and I went up to him after our own hot and hearty meal downstairs, we wore woolen clothes as well as overcoat and muffler. He was wearing a one-piece homespun cotton garment, with perhaps his white Kashmir shawl round him. But it was always we who caused the door and window to be closed. The open ventilator sufficed us.

The weekends were always a joy to him. He stayed at Balliol College, Oxford, at Cambridge, at Birmingham, at Chichester, and most enjoyable of all, perhaps, at Canterbury with Dean Hewlet Johnson.

The invitation that interested me most came from one of the unemployed cotton operatives of Lancashire, who wrote a long letter describing conditions in the cotton industry and asking him to come and see things for himself. The writer declared that his admiration for Mr. Gandhi was deep and sincere, although his leadership of the Indian movement was responsible for much of the misery of unemployment from which he and other Lancashire workers were suffering. Gandhiji immediately accepted the invitation. It was what he had long wanted. English businessmen who heard of the project visit exclaimed, "For goodness' sake, don't let your guest go up there."

"Why not?" I inquired.

"Why? The cotton operatives have suffered so much that they'd tear him to pieces."

Gandhi seemed better to understand our people than their fellow countrymen. The Sunday he spent in Lancashire was one of his happiest days in England.

There was much guesswork among his London acquiantances as to whether he would alter his style of dress to attend His Majesty's garden party at Buckingham Palace. His *khaddar dhoties* were easy to wash, not so easy to dry even on the spacious Kingsley Hall roof, but, fortunately, unneccessary to iron. One folded them up, left them, and all was well. But the white Kashmir shawl was not amendable to laundry work. When it looked off colour, it was turned. Several times this process occurred. After the royal party I asked him how he had dressed. "I just turned the shawl inside out again," he explained. ...

*　　*　　*

One day a message came from John Morris, a blind patient in the local Poor Law Hospital. "Would Mr. Gandhi came in and see him, as he could not get out to Kingsley Hall?" There was no hesitation in the manner of acceptance. Early next morning the whole ward was furbished; up to enjoy a six o'clock visit from the Indian leader. ...

The Nursery School children, hearing it was his birthday, prepared their present. It consisted of woolly lambs and other toys dear to four-year-olds. He came to Children's House to accept the gift, the only present I have ever known him to keep. On the long journey home he insisted on carrying the fragile little things himself in order to present them unbroken to the children of his Ashram school. Our children called him "Uncle Gandhi." One of them was much concerned that he had no proper shoes and socks. Mustn't he be cold? Thereafter several of them kept him daily in their prayers. ...

The neighbors noticed all his habits. A workingman who lived opposite Kingsley Hall, on his way at night shift at 1:30 a.m., often met him returning home after his long day's work. Yet at 4 a.m. his cell was always lit up for prayer. The workingman summed up his character thus: "He never missed once; regular as clockwork he wos. Now, that's wot I admire in the man. He must have got weary, but he never gave up. I'm not religious myself, but. ... "

One Sunday evening he broadcast to the United States from our sitting-room. Because he arrived five minutes late, they asked me to fill in the time with an introduction. Friends in California told me afterwards that as a sort of running accompaniment to our voices, a twittering sound was audible, incomprehensible, staccato, something like birds, but not quite. It was the children at shrill-voiced play in the recreation ground far below us. The radio people had taken many precautions to keep the ether solely for him, but in the East End, children, I am glad to say, are ubiquitous.

From *It So Happened*

When the Round Table Conference was over, a few of us were invited to travel with him in leisurely fashion through France, Switzerland, and Italy before he joined the liner at Brindisi. There was a strange scene at the Gare du Nord in Paris. People swarmed on the platforms, climbed on to engines, trucks, scaffolding, and blocked our way with their eagerness. He addressed public meetings on non-violence in France and in Switzerland, where he was the guest of Romain Rolland.

...The friendship of the two men was a real thing, though it must have been strange for Gandhiji to meet his biographer for the first time. On one of the early morning walks when the Alps towered above us in cold starlight, Pierre Ceresole met Gandhiji. The conversation soon turned into a statement of Gandhiji's beliefs, clearer than any other I had heard.

> Truth is God, and the way to find Him is non-violence. A leader must have complete mastery over himself. Anger must be banished, and fear and falsehood. You must lose yourself. You must not please yourself either with food or sex pleasures. Thus purified, you get power. It's not your own, it's God's. Look at me. Wherein does my strength lie? I am nothing. A boy of fifteen could fell me with a blow. I am nothing, but I have become detached from fear and desire, so that I know God's power. I tell you, if all the world denied God, I should be His sole witness. It is a continual miracle to me.

From *It So Happened*

...After the free atmosphere of the democracies it was queer to watch the young Fascist officials whom Mussolini sent into the carriage to welcome him as he crossed the Italian frontier. Gandhi tried to see the Pope, but the Vatican arrangements could not be made in time. He saw Mussolini, and was unfavorably impressed. "His eyes were never still," he said, trying to describe the interview. Mussolini was eager for him to visit schools, houses, and public buildings erected during his regime, but the long list of invitations was not acceptable.

By 1934 I was in India again, on my way home from China and Japan. My niece, Dorothy Hogg, was with me. Recently released from prison, Gandhi was then touring the country on behalf of the Untouchables and wired us to join him. To help and honour Untouchables, folk born outside the pale and Hinduism and despised and oppressed throughout the centuries, constitutes for Gandhi the acid test of the sincerity of his followers. "How can you demand your rights from the British when you withold the rights of those seventy millions of your own countrymen?" he asks. It is his oft-repeated and by no means rhetorical question. The anti-Untouchability campaign proved exhausting. Five or six open-air meetings and long journeys every day wore most of us down. But Gandhi himself went steadily on, the least worn though the most heavily worked of all. Each of his meetings was attended by many thousands of people, some of whom had walked many miles and waited long hours to hear him. Arrivals and departures by train or car were stimulating, if a little disconcerting. Had "volunteers" not formed cordons round us we should have been lifted off our feet by the welcoming crowds. Every time the train stopped the platform was invisible, transformed into a sea of brown faces that broke into innumerable waves. People somehow managed to climb up the smooth walls of the railway coaches and hang on to the window frames. They stared in silence into the compartment, eager to catch a glimpse of the Mahatma. Each window accommodated about eight heads.

From *It Occurred to Me*

After dinner one day I read a letter from Bengal. It reported that the previous week a magistrate had visited a near-by village and insisted on the inhabitants coming out of their houses to salute the Union Jack. As Congressmen, of course, cannot do that, trouble ensued. Inquiries should have been made, but no one was allowed to enter the disturbed area. "Perhaps they'd let a British person go. Shall I try?" I asked Gandhiji.

"You could ask Sir John Anderson's [Governor of Bengal] permission," he answered.

146

The necessary telegrams were dispatched to Calcutta while I jealously counted up the few days remaining before my ship sailed for Europe. I had promised to be home by Easter; nine months was a long enough spell of absence from Kingsley Hall. The responsiblities on my young deputies was heavy. I would just have time to get to Calcutta and back before setting out for Ceylon and boarding the boat at Colombo.

But it didn't turn out that way at all. The talk with Sir John proved too interesting, and too useful. It opened the way to many other interviews and much message-carrying. At first I worked determinedly at the jigsaw puzzle of fitting all duties into seven days, but little by little something Doris had said to me as we parted in London, assumed great significance. I had taken almost no notice of it at the time, because the idea was so alien to all my desires and plans. She had repeated several times, with emphasis, "Don't forget, if you find something you ought to do for India, you must stay on and do it."

I returned to Gandhiji. He seemed pleased with my mission. I wired to the Viceroy on my own account, asking for an interview. The reply was to be sent to Colombo. If unfavourable, I could embark forthwith and get back to work at home. If an interview were arranged, I would have to start on a five days' journey to Delhi and one thing would be sure to lead to many others. I would probably be in India for months.

It is a horrid journey from Madras down to the tipmost point of India. And I don't know any more desolate spot than where the train stops and the boat starts, except the place in Ceylon where the boat stops and the train starts. That is definitely worse because the train doesn't want to start. It seems to cleave to the smelly jetty. One walks up and down it for nearly two hours; it is scarcely surprising that no one has ever had the heart to set up a tearoom here, or a bar, or a counter for chocolates and minerals, or even a waiting-room. One stands about disconsolately. ...

The customs men had condemned the great basketful of fruit Dorothy and I had cannily brought with us for supper. Ceylon apparently was afraid of a blight on its orange crop. The meal served on the train fitted the income of the Indian Civil Service officials, perhaps, but we couldn't afford it. So we pretended we were satisfied with our biscuits and the odd bit of fruit we had salvaged when the blight experts weren't behaving too expertly.

*   *   *

Mixed up with the heat, discomfort, hunger, and guessing what Lord Willingdon's cable would be, was the slow development of an amazing new idea. If I stayed out in India I'd probably better retire from my leadership of Kingsley Hall. To return at Easter to take up my old duties had been a fixed star on my horizon. When a fixed star threatens to move, one's calculations seem scarcely worth bothering over. One thing I was clear about; I could not let the load of responsibility for Kingsley Hall lie on deputies longer than for the appointed nine months. I had intended to resign at some subsequent and not far distant date. Perhaps it would be better to cable to the trustees at once, that they might settle both problems at once, the immediate task due to the state of affairs in India, and that which was inevitably approaching, the appointment of my successor.

We drove from Colombo to the home of Mr. Ediriwara, our old helpmate in scrubbing, polishing, and other Kingsley Hall work, now the head of an interesting Buddhist school in Moratuwa. The vice-regal cable awaited us saying, "Come." I sat on the bed for hours facing the break-up of the whole pattern of my life. As I pondered, I seemed to be outside it all in some queer way. I remember how a centipede rushing across the floor made me shiver. Yet it may not have been the centipede.

I pondered every aspect of the situation for the best part of two days. Then I dispatched a cable to the trustees, airmail letters to Doris, Ben Platten, and my dear and faithful deputies.

The very air I breathed seemed different. Up till now everything I saw or heard or thought fitted into some aspect of Kingsley Hall, its past, present, or future. This was an extraordinary new world I had entered. Kingsley Hall and I were no longer one.

*   *   *

Back and forth between Britain and India went various rumours. "Gandhi is a spent force." That was wishful thinking, obviously. "The money collected on the Harijan tour is being spent on political work." "Gifts are not acknowledged." "No audited accounts are published." As I was considerably bored each week with the long columns of figures published in *Harijan*, and as one of the leading business men in Calcutta was the treasurer of the fund it seemed to be singularly unintelligent of my fellow countrymen to choose that particular stick to beat the Gandhi people with. My co-religionists worried me, too. As there were so many missionaries of various nationalities in every place we stopped at, why didn't some of them join in the public rejoicings that at long last Hindus were convicted of the sin of untouchability and were trying to get rid of it? Or if they had been conditioned to smell politics in every popular movement, why weren't they interested in turning up with the crowd for seven-o'clock prayers? Evening after evening a thousand or so citizens would come together to sit in silence while some one sang chants, hymns, prayers. If joining in these devotions seemed to them indecorous, at any rate let them call and have a friendly talk with this super-accessible, super-friendly person. But no. They mostly preserved an aloof attitude.

*   *   *

...I cooled off too precipitately one evening after a day of heat. Every part of me seemed to go wrong. I had to stay in bed when they set out on the next tour. Lots of nice young Indian doctors came and prescribed, but I knew Gandhiji's method was best—fast, fast, fast. At last I was able to move. I went to an ashram near Calcutta for Easter. It wasn't a nice Easter. Only one person, the superintendent, could speak English, and he, though very kind, had two or three hundred men to keep at work as well as a body of helpers to train. My room was a little shed. Every two hours a cup of milk, a glass of orange juice, or a glass of tomato juice was brought to me. The steamy heat at all hours of the day and night encouraged every sort of insect. A spider of intimidating girth lodged in the crack of the rough-boarded door which separated my bath shed from the rest of the sheds. When a centipede fell out of my wall, I told the superintendent, gently, so as not to appear to grumble. Unmoved, he answered, "Of course, sister, this Ashram is bounded on three sides by the jungle. The creatures naturally come through our place. It is their short cut. But have no fear. They do not hurt us. They know we are non-violent people." I smiled feebly, knowing I was not, and certain that they knew it, too.

At the end of a week's rest, I went to Calcutta to keep some engagements. I had seen Jahawarlal Nehru in London, corresponded with him, followed his development closely and with great appreciation. I was now allowed to visit him in jail. I had an hour with him. One thing he said stands out clearly. "Hornets kept flying into my cell. I killed them. More came. For weeks they worried me. Then I decided to change my tactics; to practice Satyagraha. I proclaimed an armistice. I would kill no more, and they must keep to their side of the cell by the window. Both sides have faithfully adhered to the pact." ...

It was the 15th of June when we set sail for Europe. The monsoon was due. It did not fail us. We had the most loathsome voyage home. A Bow friend met me, as unheralded I reached Kingsley Hall door. "Why, Muriel!" he said. "You've shrunk!"

From *It So Happened*

By 1936 I was back in India again for a few months with Gladys Owen, my old colleague from Kingsley Hall. We had come from East Asia where we had been making a study together of two great Japanese institutions, the one as powerful for good as the other for evil, the co-operatives, and the poisonous drug traffic. The one was Christian, and for Japanese consumption; the other devilish, and for Chinese consumption. Gladys Owen remained in India. She is still there, working among students, running a school with an Indian co-teacher, organizing a clinic, helping college folk to set up a servants' club, mixing with Moslem, Hindu, Christian, British and Indian with equal appreciation.

My fourth visit was in 1938, when I bought my passage with money I had earned by lecturing in the United States. Dorothy Hogg came with me again—niece, courier, secretary, instigator of adventures, and elicitor of laughter. We were to meet old friends in a new capacity. Former jail-birds were now honoured citizens, some of them prime ministers. ...

On previous visits to India I had made a point of getting in touch with British officials, the viceroy, governors, and others. Just because I was nearly always the guest of Hindus or Moslems, my contacts with our government officials were necessary. I had often been privileged to take to them unofficial messages from Indian leaders, or had gone to them on my own account to ask advice or make suggestions. I had often noticed their sense of frustration. "I'd like to do what you ask, but I can't," one of them would say. Or, "The Empire has become so vast that we're merely parts of a machine, no longer free agents." Or, "For years I have wanted to have a talk with Mr. Gandhi, but there has been no way of getting into touch." Or, "I have tried often to collaborate with Indians but they do not trust me because of my position. A person with no official standing can do more here in three months than I have been able to do in as many years." But now our officials, from the governors downwards, seemed less burdened. It must have been difficult sometimes for good men to hold other good men in prison; difficult to keep up the appearance of superiority to them; difficult to be prevented by pseudo-prestige from meeting them face to face and discussing affairs of mutual interest. Now officials were asking after the health and happiness of men whom I should have had to apologize for mentioning in the old days. The *Stateman*, leading British-owned daily in India, carried a leader refuting non-violence. A few days later it published Mr. Gandhi's reply, lifted verbatim from his weekly paper, *Harijan*. This new spirit seemed like a great wave rolling up. I wished there were more reconcilers to be carried on its crest.

Circling the Globe
for Peace

Following her 1926 trip to India, Muriel Lester's work began to take on more and more of an international dimension, particularly as that work related to Gandhi and the Indian struggle for independence from the British Empire. But as the international scene worsened, Lester's involvement and travels widened as she came more and more to be seen as an able interpreter of current events, a persuasive critic of both imperialism and totalitarianism, and a joyous exponent of "the things that make for peace."

In 1930 Lester made the first of many trips to the United States. The trips began, in part, to raise money for the expanded work in Bow, as well as to help interpret the situation in Britain and in India. During her 1932 trip this pattern took a new turn.

From *It Occurred to Me*

Things were going ill with China. Nevin Sayre, the secretary of the American Fellowship of Reconciliation, an old friend of mine, asked me if I would be willing to go the following autumn to Japan and China if the F.O.R. people in those countries would support my visit, arrange meetings, give me hospitality, and pay all travel expenses after my arrival there? Could I spare the time? Could I raise my fare to and from London?

This suggestion seemed to Doris and me the natural fulfilment of what we had been working for during many years. Kingsley Hall had stood for the breaking down of racial barriers and the spread of international brotherhood even in war time. At the ceremony of brick-laying for the new Hall, a Chinese representative had supplied us with a Chinese proverb to express our faith—"Under Heaven, one family."

The common sense, the inherent sanity, of our East End workmen had stood us in good stead so often and clarified so many tangled issues which intellectuals have to spend nights and days in arguing about, that I began to feel their point of view would be of value in the Far East. I had already proved its usefulness in India. Perhaps the day would come when our own statesmen would come to the East End to learn its wisdom. Now that the people of Japan and China were being sucked into the whirlpool of hate and fear, one ought to go there and give the same message to both countries, a message not of easy words and of dogmatic theory, but a sincere greeting from people who knew from experience the bitterness of war and who yet kept themselves clear of hate, held on to their faith in the way of Christ, and refused to consider any one as their enemy because they happened to have been born on a different patch of earth. Apart from all this, however, one thing made it easy for me to accept definitely Nevin Sayre's suggestion that I put in six months' work in the Far East.

Thirty years previously I had discovered a fact which history lessons at school had taught none of us. Great Britain had waged two wars to force the Chinese to buy our opium from India. At first it had been incredible. Then the burning shame was so great that it seemed to me I could never hold my head up again. I tried to think of something I could do about it. There was nothing. I found everyone eager to let bygones be bygones. The Boxer rising and the consequent European expedition had been so ill reported that many people were willing to consider that by and large we were now quits [even], China and England.

All I could do was to go on feeling ashamed. Now was my chance to make amends in some infinitesimal measure for the old outrage. I had spent most of the previous thirty years doing odd jobs in Bow. Now my friends there would speed me Eastward with their blessing and at the same time accustom themselves to carrying on the activities of the Hall without me. There were many fine workers at both Children's House and at Kingsley Hall.

From *It Occurred to Me*

We [nieces Dorothy and Rosemary Hogg accompanied her] sailed through the Gold Gate on the *Asama Maru*, and reached Tokyo in October. Only a month for the whole of Japan! My Fellowship of Reconciliation hosts and hostesses had made careful plans so that I should be quickly accustomed to Japanese ways. Dr. Kagawa called the morning of my arrival. The second day found me the guest of a Japanese baroness. There I learned to assume a new posture at meal times, sitting on my heels, not nearly so easy as squatting in India; or had the seven intervening years stiffened my muscles? The bedroom delighted me with its paper walls, tiny sunny veranda, speckless floor, and the luxurious mattress laid thereon.

*   *   *

Dr. Kagawa took me to his cooperatives, the farm, the school, the shops, and the clinics. The work most pleasing to me with my unhappy experience of money-lenders in the East End, was his cooperative pawn shop. I became a member of his cooperative hospital. It takes only twelve shillings to join, and for that one can attend as a patient at any time and enjoy free the services of some of the best doctors in the city. It was a joy to get to know Mrs. Kagawa and the children, to stay in their little house, to share their meals.

My program was heavy. I preached in churches, lectured at colleges, talked with small groups, and spoke to some hundred or so of the richest business men of the city by special request on "Voluntary Poverty in India and England." I also inspected the Buddhists' social work, and visited numerous settlements...people kept begging me for news of Gandhi's Non-Violence Movement in India and for details of the pacifist movement in Europe. Sometimes it was a little overwhelming, the sense of expectancy in a hallful of students, or among a group of college professors. They wanted details of specific actual happenings. This exactly suited my ingrained preference for facts that can be visualized rather than for theories that can be discussed. They extracted a promise from me to give permanent form to these bits of pacifist history by writing a book for them to translate into Japanese. A definite charge was laid upon me after addressing a club of particularly advanced women:

> Miss Lester, we, the women of Japan, are too recently emancipated to have been able to set up an organization of our own. We have no means to giving our message to the world. Will you

give our message for us? Please tell the world that we, the women of Japan, are solid for peace.

I was proud to have the privilege of giving this message wherever I went.

In whatever part of Japan I travelled, I knew that Government agents were with me, listening to my speeches on war resistance. I was therefore especially delighted to be asked to broadcast. I had several intimate talks with Mr. Amau, one of the Foreign Secretaries of the Imperial Government. It was inevitable that he should counter my dislike of Japan's imperialist policy in China with a *tu quoque* [Latin, meaning "you too" or "you're another" as regards Britain's treatment of India.] "Do you want independence for India as much as you want it for China?" he asked. I was glad to be able to tell him that thousands of British people were spending time and energy in working to free India from the imperial yoke, for India's sake and for our own.

The Prime Minister, Mr. [Makoto] Saito, in the course of a half-hour's talk said that Japan was carefully studying the situation in England to discover the influence of the woman's vote. They had not been satisfied that so far it had improved matters. Our policy seemed more reactionary than formerly. Therefore, he could not consider favourably the plea of Japanese women to be given more representation in the nation's councils. This excellent and kindly man, who was murdered in the army rising of 1936, tried also to explain to me that the Japanese mill girls' wages , which we deemed tragically low, were enough for her simple needs because her work was only a temporary affair—marriage was her real career.

*   *   *

We embarked at Kobe for Tientsin. China was another world. ... My host and hostess in Tientsin were American missionaries ... [who] lived near enough to the workmen's quarter to have been invovled in danger when Japanese guns were suddenly trained on the Chinese city and bombarded it for some ten days. They took me to see the industrial centre where scores of women were enabled to earn rice for their families during the weeks when the gunfire prevented the men from going to their regular work. The deft movements of their hands daintily embroidering handkerchiefs delighted us, but the faces told a story of suffering, patience and determination.

They reminded me of the women of Bow. If once more the Japanese soldiers were ordered to fire without warning on the Chinese quarter of this city, my place would surely be with these women. Remembering the Peace Army, I wrote to Mr. Amau in Tokyo to tell him what I had seen and what I would have to do, should the circumstance arise. Throughout the programs of meetings arranged for me by the Chinese Fellowship of Reconciliation, I made a point of prefacing my address with an apology for the evil that my ancestors had done to theirs by the opium wars.

*   *   *

At Cheloo University, Tsinan, I came to know Luella Miner and found she fitted into my gallery of wise women. It holds about six people. Each is marked by resourcefulness, steadfast temper, wide interests; they are people who can look at things objectively, who are rooted and grounded in God. When one dies, I don't search for her successor. She appears sooner or later. At present one of them is in India, one in the States, two in Bow, and two in other parts of England. Dr. Miner was over seventy and a lifelong friend of Feng Yu-Hsiang. This extraordinary man had already captured our imagination in Bow; a peasant turned soldier, then turned Christian as a result of watching the Christians go cheerfully to death in the Boxer rising; a great general adored by his men, a member of the Government; now in exile, living on the slopes of Taishan, a holy mountain famous in the days of Abraham, to which all China's great leaders make the pilgrimage sooner or later.

Dr. Miner sent him a message and he kindly invited us to visit him. We had to spend the night at the foot of the mountain. In pre-dawn darkness we climbed into chairs and were carried up its slopes. By the side of the steep stone paths, pines climbed. When the sun shone, green and blue birds flew from branch to branch. Every now and then on the still air we heard shouts, snatches of song, or sharp words of command ringing out. Each bend of the narrow path disclosed some new scene, wild, romantic, secluded. This mountain fastness was well guarded by devoted troops protecting a lost leader. Suddenly we found ourselves confronted by five of them, holding their horses in the bridle, ready to leap into the saddle to give the alarm. Then they caught sight of the escort General Feng had sent us. We passed unchallenged.

His officers and men numbered a thousand. They were all vowed to the service of China. They must live in purity, without drinking, gambling, or smoking. They planted trees, raised vegetables and fruit, learned hygiene, made roads, studied. They had just built an exquisite temple shrine to commemorate the soldiers who had died for the Revolution.

Once more the path wound and ended at an old temple. We were shown into a little cold, stoveless reception room. Fires were considered a luxury by this peasant general and therefore eschewed.

I thought I had never seen a face of such impressive mournfulness as Marshall Feng's. He is strong, tall, dressed like Tolstoi in a cotton blouse. His honesty has been an embarrassment to friend and foe. His simple living shames other leaders. One who built himself a palatial residence found it annoying when a humble little cottage was erected on the adjoining site for the superior officer, Feng.

He had been so deeply hurt by the British shootings in Shanghai that his devotion to Christianity had collapsed. He could have forgiven the soldiers, for militarism is much the same the world over. But he found that his special friend among the missionaries, the man who had first brought him to know Christ, justified the bloodshed, declaring that it was necessary in order to prevent something worse. Feng Yu-Hsiang proceeded to cancel the Bible classes he had set up for his soldiers. He no longer encouraged them to be baptized. He asked me many questions, seemed interested, but his look of profound suffering was not once enlivened by a smile, until I told him about the Bow children. ... He wanted me to tell him all I could about Gandhi. I proffered my usual request for forgiveness for my country's sins and began.

*   *   *

I journeyed south to Hankow. Among a variety of experiences, one stands out. Fellowship of Reconciliation members were holding a meeting in the bishop's house. Among their invited guests was a boy of twenty, Christopher Tang. He sat amazed as first the chairman and then I told of the spread of Christian pacifism in the world. It was like the Gates of Heaven opening to Christopher. He had never met or heard of a pacifist before. He had thought he was alone in his stand against militarism. As a schoolboy he had refused to walk in a certain procession because the violent spirit of its leaders clashed with what he had learned of Christ. The boys could not forgive him. They asked the headmaster to expel him. He refused, though not sharing Christopher's ideas. The boys thereupon left the school. It remained closed throughout the first term. Christopher, the cause of its closing, was repeatedly threatened, assaulted. The persecutors were the first to grow tired. The school reopened. When he went on to college, military drill was obligatory, but he could not possibly practise killing. Again a lonely witness ensued. When the examination results were published, his degree though gained, was not granted. Having never met anyone who shared his views, the discovery of an international body such as the F.O.R. was like a blessing dropped down from heaven. Those who know Christopher best, his radiant humble spirit, and his unconquerable soul, prophesy that if ever China is to have its own Gandhi, Christopher may be he.

I sailed down the Yangtse-Kiang to Nanking. If only China had an adequate news service! If only the world's press were to drop the overworked words, "chaos" and "bandit" in its paragraphs about China! There is plenty of news of a different kidney [ilk, nature] to astonish the West; a network of rural reconstruction centres spreading from province to province; a new national health service; roads thrust through mountains; railway lines bringing into contact places that were a three weeks' journey apart; training-schools for magistrates and mayors, for doctors, nurses, midwives, and first-aid volunteers; national factories with good working conditions, producing cheaply what formerly had to be imported.

* * *

Next I went into territory recently in the hands of bandits. I stayed with a woman who had refused to escape in the gunboat. She had been practising the presence of God so that she refused, on the evening the bandits were expected, to let anyone stay to protect her. Sitting alone, knitting, she heard the door thrown open, the heavy tramp of feet. A bandit held his pistol to her breast. With death so near, her sensibilities quickened. She forced herself to look into his face. To her amazement, she felt no animosity, no resentment. He was young. She felt sorry for him. Death didn't seem to matter at all, scarcely existed. She gave him her ring. He turned away and left her unharmed. Life was never the same afterwards. "Time was coloured with the infinite, immeasurably enhanced."

Shanghai was the next city on my itinerary. I detested it. ... I went into a cotton mill, by no means one of the worst. The children worked twelve-hour shifts, day or night. On night work, the shift was lengthened to sixteen hours every Friday. Some of the girls were ten years old. Worse than the weariness is the required sense of repressing one's natural instincts for joy, for leisureliness, for spontaneity. Everything is forced, hurried, rushed. It is in the small hours round about 2 a.m. that most of the accidents occur. Some of these mill girls have developed into grand characters. So eager are they to remove the stigma of illiteracy from their country and to fit her to stand up to the Japanese that after a night shift they attend classes arranged by the YWCA at nine o'clock in the morning. When they have learned to read and write, they volunteer to teach others at the same hour.

From *It Occurred to Me*

From China, Lester went to India once again and finally back home, to Bow—for three months. From there she traveled to Holland to attend the IFOR Conference where she was appointed IFOR's "ambassador-at-large." Then she went to the Soviet Union with Sherwood Eddy for a short, five-day visit.

After flying back from Russia, the weeks soon slipped by until October 9th, when my ship sailed. Before setting out, I called at the Chinese and Japanese embassies. Each encourage me. I shall never forget the Japanese official who said, "This personal method is, in my opinion, the only way in which the world will gain peace."

...I had a big program to fulfill; my lecture fees [in the United States] during these three months were to pay for journeyings and living expenses of an eighteen months' tour. The Fellowship of Reconciliation people in Japan and China had laid upon me the need of a speedy return, but made it

160

clear that there would be no possibility of their undertaking my finances as on the first visit. Then it had been a short stay, four weeks in Japan and nine weeks in China, following a full schedule all the time. But this trip was to be a long, leisurely progress, as unprogrammed as possible. I was to travel third class, go into the interior, retrace my footsteps whenever necessary, travel up and down the country as the way opened. I wanted time to absorb something of the Chinese art of life, to learn more of the Japanese way of thinking. On the previous visit the people of both countries were continually asking me to explain Gandhiji's philosophy to them. I got almost tired of relating the same facts so many scores of times. "Why don't you go and see for yourself?" I asked. "And why don't you invite one of his followers here? It seems a waste of opportunity. You are much nearer to each other geographically than I am." Of course I went on telling the same stories about India because they never lose their fascination for me, but I repeated my challenge, too. "You like the sound of life in Gandhiji's Ashram, its regular hours of prayer, its menial work, the lowly spirit of its leader daily performing the dirtiest jobs. Isn't it time you started an Ashram yourselves? Any one can, you know."

So it happened that one of the outstanding Chinese Christians, a brilliant Confucian scholar and stalwart member of the Fellowship of Reconciliation, wrote to me while I was still in the States. "When you come, will you join a few of us who want to set up an Ashram during August? An experiment, of course, but it may lead to something permanent."

I received another letter from China at about the same time, a cyclo-styled letter [made by a machine that makes multiple copies by utilizing a stencil cut by a graver whose tip is a small rowel.] Dull-looking as such always are, it altered the course of my life. It was from a trustworthy traveller, and among other things it told in a few objective sentences about a town in North China where Japanese influence was supreme. As a result, the Chinese magistrate was witnessing a sudden influx of drug traffickers. These enjoyed extra-territorial rights as Japanese citizens and in this way were able to ignore the magistrate's authority. He had a good reputation; in fact the whole district was well governed and self-respecting. Opium was smoked, of course, but this heroin and cocaine trade was far more dangerous; traffic in poisonous drugs had been practically unknown in the district before the Japanese took Manchuria. Now, two years later, there were some thirty-nine illegal drug shops in this town alone, and over a hundred others in the surrounding district. They were on the increase all the time. The magistrate therefore had told his police to watch out for any Chinese employees of these firms. One of them had been arrested with five hundred dollars' worth of drugs on him. The magistrate confiscated the stuff and sent it to the capital, Nanking. Thereupon a gang of ruffians had forced their way into the magistrate's office, demanded the release of the Chinese employee and two thousand five hundred Chinese dollars as compensation for the confiscated drugs. When he refused their request, they kept him prisoner in his own office. Eventually he paid part of the amount demanded and went home. They next day they turned up again and insisted on his paying the balance out of his own pocket. The letterwriter said it was well known that Japanese policy was to weaken the Chinese nation by protecting the many hundred Korean, Formosan, and Japanese drug traffickers who were setting up this illegal trade all over the country.

I read and re-read this paragraph. I saw our last century's sins brought up to date and committed again by a nation that was in close alliance with Britain, whose policy we encouraged, however nefarious, giving way to her all the time so long as our own trade interests didn't suffer. I longed to disbelieve the letter-writer, but could not. He was the author of several reliable books. After much pondering I decided to follow the vow of truth and put the situation to some leading Japanese as soon as I reached Tokyo.

My last month in the States was spent in California. I had a week at Asilomar among six hundred students. The conference grounds stretch down through pine woods to a rock strewn headland on the Pacific coast. I talked to them the first hour every morning, and after a short break I had another hour for questions.

* * *

After the last evening service, we went out of the chapel, a long silent procession in the dark, carrying tapers to throw on to the gigantic bonfire which was soon flaming and flaring into the night sky. We stood round it, pledging ourselves to fellowship and service.

In the California colleges I found a quite different atmosphere from that of 1933. Then I had been invited to lecture to the whole assembly of one of the leading colleges. The president had taken the chair and afterwards asked me to consider coming back and delivering a six weeks' course to the students. This time I wasn't allowed to speak on the campus at all. It was made clear that this was not the result of anything I had said or done in the interim. The communist scare, with all its fakes, its black list, and its red network had made even quite sensible people jumpy. I was advertised to speak just outside the campus. It was sad, though gratifying, to hear that the president had taken some trouble sending out messages to the students urging them to go and hear me.

*   *   *

On arrival in Tokyo I sought out an old Friend whose life has been spent in Japan. He read the paragraph in my cyclo-styled letter with a weighty seriousness. He said that the only thing to do was to ask Japanese advice. With his help I was given an interview with one of the elder statesmen. He asked me to state my case. I reminded him that it was scarcely a case, only hearsay. I was half ashamed to give voice to it. Calmly he bade me start. At the end of the short recital he proceeded serenely to give me a detailed account of the past and present Japanese policy regarding opium and drugs. It reminded me of many a formal statement delivered by responsible British Ministers regarding India, Africa, or other parts of the Empire, when they were trying to reassure the public that what looked wrong was really right. As his voice went on and on, a moment or two of disillusion and hopelessness overwhelmed me. What was the use of trying to keep the vow of truth? Then I bethought me...that this good statesman had no idea that I was trusting only to truth and had no desire to dispense blame or praise. He did not even know I was ready to confess our share of responsibility. I waited. The confident official voice ceased. He looked at me to see if I was reassured. I could only bow my head, wholly unconvinced. Then I shot my last bolt. "You know, sir, don't you, that I am not here in any way to blame Japan. Even if everything in this letter of mine proved true, I could not lift a finger of blame against you. All the time I am conscious of the grave sin we committed against China last century in the opium wars. Our sin is greater than yours."

As sudden as an April change of weather was the difference in the atmosphere. His face lost its polite, impersonal expression. He turned to me as one human being trusting another. "Are you going to China?" he inquired.

"In a few weeks," I answered.

"Will you then please keep a careful watch? If you see anything that seems bad, go to the nearest Japanese official and tell him all about it. I will see that they are all prepared to give you every facility for investigation. Whatever you may discover that is wrong, get proof of it and reliable witnesses, Japanese if possible; if not, British or American; best of all if you could return here yourself and bring your evidence. I would see to it that your reports reached the highest quarters."

We made our way home, amazed at the outcome of our mission. Part of me, however, was concentrating on a passionate hope that I should never notice or hear of my drug misery.

*   *   *

I arrived in Peiping the day after Palm Sunday, fervently hoping that if there were any signs of the Japanese drug traffic, I should not notice them. Dislike of responsibility may make one immoral.

Five days later I gave my first address at a YWCA. I had been asked to speak on a completely innocuous subject, Kingsley Hall, not at all likely, I thought, to stir up any unpleasant facts about Japan. The question time was safely over. The audience melted away into the tearoom. But a tall Chinese woman with a strong face of almost masculine type detained me. When we had the room to ourselves, she burst out with her question, "What would you do," she asked, "if you were in my place and saw the Japanese ruining your fellow countrymen with drugs? They entice our young people, too, even children. They give them a taste of the poison free. I'm a doctor. I know what it leads to. What can I do?"

It was strange to see an impassive-faced Chinese woman weep. My hour had come pretty promptly. I asked for names,

164

addresses, proofs. I told her what my job was. A day or two later I found myself right in the middle of the melee. My friends explained that they were having trouble with a Korean drug-trader who had set up his shop immediately outside the university walls. He could not be permanently dislodged because he claimed extra-territorial rights as a Japanese citizen.

Shortly after I made my way to Changli, the place described in the cyclo-styled letter. Japanese barracks were at Changli as at other towns. As more soldiers had arrived, more prostitutes came, too, of course. The county has 400,000 inhabitants, the town 15,000. I was furnished with a map of the country, showing the positions of a hundred and forty-one drug shops, all illegal, Japanese or Korean owned, set up in the last year or so. They had all countered the magistrate's closing orders with the claim of Japanese extra-territorial rights. Nearly all these drug shops were situated in this self-respecting little town, accustomed to good government, wherein a social conscience had been fostered for generations.

Public opinion is too strong and socially progressive for property-owners in the city to lease houses or land to the drug-traders. Consequently nearly all the shops are just outside the walls, some of them disreputable-looking shanties, clinging to the mud bank at the foot of the wall like parasites infecting and reinfecting a fever-stricken patient. Much of the drug trade is allied with other antisocial activities — brothels, gambling-dens, unlicensed pawn shops where dope is offered instead of cash. If an injection is desired, a syringe is rented to the customer on the deferred-payment system. The first dose of heroin is obtainable at a low price, which rises stiffly as the customer becomes an addict. Lotteries were something quite new in the people's experience and the decrease in prosperity which had occurred during the last two years, due in a great measure to the Japanese evading payment of customs duty on imported goods, had made the idea of getting something for nothing specially attractive. One can purchase drugs for five cents (about three-farthings in English money.) Young people are freely served.

The city authorities have had to open a clinic for drug addicts. The magistrate was engaged in his office when I went to visit the clinic, so without waiting to see him I asked to be shown in. There were twenty-five men, mostly young. Often the number is larger. There is no accomodation for women, though they have come asking for treatment.

Those who do not know and love the Japanese must remember that the citizens in that great country are as ignorant of what is being done in their name as the people of Germany and Italy, or, should I add? as my own kindly fellow countrymen. Our English newspapers never tell us details of the raids our airmen make on the northwest frontier of India. It is only if one has the opportunity of hearing the airmen themselves talk that one comes to know what they have to do.

I came back to Peiping with the names and addresses of each of the traders in the county, well aware that this specific information applied only to one comparatively small area. The other cities in the demilitarized zone were much worse, but it was in Changli that the quality of citizenship was such that several people, both Chinese and foreign, were willing to risk loss, imprisonment, and life itself rather than witness in silence the progressive poisoning of the population.

According to my initial instructions from Tokyo, I got in touch with the consul-general in Tiensin, Mr. Kawagoe, the present Japanese ambassador to China, and heard he was expecting me. He welcomed me with great politeness, and through an interpreter we pursued the subject of drugs along a rambling route which continually led us away from our quarry. But the fact that I had been invited and welcomed seemed to me a great thing. In a few days I had a letter promising that stricter control would be exerted in the future. As in all subsequent talks with Japanese Ministers on this subject, the outstanding fact was the unworkable, equivocal, unjust damnability of the doctrine of extra-territoriality. I wonder if any other country has benfitted by it as much as my own.

I dispatched to Tokyo an account of what I'd seen and offered to come back for ten days in July if my evidence was wanted. Mr. H. Tymperley, of the *Manchester Guardian*, was meanwhile helping me in numerous ways. It was a joy to find he definitely favoured the method of going straight to the Japanese officials, without apportioning blame. He gathered a roomful of journalists to hear the details of what was happening in North China, and within a few days the news had gone round the world. Now wherever I went, some foreigner or other was sure to impress on me that I mustn't imagine that North China was the only place where this sort of propaganda was going on.

One observer said, "I've knocked round the world for a good many years and seen plenty of human hate, but I've never seen anything equal the bitterness the Chinese feel toward the Japanese on account of their drug trade." ...

It must not be imagined that Chinese, American, and British have no part nor lot in the drug traffic in China. The vast ramifications of the trade spread all over the world. Its clandestine methods are well known. The point of my report was the fact that it is continually protected by the presence of Japanese troops and the civilians' claim of extra-territorial rights to permit them to break Chinese law.

*   *   *

Down in Amoy, I found there were three hundred and seventy-eight Japanese opium shops operating illegally and quite openly. The Chinese magistrate, unable to touch the shopkeeper, instructed his police to follow the Chinese customers on their way home and arrest them quietly so as not to precipitate an incident. The drug-traders retaliated by setting up armed protectors outside the shops to give safe conduct home to each of their clients, a new result of extra-territoriality.

Yet there is a marked tendency among the comfortably placed to make light of it. I suppose generation after generation of British people in the East have echoed the refrain, "It is impossible to keep the Chinaman away from his opium so what is the use of trying?" With the easy tolerance that comes from personal immunity, one official said to me, "The addict asks nothing better than to be left to die in peace. We've no right to deny him this pleasure."

It was my job to point out that, unfortunately, he didn't die. He sold his wife or forced his children to work at an early age to provide him with the means of buying more dope. ...

In Canton I found that in some streets every other shop was fitted up with wooden berths like those in a ship's cabin, and in most of them smokers lay. All day long this goes on; children run in and out freely. A special launch is put on from 10 p.m. to 4 a.m. to bring smokers over from the business part of the city to the other side of the river. Near each opium and gambling shop is the pawn shop. On the launch one can sometimes see men holding tightly to a little bundle of baby clothes which will soon be exchanged for the price of a pipeful. ...

There is little that can be done as regards the drug traffic until the aims and ambitions of beneficiaries under the present economic and imperialist system are reorientated. Callousness, open and unabashed, may be preferable in the sight of God to our Western methods of allowing nefarious trades and then assuming a posture of horror and sympathy when the condition of our victims comes to light.

I soon received the invitation to Tokyo, and set out with my evidence. It was a strange week that I spent there, going wherever I was asked, from one statesman to another, one Ministry to another, giving report. It would be a pleasure to describe some of these interviews, but the impossibility of doing so is self-evident. The amazement and distress of many was obvious. Some awoke to a new sense of duty as regards the drug traffic. In between these appointments I told the story to many groups of fine, public-spirited citizens.

*   *   *

Nine years ago, when I first came to India, I was not exempt from the wretched shame one feels, the dishonour, here, of being British. But this time it is much worse. Probably it is the result of those months I spent with the Chinese people, feeling more firmly every day the heel of Japanese imperialism pressing down upon us. China's sorrow, China's insults, and China's bondage are so real that they are a burden even to her foreigners. Filled with the atmosphere of these months, I come directly to India and find myself more alert than on either previous visit to what is going on. It is much clearer to me now, the depth of spiritual havoc that is being wrought. Should one grain of humour be allowed entry into the official mind, I don't believe the present way of governing could persist. A sense of the ridiculous would make it impossible for us to keep adorning Indian cities with large-sized statues of British gentlemen of full-bodied habit in frock coats. A shred of psychology would prevent us from continually irritating so many fine young people with our attitude of conscious, even self-trumpeted, rectitude. A little science would change the technique of our detectives. They stand for hours outside one's gate, pretending to admire the view, while the householder and all his guests know perfectly well which of them is being shadowed; they know also the complete innocence and integrity of the suspected ones; moreover, they know that the detectives know it too.

Spying is always an expensive method of acquiring information. Friendship elicits all one needs much more quickly. And it's definitely more reliable. So long as our officials in various parts of the world live in British style, high and lifted up, they must depend on their paid dependents, spies and otherwise, for information. But what they get for their money is sometimes far removed from the truth. We spend thousands of pounds on paying men to spy and lie all round the world. It is a calamitous procedure to subsidize the breaking down of confidence between man and man. It was a good many centuries before our ancestors dared to trust each other. Civilization is built upon this trust. Without it life would have few values.

Muriel Lester returned to England from Asia with a great deal of documentation about the drug problem there. Not long after returning home, she wrote:
...I soon had to pack up my briefcase and go to Geneva. Mr. Leonard A. Lyall, chairman and Assessor of the Opium Advisory Committee of the League of Nations, and one or two other experts had seen my letters from China and wanted to talk. Malaria laid me low as soon as I arrived. It was my worst, seventh, and last bout. How well I understood now the Psalmist's declaration, "My bones are consumed within me. My strength is become like water." The evidence I took proved of some value, and Mr. Lyall used it in his speech at the Opium Advisory Committee during the annual session on opium which was held a week or two later. He appealed to Japan in the following words:

> ...If the Chinese people once become convinced that Japan is chiefly to blame for all the lives that are wrecked by heroin, the amount of hatred that will be engendered may last for generations.

A hundred years ago much the same thing was going on in the South as is now happening in North China. But in those days it was opium, not heroin, that was being smuggled, and this opium came from India. Most of the opium was actually smuggled by Chinese, but it was imported into Canton by British merchants, and behind the British merchant stood the power of the British government. When a courageous Chinese Viceroy confiscated and destroyed twenty thousand chests of opium owned by British subjects, China was compelled to pay six million dollars compensation and to dismiss the Viceroy for his anti-British attitude. And the smuggling continued.

> The political differences between England and China did not cause much ill feeling and the fight that they led to was very soon forgotten. But for nearly a century the relations between England and China were poisoned by Indian opium. This was what Consul Alcock wrote about it in the middle of the nineteenth century:

> The Chinese regard the British as the great producers, carriers and sellers of the drug, to our own great profit and their undoubted impoverishment and ruin. Hostility and distrust can alone be traced to this source. No other feelings flow from it, and the consequences will meet us at every turn of our negotiations, in our daily intercourse, and every changing phase of our relations. It must be seriously taken into account and calculated upon as an adverse element in all we attempt in China.

> England made the mistake of allowing a moral question, in which she was wholly in the wrong, to get mixed up with political questions, in which she had a great deal of right on her side. For the sake of China and for her own sake, I hope Japan will be wiser than we were.

It was a happy homecoming for me, conscious that at last I had handed over to a permanent body of representatives of many nations much of the responsiblity that had so long burdened me.

* * *

The International Fellowship of Reconciliation held its conference in Cambridge. Dictatorship had taken its toll of our membership. The shadow of war was upon us. We learned much from our Belgian, Dutch, French, German, and Italian members. The courage of our continental friends was superb, their lack of bitterness a miracle. Their quiet confidence in God and the future profoundly impressed all of us Americans, British and Scandinavians who were comparatively safe. The outcome of this week of intimate fellowship was the formation under the clear direction of God of "Embassies of Reconciliation." A panel of men and women are going from country to

170

country throughout the world in unofficial peacemaking. George Lansbury visited nearly all the Prime Ministers of Europe as well as President Roosevelt and Herr Hitler within twelve months. His messages were given in the name of ordinary people like ourselves.

The previous December (1935) in Hong Kong, a cable had reached me from the States asking me to join the National Preaching Mission. I didn't like the sound of it. I'm not keen on sermons. I cabled back a refusal. A month later in India, letters arrived telling me about the format of the Mission and explaining its program. This sounded good. I liked the idea of a nation-wide movement, ignoring denominational differences and touching every strata of the population. I was allowed to reverse my decision. In October I set out for the USA and joined the Mission in Montana. It was a stiff bit of discipline at first to speak on a platform with certain of one's colleagues who held contrary views to one's own about nearly everything. But very soon we became a unit. We experienced miracles of grace among ourselves; it accounted for the potency of messages to the daily audiences of twenty to twenty-five thousand.

When it was over, I went down to Mississippi to spend three weeks on the Delta Cooperative Farm where cotton share-croppers, white and coloured, work together in amity. I knew the superintendent, Sam Franklin, well. It was he and his wife who were responsible for Fellowship House in Kyoto, one of the best bits of work I saw in Japan. Even when they had given me hospitality there in 1933, Sam was debating whether he, a Southerner, of farming stock ought not to be tackling the harder problem in his own country. Mississippi depressed me abysmally. The psychological atmosphere reminded me all the time of India.

I was sitting there in winter sunshine on the bottom step of my wooden cabin, cotton-fields stretching illimitably in every direction, when I started this book. I finish it in my one-roomed home in Bow, this last day in May. Life grows richer and richer. Very often I cannot imagine greater joy. Queer but true!

Yet all the time the dead weight of Spain, of Ethiopia, of drugs, of child slaves, of the north-west frontier drags at one, a bearing-down pain. Early in 1918 we were told to trust our fighting forces. Only complete victory could make us safe. The knock-out blow must be administered. When victory came, we were to squeeze Germany "till the pips squeaked." We obeyed our leaders and did that, too. We were to trust the peacemakers at Versailles and all would be well. Some of us suggested forgiveness as the only force that heals old wounds. Punishment, we said, would surely bring revenge later on. But, no, our leaders emphasized the fact that we were the victors, the enemy wholly at our mercy, her women, too. We must disarm her, dismember her, drain her. Regrettable, perhaps, but necessary to ensure future safety.

Now, eighteen years later an East End child came running out of her house, anxiety writ large on her face. She saw Mary Hughes passing up the narrow street. She'd never seen her before, but fear made her bold. "Please, Miss, can you tell me," she said, "is it true that the government has enough gas masks for everybody?"

"Yes."

"Babies, too?"

"Yes, babies, too."

"I don't see how," persisted the child, "'cos we've got a new baby indoors and don't think the Government knows."

I can't dismiss this anxious, logical child from my mind as exceptional. She symbolizes the world's children. Childhood robbed of its carefree gaiety—this is the fruit of victory.

I learned something yesterday. Two neighbours, splendid people, were giving up their home which was everything to them, to oblige a brother-in-law who in the past had treated them scurvily. The old Adam in me is nearly always on the spot first, and said, "What a shame! I hate to think of it. Those two dears moving, for him who behaved so abominably!" My informant, surprised at my bitterness, said, quietly: "But that's just the beauty of it. Don't you see?" After she had gone I pondered on her words. They illumined the cross.

> He is the lonely greatness of the world,
> His eyes are dim;
> His power it is holds up the cross
> That holds up Him.

Christ could have evaded the issue. He wasn't dominated by the men who killed him. He cooperated with them, cured their hurt, comforted them, made excuses for them instead of feeling bitterness. It was by His help, His will that they wreaked their will upon Him.

Some of us personally fear Fascist and Nazi persecution. Some of us have experienced their ruthlessness, have had warnings of what imperialist displeasure may mean. We are afraid of being afraid, of giving way, of letting down other people. Brutal people can dominate timid ones. They can wreak their will upon us. But is it really their will? Is it not our own will that puts us into their power? It is by our permission that they do what they like with us. We could have chosen the coward's way, their own way, or the way of sitting on the fence, a popular attitude which appeals to many. It is by our own choice that we have taken a position which puts us into danger. To be one with God is to be in a majority.

It Occurred to Me ends with this postscript:

.....As I wanted to make an objective study of how an army in action affects soldiers, women, children and non-combatants, I set out for the Far East and reached Japan on Christmas Day, 1936.

I found no Japanese enthusiastic for the war, though there was plenty of organized flag waving, victory marches and advertising propaganda. Refusal to serve with the forces was almost unheard of. Such a stand would bring disgrace on one's parents, one's family and one's ancestors; but numbers of men had joined the China draft, determined to drop their rifles at the first battle, preferring to be shot by their own officers rather than to fire on the Chinese. This attitude is widespread. I was more deeply impressed than ever with the selflessness of the Japanese character, its loyalty and courage, its devotion to duty. It is a privilege to be able to call so many of them friends.

Hundreds of individuals who cherished independent thought had just been imprisoned. A teacher had boldly declared it unseemly to call school children out to triumphal processions which each victory meant death and pain to thousands of good men, both Japanese and Chinese.

When I urged upon a leading statesman the basic injustice of letting their soldiers loose in somebody else's country, he reminded me that for years there had been more American and British soldiers than Japanese in China.

Evidently the army held complete power. What could civil ministers do? When a few years previously the Minister of

Finance had proposed cutting down the appropriation for military purposes, his assassination had almost immediately followed.

"Come back to us on your way home from China and stay longer," said my Japanese friends in both humble and exalted positions. So I promised.

On New Year's Day we steamed up the Yangtse-Kiang past shattered buildings, the ruined University, and the Japanese flag was flying everywhere. So this was war, plain unvarnished war. From our house in the International Settlement we could see the uninhabited area on the other side of the river that had recently been a specially cheerful city.

*   *   *

I left the shelter of the International Settlement which looks the same as ever, and reached the desolation that was once densely populated Shanghai. On three previous visits I had seen the gay and crowded streets, a veritable network of narrow roads lined with little houses where tradesmen, crafts-men, and their families lived, each a hive of good-tempered industry. Now it was desolation. No house that I could see had four walls and a roof. None was inhabited except by the dead soldiers and a pack of dogs. Queer to call them a pack, but they ran together like wolves and they looked over-nourished and bold, puffed up with pride, perhaps, at their unaccus-tomed human diet. I roamed about for an hour or two, then I found myself in a part to which the dogs had not yet eaten their way. Chinese soldiers lay all over the ground. They lay as they had fallen, as though asleep, arms flung out, hands relaxed, a peaceful look on their faces. I went from one to another, linking them in thought to their mothers, to their homes and to God. Then I forced myself to act. Strewn all around them were bits of shrapnel. I picked one up and gazed at it.

Was this our scrap iron, British and American scrap iron, for which we were getting three times its normal price, out of which we were growing prosperous, like the dogs? I brought the piece home with me to show to those double-minded people who indulge equally in moral indignation against the Japanese, and in personal gratification for the high price they are getting for their old iron.

174

*   *   *

The alien soldiers in Shanghai reminded me of our Black and Tans in Ireland. They were lonely, knew themselves to be hated, wanted to go home. How glad they were if we said "Good morning" to them in Japanese, or after asking them a question, gave them their own word for "Thank you!" They were bewildered too. They would enquire of Press Men, "Is there any news? Shall we get home soon?" They had been sent out from Japan as noble warriors, "to go and save the poor Chinese from the wicked tyrant, the generalissimo, Chiang Kai Shek." They had knelt in the pine encircled courtyard of a Shinto Shrine or a Buddhist Temple, surrounded by their family and friends all praying a blessing on their chivalrous arms. ...

Soon bad news came through from Nanking, from personal friends, from missionaries and other well-known foreigners. Month after month, rape, torture and terror reigned. Inside and outside the refugee camps women were seized by soldiers, made to do laundry by day and play the immemorial prostitute's part by night. Such horrors tempted me to pick up the stone of condemnation to hurl at the Japanese. But it dropped from my hand when I remembered the German Rhineland towns after the war where the Mayors were forced by the French army to set up brothels and provide German prostitutes for the satisfaction of the victorious troops from Africa.

*   *   *

During the fortnight I spent in Japan on my way home I had talks with a good many people, including General Araki. Many were deeply concerned at the news I brought, for *truth* is rare and precious in a country mobilized for war. I had ample opportunities to put forward alternative programs to the militarists. I reminded several of their statesmen that if Britain or America came into the war, it would be the inflammable slum areas of Tokyo and London that would go up in smoke, not the well-guarded homes of us privileged people.

From *It So Happened*

The police were arresting folk for "dangerous thoughts," detaining them for questioning, commandeering Bibles which they studied from beginning to end to see whether this foreign religion was against war or not. Yet there were Japanese who somehow contrived to send fraternal messages to their Chinese friends. Some regularly sent money. Kagawa also sent apologies. "Dear brothers and sisters in China," he wrote. "Though a million times I should ask pardon, it would not be enough to cover the sins of Japan which cause me intolerable shame. I ask you to forgive my nation. ... I beg you to forgive us especially because we Christians are not strong enough to restrain the militarists." I was staying in the guest house when Kagawa's secretary found a poem on his desk one morning, addressed to the Chinese. It was entitled, "Tears," and was blotted with his own.

A serious-minded American once wrote to Kagawa, "I want to know how you manage to go on living when you know what terrible things your countrymen are doing in China. How can you bear to go on?" "I couldn't," came the reply, "were it not for my habit of waking every morning at two o'clock for prayer."

From *It Occurred to Me*

A heavy lecture programme awaited me when I reached Seattle from Japan. Everyone wanted first-hand news about China. I heard that the biggest shipment of scrap iron ever to leave the Pacific coast was just starting for Japan. That meant I had to go to the exporting firm and see its representative. I showed my bit of shrapnel and told him where I had picked it up. He looked embarrassed. Evidently others had gone to him on the same errand.

"We didn't want to send the stuff. We had to," he said. "We're no worse than the cotton people, the gasoline and auto people." Later he added, "Besides if *we* didn't send it to them, somebody else would."

Note these three different avowals of spiritual impotence, to accept which would amount almost to blasphemy. The first, the "necessary evil" idea is a lie which was nailed to the Cross a long time ago. The second is an excuse that every child discovers can never shield one from blame. As for the third, "If I didn't, someone else would," it is strange that anybody can be deceived by such argument.

An average of one hundred people are killed every day on the roads in this country. If you were driving in the country and a child ran in front of the car, would you clamp down on the brakes at the risk of your life, or would you begin to excuse yourself and say, "After all, if I didn't, someone else would?" Isn't it Pharasaic to let Japan get the hate and us all the profits?

At the close of a meeting in Oregon a thin, ill-dressed woman came up to thank me. "I am so glad now," she said, "that I refused to sell my old iron. They offered me a lot for it but I had a feeling they were going to do something wrong with it."

From *It So Happened*

The missionary societies mobilized their resources. Resolutions were passed, messages sent. ... My friends sent letters and memorials to cabinet ministers in Washington. I wrote to Downing Street and Whitehall. Every now and then a British cabinet minister announced that we had no quarrel with Japan; that we should not interfere in China so long as British interests were not involved. Doom impends when Christian statesmen adopt anti-Christian standards in foreign affairs.

I was weary when at last I reached Washington. But the First Lady of the Land, who had invited me to lunch at the White House, gave far-reaching comfort. Many individuals have received new confidence through Mrs. Roosevelt's unfaltering courage and directness of approach.

Traveling Secretary
of the
International
Fellowship
of Reconciliation
The War Clouds Gather

Ominous events were casting the growing shadow of war over the world as totalitarianism gained strength during the decade of the 1930s. Muriel Lester, ambassador-at-large for the International Fellowship of Reconciliation (IFOR), came face to face with the impact of militarism and the drug trade on people's lives as she traveled up and down the vast territory of China and Japan. But the crisis was deepening in Europe as well, and the London office of IFOR sent an unexpected invitation to Lester.

From *It So Happened*

From Europe came a cable that altered the pattern of my life. It was from Nevin Sayre, then attending the Council meeting of the International Fellowship of Reconciliation. There was to be a rearrangement of staff. When the International was founded after the 1914 war, Kees Boeke and Pierre Ceresole were its secretaries—its office in Holland. Later Oliver Dryer became secretary and the office was moved to London. Donald Grant and Kaspar Mayer were in charge when it was Austria's turn to provide the headquarters. In 1933 it went to Paris,

179

with Henri Roser as secretary. Now the decision had been made to employ four people—Henri Roser, Percy Bartlett, Siegmund Schultze, and myself, with the central office in London. I had never dreamed of such an invitation. Doris and I had to walk miles, think hard, experience a tussle of wills, look at it from every imaginable point of view, pray over it, and sleep on it. Having never worked under a committee, I'd have to undergo a new sort of discipline. Though a travelling secretary, I'd have to fit into the routine of office life. I guessed my casual ways would prove annoying. But I cabled back proud and joyful acceptance, and have never regretted it.

It so happened that, shortly after her appointment, Lester was back on the continent of Europe. A long-planned for speaking trip to Germany coincided with Neville Chamberlain's fateful 1938 meetings with Adolph Hitler; the trip gave her an opportunity to see the influence of Nazism firsthand. From Germany she proceeded to Austria.

Vienna still showed the signs of the recent riotous bonfire ceremony outside their old Cathedral of St. Stephen's, during which young Nazis had been encouraged to set up ladders to the first floor windows of the cardinal's house, enter his rooms, despoil them, and throw down into the flames pictures, books, a large crucifix, and last of all the cardinal's secretary himself. An English journalist had seen it all happen, slipped into a telephone box and got the story through to his editor before he was found and taken by the police. Now I passed the smoke-blackened walls, saw the battered window frames, heard that the priest was not expected ever to leave his hospital bed and, later, that he had died of his wounds.

A big exhibition was in progress in Vienna and crowded from morning to night. It demonstrated by greatly enlarged photographs, posters, and pictures, all the bad things Jews had ever done, all the highly paid jobs they held, all the honours they had won in music, literature, art, drama, philosophy, and every branch of science. The massing together of so many proofs of genius seemed to reflect discredit on us Gentiles rather than on them, but it had the desired effect on the young Nazis, who conducted ever fiercer pogroms. Jewish synagogues were broken into, sacred scrolls of scripture seized, worshippers forced to scrub the floors with them. What a young rabbi of Chicago said to me once on the Atlantic, came back to mind, "We Jews are accustomed to suffering. It's no new experience for us. For centuries past we have had to run from persecution, shut outselves up in our homes, pull down the shutters, and, united with our families, commit ourselves to the power of God for protection. That's how we got through, but now! When our folk have to face the same sort of thing today they've often enough nothing to hold on to, poor devils! Perhaps not even a home, only rooms in a hotel; perhaps not even a family, only two broken halves sharing the children alternately between the divorcees and their new partners."

In one town a hostess discovered I was craving for music, did some phoning, and then informed me I was to have a treat that afternoon. An old artist of her acquaintance, a Jew, was to give us tea and perhaps play for us. Near the tram terminus we found him waiting, inside his, car, a necessary preparation. His wife was incapacitated, grappling with despair and the idea of suicide. His son had become insane. He had to do all the work of house and garden but not a shred of self-pity was in him. White-haired, gentle, and sensitive he foresaw our every want. Then he asked me to choose the composer, sat down at the piano, and set Bach and Beethoven free in that stricken house, to bring their strength and their sorrow, their joy and their wisdom to a spiritually bankrupt world.

*   *   *

From Vienna I flew to Prague. It was the sort of week one would like to blot out from memory.

The city seemed paralyzed by the blow it had just sustained. I soon learned to keep silence while in bus, tram, or shop. The English tongue caused a tremor, a shock. Folk did not strink away from me or look antagonistic but profoundly sorrowful, amazed, and distressed. Some of the best citizens were quietly slipping out of the country by devious routes. There seemed to be many grey shadows flitting about. People wanted to be unnoticeable, to pretend they were not there. Outside the British and American Consulates, long queues formed before breakfast. Only a small fraction of them could get the longed-for visa. There were other English folk like myself in the city, an unhappy group.

181

Prague's Children's House stood a little way out of the city, a well built, unpretentious, friendly sort of place. Grown-ups could join some of its groups, classes or clubs but only if they were introduced, as it were, by their children. I was proud that Premysl Pitter, the leader of the FOR in Czechoslovakia, had founded the House. He and six or seven other youngish men or women were responsible for it and lived on the premises. They did not have the boring job of collecting subscriptions for their maintenance and pocket money. They held remunerative half-time posts in the city and pooled their salaries. This fund was more than sufficient for their needs.

I was entertained by another FOR member, Elsa Tutsch. She had been working for reconciliation in her own quiet way for years past through a hospitality scheme whereby Sudeten German children were given holidays in Czech homes and vice versa. Remembering how much the ex-enemy child, Marie, had done to break down war bitterness in Bow when she arrived as our guest in 1919, I could understand the high regard Elsa Tutsch was held in.

*   *   *

The only other conversation I can remember which salvaged a grain of faith or strengthened a shred of hope, was with a Swiss friend who turned up unexpectedly one evening at our hotel. He and I had worked together in America. Because he was not so weighted down with responsibility as I, conversation with him was bracing. I confided in him my old belief that we Christians ought to have done what St. Catherine suggested long ago and stormed heaven with our prayers for the poor, battered, distorted personality of Adolph Hitler, twisted with inherited grievances, inhibitions, hunger, pain, and shame. He, too, is only a child of God and certainly not strong enough to resist spiritual power if it were mobilized. To my deep delight this man, one of the youngest permanent officials of the World Council of Churches, assured me that he had also been seized by the same conviction. He had written to certain well-known leaders in different countries suggesting that this should be done. One or two welcomed the idea. Some were indignant. Others owned they could not bring themselves to pray for such a man.

Later that fateful year of 1938 Lester went back
to India again. She was there at the time of the great
world Christian conference in Tambaram. She made
arrangements with an international and interracial
group of women from the conference to meet with
Tagore, Gandhi and others. The group went to Sevagram for meetings with Gandhi and to villages and
schools where Gandhi's ideas were being propagated.

From *It So Happened*

We were entertained one evening at a women's ashram
school, where girls and young widows were being trained for
useful citizenship. After the evening meal they took us up to
the roof, seated us on mats, and then asked each of us in turn
to say why we had come to India, what was our work at home,
and the nature of our hopes, aspirations, and convictions. Our
hostesses were amazed to hear how widespread and established was the non-violence movement in the West, having
thought apparently that it began and ended with India. I
remembered the India woman leader who, when she first
heard of the world-wide movement in 1926, had remarked,

> This is great news. I am a convinced follower of Gandhi and my
> non-violence is a principle, not a policy, but there have been
> moments during the last seven years when I've asked myself,
> (Can it be true? Supposing we Indians have got a queer kink! Is
> it credible that we could be right and all the rest of the world
> wrong?) Now I shall never again have such qualms.

We told these ashram students about Mathilde Wrede of
Finland, one of our members, who, as a young girl, began
making friends with brutalized criminals, murderers some of
them, and was more successful in her influence than warders
who depended on violence for their safety; of Siegmund
Schultze of Berlin who from 1914 to 1918 continued his
pastorate of the Lutheran Church to which the Kaiser belonged, though he refused even verbally to support the war or
pray for victory; of Jane Addams of America, born of ruling
class family, steady in spirit, travelling from one European
capital to another to testify to rulers of each country that four
years spent in slaughter was both folly and sin, that instead
of creating lands fit for heroes it would produce a world unfit
for babies.

Before leaving Sevagram, I tried as I'd often done before, to convince Gandhi's chief helpers that it was a pity not to include non-violence experiences of common folk all round the world in their curriculum of training. Non-Indian pacifist leaders, I told them, studied the great Indian movement and read countless books and pamphlets about it which deepened their faith. Wouldn't India study ours? But I was unsuccessful. I was asked to speak at big meetings where famous citizens kindly took the chair. Scores of people would be standing crammed into corners, crowded on window sills — even the sills near the ceiling held eager, squatting figures. They showed that they liked my way of living, that they felt at home with me. But the movement I represented, the IFOR, did not appeal to them. "It will crumple up when war comes," they asserted. Then I saw sparks. My voice acquired its horridest tone; my hands grew cold; my tongue let fly. And all the time I knew that these symptoms, detestable enough to me, were to them the signs of an ungodly person. Their criterion of devoutness is serenity. Thus in but a few moments did I disprove, poor advocate that I was, the very truths of which I so passionately longed to convince them. ...

Then came our visit to the poet, Rabindranath Tagore. When Gandhi had been told the date of our impending visit to Sevagram he had wired, "Six foot three of ground space reserved for thirteen travellers." From the poet came a beautifully worded message of welcome through C. F. Andrews. After the night journey from Calcutta to Bolpur, we reached the peace of Santiniketan, where we fed, bathed, and were summoned to the red-stone, one-storied house designated for the poet's receptions and the reading and rehearsing of his plays. As I presented each friend in turn, Tagore had an appropriate and kindly message for each, reminiscent of his own visits to China, Japan, and America. His voice was clear, rather remote, his enunciation slow and perfect, his look far more beneficent than I had ever seen it. I felt he appreciated this small attempt at race reconciliation and really wanted to encourage us all. His welcome was so generous that we felt bound to shorten it ourselves, for he was an old man. Moreover, a reigning prince, ex-scholar of Santiniketan, had just been paying a visit with much blowing of conch shells and long, honorific addresses. So we thanked him for the comfortable rooms he had assigned to us, expressed our sense of special good fortune at the prospect of seeing the students perform one of his plays that evening, and left him.

What a rich delight to be able to roam at will through Santiniketan's library, art school, museum, school-house, theatre, and garden! To "stand and stare!" To converse with this professor and that! To meet the gifted dancer who was to take the leading part in the play that night and discover that she was the daughter of an old friend and hostess, Mrs. Swaminadhan, whose gift of a gracefully poised stork carved from horn has lived on my mantelpiece in Bow for years!

I have not skill enough to describe the play. Nor is there space to do justice to the poet's special pride and joy, the rural centre which Santiniketan has built up in the next village, where students teach handicrafts, and do research work along many avenues of national service.

Gandhi does not like people to embroider their saris. Even the immemorial painted patterns on the wheels of the village carts he calls a waste of time. But the poet glories in beauty as a manifestation of God, and possibly underrates some of the drastic discipline that Gandhi demands. These different strains blend noticeably in Gandhi's two grandsons who soon made themselves known to us. They were among the best painters and designers of the art school and full of enthusiasm for their work. But unlike most of their fellow-students, they held to the stern discipline of their upbringing. If a saint like their grandfather needed the discipline of 4:00 a.m. to 7:00 p.m. prayers every day, then they were sure they did also. Besides, they had kept their eyes open during their sixteen and seventeen years of life. They had seen enthusiasts come and go, zealous men and women of various races turning up punctually at each prayer time, thoroughly enjoying the rewards of abstinence so long as the Mahatma was there to stimulate them but decidedly inconspicuous whenever he was away for a few days. They had seen artists whose sureness of touch, strength of line, and awareness of life had wilted as a result of moral decay. How easy it is to divorce oneself from the mass of one's fellow-countrymen by imagining one is of rarer clay, and therefore excused from self-discipline, menial work, and simple living! How certain is the deterioration of spirit that follows such pampering of self! How lamentably obvious it is in the things one creates!

Before we left for Santiniketan Gandhi had said, "Be sure to ask Mallikji to sing for you. He always does for me when I am there." As soon as this man met us at the station we realized that we had acquired a new brother. He accepted us all with very few words. As he helped the coolies put the suitcases on the cart it was obvious that they, too, were brothers. He was behaving as if our holiday were his own, his eyes sparkling with joy, but soon we knew that he counted every day a holiday and every job as enriching pleasure. He accepted life and found it good. His serenity was blended with the grace of Christ. He knew our hymns as well as the hymns of other faiths. He knew the Bible better than we did. As we walked under the trees with him none of us felt tired. We even forgot the heat. We were with someone who had arrived. "Gandhiji says you will sing to us," I suggested. "Certainly. When?" was the response. We fixed the cool hour after supper and sat quietly while the brief Indian twilight vanished into blue darkness. Then he sang as a bird does, in pure rapture, in Hindi, in English, in Bengali, songs from our scriptures, from Sanskrit scriptures, peasant songs, and true love songs. Something of eternity touched the dullest of us that night.

Mallikji explained that Charlie Andrews was a very special brother of his. After the Amritsar episode, when the British order to shoot into an unarmed crowd was followed by the notorious Crawling Order, a physically painless but psychologically damning form of punishment, these two brothers had set out together to wander up and down the shocked and horror-stricken countryside, trying to strengthen men and women, particuarly the young, trying to help them to accept the blow as of temporal significance only and fated to bring far more suffering on the race that inflicted it than on its victims. They tried to keep them from giving way to bitterness and perpetual resentment. The evidence they collected forms a valuable, unpublished document. I wish I had noted Mallikji's word for word description of one incident. He and Charlie had come across a man who looked psychologically bruised. His attitude and his despair filled the brothers with horror and burned fiercely into Charlie's British conscience. The poor man's eyes seemed to be fixed in anguish, at a stage far lower than sullenness, at a degree of smouldering hate that could find no relief in action on the time plane. He would not even look at Charlie, but Mallikji's gentle persistence eventually elicited his story.

He was a policeman and had just been dismissed. Indians in government service are carefully conditioned to feel intense pride in their position. They need it, for they lose many old friends when they work for the British Raj. This one had been loyal and trusted. But his conscience had revolted against the Crawling Order. Was it possible to order a Brahmin to crawl along a street on his belly like a serpent? He had looked the other way, refusing to humiliate a fellow Indian. So he was dismissed. For some time his story got no further than that. Then Mallikjni guessed something and asked a question. The man, still with a face of stone, nodded. Mallikji gently pulled at his shirt. The man let it fall from his shoulders. Broad red welps of the lash were flaming across his back. All Charlie could do was to make India's gesture of deepest reverence. He took the dust from his feet.

*   *   *

Our tour had come to an end. We were all tired. We had lived too fast. But we had been enriched. Most of the good-byes were for me only temporary. When the others had left us, Dorothy and I started off for the Punjab, en route for the Northwest Frontier. ... Since one must try to make amends for national as well as personal sins, a pilgrimage to Amritsar was necessary. Then on to Peshawar and the Northwest.

*   *   *

At last came the longed-for day when we set out for Utmanzai, the home of Abdul Gaffar Khan. This man stands six foot four without sandals, a figure of great gentleness and humility, an Indian medievalist, reminding one a little of St. Christopher. It was easy to understand how deeply he had perturbed the Government in 1931. The patriarchal condition of his upbringing; his vital faith in what he held to be Allah's will; his love of the common people; his passion to set up for them schools free from imperial patronage, commercialism, and militarism; his discovery of Gandhi's creed of non-violence and his plan to convert his warrior brothers to it; the adoption of the name "Khudai Khidmatgars," Servants of God, and of the white homespun shirt as the unifying sign;

the change-over from white, which in that dusty country becomes unsightly so soon, to the brick-red dye that is easily procured locally; the simple, direct speech of the giant leader that could easily be interpreted as dangerous: all these developments soon provided London dailies with scare headlines about "the Red Gandhi of the Frontier!" His imprisonment had of course given him added prestige. He was still quite circumscribed in his movements, but was allowed to carry on with some of his work, serene in the knowledge that he and his brother Pathans have taken a big step forward in realizing that violence does not secure, but is likely to destroy, freedom. As we wandered about near his home, talked to his friends, listened to the children chanting their lessons in his schools, and watched them at play, we became more eager than ever to be allowed to mix with these people's neighbours and relatives in the adjoining areas. What damning names these areas own! Fancy being born on a spot of God's world called No Man's Land and labelled on maps as Unsettled Territory or Unincorporated Area! An ex-viceroy told me once that he thought it disappointing that Pathan folk showed so little appreciation of such government schools as had been setup for them, even sometimes set fire to them. But Pathans never forget that those who built the new school and chose the teachers had also sent the bombing planes, and were even now encircling them with military roads.

*   *   *

...the time had come for us to leave India for Palestine.

Nearing Europe one caught something of the tense mood, taut nerves, and strained attitude of a victim waiting, grim and without hope, for judgement to be pronounced. Would this be the end of her civilization? Of her Christianity? Some of us felt that we Europeans had brought on ourselves the coming judgement. What was morally wrong could not be politically right, but we had argued ourselves into imaging the contrary. Were we not even now still helping the Japanese to starve and kill the Chinese? How could we hope to escape the net we were weaving with our own hands?

Jewish friends had invited me to spend a fortnight in Palestine—where Doris joined me—and had arranged a full programme. They wanted me to see the Arab viewpoint as well as their own, and as I went from one troubled group to another my confusion increased. The Jews had accomplished wonders through their hard manual work, scientific skill, and organizing power. Bare, arid spaces that I had seen in 1910 were now blossoming like the rose. Land once denuded of trees because of the Sultan's tax on them was well wooded again. Miles of malarial swamps had been converted into healthy areas. The finest oranges grew in plenty.

Close by the flourishing Jewish settlements lived the Arabs, in their immemorial manner. Bedouin tents shielded the women at home, veils when they walked abroad. The men folk gazed with disgust at the sophisticated Jewesses in their short and skin-tight skirts. When the zeal of a Jewish worker induced her to interfere with the age-old conventions of the East, sparks flew. An Arab rides the ass while his wife walks behind carrying the baby or any other burden. It was silly to think such a custom could be altered by pulling the man off the ass and lifting the woman into his place. One can imagine the scene at home afterward, the rebukes, tears, and reproaches; the mix-up of emotions, the aftermath of suspicion.

Discord was everywhere. It was unpleasant to hear responsible British residents gravely asserting their belief, reluctantly acquired after months of observation, that the Mandatory Power was taking few if any steps to lessen the friction. Some even claimed that it seemed to suit the imperial programme to have just enough trouble to justify keeping an army in the Middle East. "But what can we do?" said a friendly colonel trying to justify us. "We can't afford to offend the Jews, but we mustn't offend the Arabs either. We shall probably be needing their help soon."

On all sides one heard of foreign Arabs from the East penetrating the country, settling down in villages, introducing illicit arms, terrorizing inhabitants both Arab and Jew. These were practised agitators, some impelled by pan-Islamic passion, some in the pay of one of the Great Powers.

"I can't understand your present policy," said a young Jewish intellectual. "My brothers and sisters and I have from babyhood been accustomed to playing with the Arab children from the near-by village. We had no secrets from each other. There was mutual respect between their parents and ours. When the troubles began and foreign Arabs began to enter the country from Trans-Jordan to stir up strife we vowed we'd keep them out of our village. We knew their methods: first subversive talk with individuals, then the loan of a gun or two, then the dragging in of religious dogmas, the whisper of promotion, position, power. We kept a strict watch. When one eventually arrived secretly armed we communicated immediately with the British official responsible. We told him we knew trouble was brewing and asked to be relieved of the stranger's presence and propaganda. To our amazement no action was taken. Two days later a murder was committed. Communal passions were released which have never abated."

*   *   *

At one settlement a little group of us, mostly teachers, were talking over our coffee one evening about the world, the IFOR, and the importance of discovering each other's spiritual experiences and sharing them, whatever our particular religion might be. Next day my hostess told me of a queer thing that had happened after I had gone to bed. Continuing the conversation, one of them had said, "Yes, I suppose we ought to realize that Jesus of Nazareth was our greatest prophet." At this a Polish teacher almost leaped out of his chair, his face flushed, his voice emotional. He violently repudiated the idea. As he was ordinarily a calm person the others tried to hide their surprise. But he couldn't hide his own. He sat there silently analyzing his outburst. After a time he reached its origin and asked leave to explain. When he was a small child in Poland, he and his grandfather were walking home one day, hand in hand, when they saw a mass of people pouring out of a building. The foremost carried a long bit of wood, cross-shaped. The crowd seemed queer, excited, frightened. They were shouting things. Suddenly some of the men broke off from the rest and began to run toward him and his grandfather. Their shouts grew louder; they looked very angry. So the two quickened their pace, then began to run. They had only just managed to get into the house, bolt the door, and let down the shutters when they heard stones rattling against them. These people were Christians, followers of Jesus of Nazareth he was told, and this was their way of celebrating a festival they called Easter.

*   *   *

We came to know a good many of our soldiers, perplexed and worried as they were. Climbing the ruins of the tower of David one morning, I saw khaki shirts fluttering over the crumbling stone steps. A young Lancashire lad with very blue eyes was whistling to himself as he leaped up two at a time.

"How do you like the people here?" I enquired after a little conversation.

"Get on all right with both sides. We're only here to protect British interests. We know that."

Off he went with a towel rolled under his arm, intent only on finding his pal and going to the Y.M. for a swim.

I made friends with an officer stationed near. I noticed he was much alone and habitually wore a queer, rather baffled, look. He seemed to be brooding about something. Sometimes he tried to explain. "You know there are men who can't stand it—these long evenings and nights, kept behind barbed wire, miles of it, month after month." Once he confided, "A sergeant shot himself the other day. He couldn't bear the monotony. All that barbed wire shutting us in."

"This sort of war wears you out," said another.

> You plan your off-duty, perhaps to go to a show with some friends. Just as you're ready to set out one is missing. You make enquiries and find he was picked off an hour before by an Arab in one of the villages. Mistake, maybe. Got him instead of a Jew. But it makes us mad. Seems such a rotten way to fight. Just murder. Of course we know they can't use any other method while we're here in full force. But you don't think of that when your blood's up. How can you go and look at a Mickey Mouse when your mate's stiff? Makes you break out, and then afterwards you feel worse than ever. Once when a pal was found shot we ganged up on the corporal in charge of the arms room, got him down, opened it up, took what we wanted, and did a bit of violence on our own account. Felt fine at the time, but it didn't last.

A different reaction, thoroughly surprising to himself, was experienced by another. Quite free of any pacifist tendencies, he suddenly found himself swept into non-violent action when his best friend's murdered body was brought down from the hills. He'd been on duty on a particularly sticky stretch of road within range of a much hated Arab village. There had been several casualties and many, many narrow escapes from the guns of hidden marksmen. Now his mate was dead. Suddenly the hate and fear of this village burnt itself out. How futile to go on like this! A village was a place where children played, young mothers gazed at their first-born, men dug and planted, women wove and spun and told each other stories and sang and recited the Koran. He decided to break the regulations which kept interfering with elemental human relationships. He wasn't religious, but he knew the first two words of the Lord's Prayer. Leaving his weapons behind, he set out unseen in the direction of the village. When he knew he was within gunshot range, he held out his empty hands. Soon he thought he could seen the gleam of metal, but he didn't care whether he lived or died. It was as if he were entering a new life. Yes, the miracle was going to happen. It was true. People were coming toward him with their courteous Eastern ceremony. The leading man was embracing him. He was taken to a feast. After that experience he spent all his time off with these new friends whom the old one had bequeathed. The revolution in his way of living led to so many readjustments that he could no longer be fitted into the machinery of military security in Palestine. He made his way home.

My best afternoon in Jerusalem was spent in the Hebrew University. Its philosophic and scientific work is enough to make it famous, but it was the archeological department that specially appealed to me. There one could see the valuable results of years of digging, and realize afresh the sense of achievement in having initiated and carried through this research with manual toil as well as precision and imagination.

At the long, narrow tea table I was asked to speak, and discussion followed.

"Your dislike of British imperialism doesn't appeal to us," they asserted frankly.

"It isn't only British imperialism," I replied. "I hate the Japanese and American type just as much, the economic cruelty and the racial pride."

"Yes, but it's the British type that we know. It's infinitely preferable to any other. We want its protection."

"Does it protect in the long run?" I queried.

En route for home I stopped in Zurich to spend a day with Siegmund Shultze. The great exile gave to me what he dispenses day in and day out to refugees, exiles, and visitors from all over Europe.

He breaks the bread of life for us.

* * *

We reached home in time for an English spring. I had missed this quintessence of delight for the previous five years. Soon the glades of Epping Forest enticed me to forget all man-made misery and roam by the hour among its winding paths. Once more straggling wild roses caught hold of me as if beseeching me not to leave again too soon. Each twist in the track brought a new vista of green and gold. I was introduced to the bride of the season, a hawthorn which stood a little aloof, waiting breathless in the twilight. It was dressed in myriad blossoms, each holding its fill of white light.

Either solitude or a comfortably shared silence is necessary if one is to absorb the wholeness of spring. For some, birds are of its essence. When the nightingale takes charge of the situation, one can ask for nothing more.

The fifty-minute journey back to Bow from the forest seems like the descent into hell. Isn't it rather mad, as well as wicked, to leave perfect beauty to the birds, the deer, and the trees, and burrow into a box of a house on a metal road in a neighbourhood which is permeated with fumes from chemical works, breweries, and bone-manure factories? In prospect, stepping out of the bus on the mess of tar and concrete is always painful, but something always happens. The people of the East End change one's mood. A Bow friend passes and calls out a greeting. The conductor says one of those silly things that Cockneys like to say with a straight face. The worried look of a passing stranger turns to one of content as he catches sight of the honeysuckle brought back from Epping as a pledge.

There was a queer atmosphere in England during those months. It was widely believed that war with Germany was inevitable. Industrialists were importing scrap iron from the USA and selling a lot of it to Germany. Refugees were still arriving from Germany, Austria, and Czechoslovakia.

*   *   *

Cynicism had captured a good many people. Cheery youths were saying, "How can we bring ourselves to kill Germans? We've stayed in their homes, swum with them, played tennis with them, sung in choirs with them. If war comes, I shall have to join the Navy. Then I shan't see the chaps I kill."

Meanwhile the news from China was growing worse, though the public heard little of it. Many of those who owned shares in newspapers were drawing profits from the sale of war materials to Japan. Now and again, to still incipient anxiety, leading statesmen would announce that British and Japanese interests were identical. Photographs of hungry Chinese children and their distressed mothers were put in cold storage until 1942 when acres of advertisement space were covered with pictures of Chinese men, women, and children under the caption, "Help China." The public which later responded so generously did not stop to enquire who helped to furnish the aggression that these hungry ones had been withstanding so bravely since 1937.

Japan's poisonous drug traffic was spreading over China, a new sort of warfare by which the enemy is incapacitated and demoralized while he produces steady profits for the trade. We were roping in some fine men and women from various parties to help rouse public opinion in the situation. The Home Office Poisonous Drug Department was always helpful when I called to ask whether British delegates to the League of Nations Opium Commission could be induced to take a stronger line. But little progress was made. War was too near.

*   *   *

Hitler's anti-British speeches were getting careful attention. He broke through all the taboos of Foreign Office conventions. He said what he wanted to say, what he felt like saying, and what he obviously enjoyed saying. He knew exactly where the chinks in our British armour were. He knew how to refer to India, what to say about Palestine, how to display the bad state of affairs our royal commission had found in the West Indies. It is easy for us British to listen to the criticism of friends and the ravings of enemies and to remark of both, "There's probably something in what they say," and remain quite unperturbed. So it happened Sunday after Sunday that summer. Hitler made devastating analyses and pointed out the moral—his moral, of course. Whether there were extenuating circumstances or not mattered little to him. He splashed on the colours to make a dazzling picture. But there seems to be one certainty about human nature. If somebody is always finding fault with another and obviously enjoying it, the animus aroused pretty soon turns against the fault-finder. Young sportsmen began to feel that though it would still be detestable to fight their German friends, it might do them a kindness to rid them of this egregious boaster.

I wished our Foreign Office would free itself of the frigid conventions of diplomacy. It would be good politics to let the world see that we, as well as Hitler, have vitality and initiative enough to get out of the old rut and talk about international affairs in the language of the common man. Why couldn't we own up cheerfully that we have often made a mess of things; that we are not really happy about all the methods our ancestors used in acquiring the Empire; that though we do not know any other empire in history which has done better, that does not exonerate us from guilt? Taking the words out of Hitler's mouth, we might have spoilt the effect on Saturday of the diatribe he had prepared for Sunday. And we could have pointed out that it is no worse to cleave to empire than to covet one.

I suggested to those Cabinet ministers I knew that something of this sort might be useful. I reminded them of the baleful effect of the official attitude in India with its aloofness, air of conscious rectitude, and rigidity. I suggested that in a difficult situation such as a family quarrel or a church dispute, when both sides refuse to move from antagonistic positions and the conflict is hardening through pride, true Christians would use the common sense and Gospel-required technique of being the first to own up to a share of responsibility for the evil, thus paving the way for others to do the same without losing face. Christians have no need to save face. It should be our job to be the first to confess our human inheritance of sin and the extra follies we have personally added to it. But in the numberless speeches and pronouncements of our rulers one finds little of this grace.

*   *   *

The contribution of the French section of the IFOR has always been different from that of any other of our national groups. Its leaders have several times had to warn us Anglo-Saxons against an optimism so easy-going as to appear superficial. They have been chary [wary, reluctant] of using fine phrases which they felt they could not live out in their actual surroundings. They have clearly seen the danger of lapsing into a negative pacifism, a negative Christianity of the devil's own brand. This has led them to settle in industrial areas, living in workmen's dwellings in a steel-producing city, or to identify themselves with struggling farmers and labourers in rural areas. Set down amidst the strain and stress of insecurity and frustration, disillusion and propaganda, they have learned how to use to capacity their physical, moral, and spiritual powers. Nothing else could have kept them going in the France of 1919-39. Their leader, Henri Roser, was the adamantine opponent of all sentimentalism and shallow thinking. He had gathered a group together in Aubervilliers, an industrial section of Paris, and taught them in the spirit of his great ancestor, Oberlin. Many a night he would be called out to save some dope-maddened victim or prevent some suicide. He was always available to his neighbours. That the church authorities would not recognize his position was a pity, but nothing to worry about. When God is with us, time as well as eternity are on our side. He was beloved by Protestant and Catholic alike.

He invited me to France for a fortnight to speak at a series of meetings. I had been to France again and again, sometimes for months at a time, but always in hotels. Now I was to be with the people in their homes, churches, schools, and colleges. It was a revelation. I sat in conference with working men and women, was asked to tell about our struggle in Poplar for decent social conditions, and had to answer searching questions. We shared frugal meals and searched together for some manifestation of the Eternal in Time, by which the power of God might work through our conscious weakness, His wisdom through our crudeness, His great love through our mean little selves.

*　　*　　*

I spent a memorable weekend in Le Chambon [the village where hundreds of Jews were rescued during World War II through heroic non-violent efforts led by Magda and Andre Trocme], a village on the Loire. Smiling fields, friendly woods, and gently sloping hills surround a big parsonage where two members of our Fellowship live with their big families. The families are partly synthetic: small salaries make it necessary to take in other people's children who attend the excellent school attached to the church. When a spate of refugees inundated France, they adopted another twenty-five. The church is wholly supported by farmers and labourers, some of whom are the great grandchildren of those who contributed the work of their hands in building it. Its strong, tall pillars are trees lugged in as gifts a hundred years ago.

This fortnight in France, of which nearly every night was spent in a different home, taught me a lot. This was the real France, different from the one I imagined, seen, or read about. The clear thinking of these friends of straitened means shamed me. They had no illusions about their beloved country. I think they felt that Hitler could take France whenever it suited him. They were already looking past that grim episode, when the things that were ready to perish would disappear. They were training themselves in spiritual resistance and practising it all the time. They were withstanding the present tyranny of evil—the French brand, the American and British brand—all the appeasement of wrong, the scramble for profits, the pride of material power, the things which were rooted in illusion. They told me of a woman who, centuries before, was shut up in a tower because she "would not bow to insolent might." She could have gained her freedom at any time by yielding to contemporary authority. She lived long, deprived of amenities. After her death, a word was found scratched again and again with her nail on the stone walls— *"Résistance."*

*　　*　　*

....the IFOR summer school and annual council meeting...was held in Denmark that year [1939]. We had taken the whole hotel on a lonely stretch of sea coast called Fano. Between sessions we had not even to cross a road if we wanted to run into the sea. We soon learned to walk warily on the wide sands. They were a sort of maternity ward for birds. Parents would circle and screech around our heads just in time to arrest the careless foot in mid air. Stumbling backwards or leaping sideways we would gaze down on the neatly laid eggs. Their exquisite shells, brown and sand-coloured, were a perfect bit of camouflage.

We needed the long, bracing sea-walks as we studied, listened, and planned. This might well be the last meeting before war came and changed the face of the world. One thing we knew in our bones, that war could not shake our confidence. We *knew* we were actually one family, God's, and that all were equally precious to Him. Hitler, Mussolini, Roosevelt, and Chamberlain were temporary, almost irrelevant.

In the plantation nearby we used to spread rugs in the afternoon, intending to read or sleep. But instead we would get the Chinese woman delegate, En Lan Liu, to tell us about her people; or the stalwart women with whom I had stayed the previous autumn in Germany would tell us of phrases coined in times of danger which aptly served them when the peril was passed; or our Danish members would explain how these plantations were part of their national policy, learned last century in the great defeat when land, capital, raw materials, and universities had been reft from them after a war. Then it was that Bishop Gruntwig had roused people from stunned despair with the slogan, "We have each other still." Confidence spread, and hope. The people of Denmark worked out new methods, decided to improve their education. Folk schools were set up in village and town. The people of Denmark worked out new methods, decided to improve their education. Folk schools were set up in village and town. Run co-operatively, these remade the country. At the same time an immense land drainage and development scheme was started. The slogan for this was not easy to translate, "What we have exteriorly lost we must interiorly gain" is its ungrammatical English form. Marshy land was transformed, trees were planted, crops raised by intensive culture, co-operative distribution and marketing were organized.

Our Council meeting after the school was clouded over. It was not only that some among the fifteen present were old and unlikely to survive the war, nor that we had to keep in view the grim possibility of prison and concentration camp for a number of us. The knowledge that we were only a poor lot of human beings lessened our courage and confidence. Our chairman grew more and more grave and serious-looking as the hours passed.

Dr. P.C. Hsu stirred our imagination by suggesting that there should be a second central office for the international Fellowship—in Asia. It should be in China, staffed by one Chinese, one Japanese, and one Indian, and work in closest union with the European office. An American or English member already known in the Orient should be lent to it for two years. The idea commended itself to the whole council, but the approach of war made immediate planning impossible.

After the Council, Lester returned to America to join a team sponsored by the Federal Council of Churches to speak in colleges and universities. She was accompanied by Clare Bedwell, a former helper at Kingsley Hall. First they went to New England for a retreat with Dorothy Day and others at the retreat house of the Companions of the Holy Cross.

These were fateful days leading to the declaration of war. The radio in the near-by cottage kept booming out the news for us. Like millions of other British far away from London, we strained and struggled to get the true picture of events. What was really happening at home? Sleep evaded us. The path of the constellations across the serene heavens became a part of one's own life. So did the vivid-coloured pageant of the sky above us long before the sun's rim appeared in the east below. Thus the fatal Sunday morning dawned. England was at war. The first air-raid warning had sounded. Every few hours the radio announcer gave us more details in grim, excited tones. At last we slammed down all the windows. We couldn't bear the pepped-up, sensational tones, assumed though they may have been. It was our precious country he was describing. England. There is none like her, none.

What should we do? Dash back? Wire for instructions? Ideas swirled about. The ground seemed no longer solid under our feet. It was as though surging waves, huge rollers, were dashing themselves against us. Their impact was terrific. Cross currents hurled themselves sideways. Nothing to be done but hang on to one's own bit of rock and wait for the stormy conflict to die down. But suppose the handlehold were really egoism! Suppose it were just a shrinking back from danger, or from the long-drawn-out frustration of a pacifist's daily life, cut off as we inevitably are from the rest of the nation. A day at a time was too difficult a way to live now. It could only be an hour at a time. This new pattern helped us both through.

We were due to foregather in a day or so with folk from all over the country at Haverford College, for the annual conference of the Fellowship of Reconciliation. Before reaching it I made a decision. I must and would respect my position as travelling secretary of the International Fellowship of Reconciliation. I was employed and trusted by neutral and so-called enemy members in a dozen countries, as well as by members of allied countries. The other secretaries would be frozen in their homes: Siegmund Schultze, our German secretary in Zurich; Henri Roser in Paris; Percy Bartlett in London. I alone was free to travel. How would my American friends interpret the situation, I wondered. I found that they had taken this position for granted.

It was rather an agonizing job giving the interview that the press demanded. I hated seeming to stand apart from my countrymen, yet I could not avoid the issue when leading questions were put to me. I had good grounds for loathing Hitlerism, I told them. But I had studied the steady process by which year after year Hitler's power had been built up: the financial groups in America, France, and Britain which had aided him with loans on favourable terms repeatedly denied to the Weimar Government; the relief felt in certain circles that he could rearm Germany and protect us from Russia; the open admiration of his efficiency in bringing orderliness back to Germany; the appreciation in some quarters of his anti-Semitism; his real concern for the common man provided he was Nordic, German and docile.

There had been moments during the previous decade when he was climbing to power, moments pregnant with decision, when the democracies could have taken the initiative from his hands by confessing past mistakes and setting up a better world order. Britain need not have sent Lord Londonderry to Geneva in 1932 to persuade the League of Nations not to abolish bombing aeroplanes. America need not have torpedoed the Economic Conference and drive other nations into autarchy. Lord Simon need not have helped the Japanese to whitewash their aggression in Manchuria. President Roosevelt's eleventh-hour attempt to call a world conference could have been encouraged instead of frowned on in Europe. Most of us had contributed to the power of Hitler.

There is in us all not only something of the strutting dictator, but also a bit of the aggrieved, resentful, self-pitying, unconsciously vengeful victim of a feeling of inferiority. It seemed to me irrational to expect to overcome these world evils by killing each other's wives and children. This generation, though liking to appear hardboiled and realist, was being naive, romantic, unscientific.

But far more potent an argument had been given me than anything I could draw from these considerations. Given is the word. Given publicly, on the first Good Friday, on a hill, in the sight of all, was the visible demonstration of the only permanent way to overcome evil. Human nature demands something more enduring than the unquiet equilibrium of rival powers. ...

Happily for me, a Briton, Richard Roberts, ex-Moderator of the United Church of Canada, had been chosen months previously to lead devotions at the conference each morning. After silent worship, hundreds of us waited in deep need and expectancy for his guidance. He faced his fellow Christian pacifists and gave us our keynote. He declared he could not tell us what we ought to do. But he was sure of one thing. Each of us must spend a much longer period each day than ever before "in exposing our minds to the light and wisdom of God." I wonder if that sounds a small thing to anyone. I believe it spells revolution. ...

While preparing for her speaking trip across the United States, Lester was asked to write a book. Finally, a title — Dare You Face Facts? — and a publishing deadline were agreed on. After the University Mission was completed, she began on the book in earnest.

Now I was to stay still in one place, in Hollywood, for six weeks. Delicious prospect. The book I had promised to write could do what it liked. Let it work itself out in one pattern after another, discard each tentative shape if such was its whim. So long as I could sleep in the same bed and be with the same people every night, I would become its faithful servant, alert and receptive, on duty all the time. Close to the Hunters' house [Allan Hunter, a prolific author, retreat leader, vice chairperson of U.S. FOR and pastor, and Elizabeth Hunter, a poet, church worker, and home maker were among her closest friends.] I found an unfrequented hillside covered with shady old olives. To these I would daily report myself. I would place my travelling cushion on the grass, take from its capacious pocket a bottle of ink and a couple of fountain pens, settle my writing board on my knee, tilt my sun hat well over my eyes, and scribble. Hours later I would stumble home, dazzled by the light bouncing off the walls of the glaring white houses, wash, eat, and rest, and set off for an hour's walk.

But I lost my self-respect as the weeks passed. For the new book hung around my neck like a scratchy, heavy blanket whose voluminous folds entangled my feet, heated my blood, obscured my sight. Day after day I sat beneath the olives, ankles aching as I squatted, finger muscles tense with grasping the pen, scribbling, and crossing out. I heaved great sighs. All around me was carefree beauty, child of joy. Near-by were rows of bright-coloured California poppies dancing in the breeze. Behind them, a group of tall eucalyptus trees which negligently draped themselves and their neighbours with long strips of peeled-off bark. Their shimmering branches, slow-moving in the wind, were soothing companions, and tolerant. As evening followed evening the olives cast their shadow to the east, but no clear line of writing came from my pen. At length I wanted to cry. I did one afternoon in the darkness of a carol service where pictures of Bethlehem were being thrown on the screen. It was the first Christmas of the war and the contrasts between traditional and present-day Bethlehem were too poignant. But this was getting silly. Tears are strange to me. My head felt hot. It began to ache, a notable occurrence. I had a talk with my wise hostess, crept into bed, and stayed there. For two whole days I lay and slept. Then, with my temperature down again, and feeling elated and expectant I once more sought the olives' shade. Now all went well.

Every Monday, soon after midday, we used to drive up to the room in Beverly Hills where Gerald Heard lived, pick him up, and go on to the fire break. There we spread our rugs, unpacked sandwiches, salad, and fruit, stretched ourselves in the sun, and looked down over miles of hillside to the sparkling blue of the Pacific. We didn't leave these delectable mountains until about five o'clock. It was sheer bliss. Allan Hunter and Gerald did most of the talking. Allan's wife, Elizabeth, occasionally cut in with a bit of woman's wisdom that outshone theirs. I sometimes interrupted to ask a question, or grunt disapproval if they forgot the profound wisdom of the poor. Very often Gerald would descend from fascinating intricacies of philosophy to take an example from everyday life. He would act out the situation, assuming the exaggerated voice of each actor until we were rocking with laughter. How inadequate are our words to convey the effects of humour! How can one sum up such exquisite subtleties in so banal a phrase?

We promised ourselves a treat after Christmas. The children should be parked out [farmed out] and we four grown-ups would drive to the desert and stay two nights in Death Valley. We engaged one of the numerous wooded huts which America supplies at a cheap rate for her nature lovers, packed hampers, and set out for this strange, arid district, where, before the coming of cars, so many had lain down by the roadside to die. The majesty of the deserts of the West is tremendous, their peace sublime. The surrounding mountain peaks in the distance seem to work miracles of light and shade, especially at dawn and twilight.

Gerald was preaching one Sunday each month at Allan's church. The place was packed to the doors. It was very good, this series of sermons on the Lord's Prayer, but I liked Allan's just as well, and used to look disgustedly at the semi-filled pews on the days he preached. The two men complement each other excellently. Allan has more experience of ordinary people and knows more about the unintellectuals who form the majority of the world's population. Gerald's range of scientific knowledge is immense, as those who heard him broadcast for half an hour every week for over two years will remember. The many hours a day he spends in prayer have given him insights which throw clear light on problems that trouble the ordinary, humble Christian. His deep humility shames one.

The book was finished at last. Allan and various members of his church polished up its gaucheries and got the whole thing into neat typescript. I waved them all good-bye and sped east to New York City.

Internment
in Latin America

Travel abroad during wartime, especially for an outspoken pacifist like Muriel Lester, was becoming increasingly difficult. Renewing a passport and securing visas and travel tickets were time-consuming and frustrating. An invitation to come to Latin America was accepted and an exhausting itinerary down the Pacific side and then back up the Atlantic side was finally undertaken, despite warnings from many quarters and wild rumors that Lester was pro-Nazi! The much publicized trip, ending with incarceration on the island of Trinidad, really had its beginning several years earlier in a Sunday school in Uruguay.

From *It So Happened*

Two or three years before, Earl Smith, an American missionary in Uruguay, was wanting a fresh illustration of Christian citizenship for his lesson series. Having recently read about the Children's House, he made it and Kingsley Hall into a story. Noting the children's close attention, he remarked, "What a pity Miss Lester isn't here to tell us more about it." Whereupon a ragged, under-sized boy piped up, "Can't you write and ask her to come?" Acting on the principle that one must never quench the smoking flax, Earl Smith wrote. But the letter got lost. Two years later, when the European war had started, he sent a message to Nevin Sayre saying that he and his friends were eager for a strong witness to be made by a pacifist, since their country was being invaded by a spate of visitors who were lecturing all over Latin America on the necessity of supporting the Allies. Well-known Christian leaders from the United States were strengthening the idea that to fight was a Christian duty. Could Nevin come, or someone?

Nevin read me his letter one evening. "One of us must go," he said. "I suggest it's you." I took a long breath. It seemed so very far away. I felt I'd never be able to keep up with the hosts of friends and problems that soon engross one after entering new territory. Besides, peace might come suddenly, or disaster to Doris or to Kingsley Hall. I might be needed at home. Could I possibly embark on such a voyage, down the Pacific side of that vast continent and up on its Atlantic coast? Nevin left the request to simmer in my mind, promising that at any moment I would be free to go home if a crisis occurred.

Eventually Lester began efforts to get travel documents for journeying to Latin America. After much difficulty, she received the new passport she needed for her trip, but only after long delays and warnings from the British authorities about the delicacy of such an outspoken pacifist traveling about during wartime.

She made fact-finding visits to Peru, Chile, and Argentina before reaching Uruguay, where she spoke to various groups and held a four-day prayer school. Her visit culminated in a meeting to consider setting up a Fellowship of Reconciliation branch, but she played a cautionary role.

I stressed the demands it makes. It wasn't just another society to join and subscribe to. It meant ceaseless vigilance, though all its members fell far short of its claims. It was easier to love a far-away enemy that the friend who kept the radio blaring out an inferior programme when one wanted to listen to Bach chorales. I showed them our cheap lozenge-shaped, lead-coloured badge with the word, *Eirene,* in Greek letters at its centre. I told them how I had seen members hurriedly unpin it and put it away when they felt themselves getting involved in a squabbling altercation. I said that non-violence or pacifism meant breaking down or ignoring barriers of class and race as well as of nation, that it implied identification with the lowliest, the ugliest, the dirtiest, and the stupidest.

After mutual heart-searchings, the first Fellowship for Latin America was formed. No one in the crowd of us that approached my boat next night will forget it. We were singing and laughing, and I'm not sure that we didn't do a little dancing on the way.

Lester had to return to the United States via Rio de Janeiro in order to obtain a visa for what had become a controversial reentry into wartime America. But even getting there was not easy.

...the British authorities asked for a promise that I would not lecture, or give a press interview, or talk about the war while in Brazil. Actually there would have been little time to do anything but pick up my American visa, but I could not give such a promise. If asked about the war and its relation to Christianity I should have to refer to the classic opening words of the Lord's Prayer, the "Inasmuch" pronouncement, or the demonstration or Calvary that God's way of overcoming evil was more practical than Roman or British imperialism.

The British authorities knew all about these Christian fundamentals, saluted them with respect, but said they could not be carried out in wartime. I must give my promise if I wanted to go to Rio. I said I couldn't. They persisted. So did I. I asked how an idea, a philosophy, or a religion, could be eternally true if it changed its nature according to the temporary activities and policies of men.

Finally, the authorities relented and gave Lester permission to take the plane to Rio de Janeiro from which she then took a ship bound for the United States. When the ship docked in Trinidad, British authorities boarded the vessel. Lester's books and papers were taken for examination. Her diary records the events that followed.

This major does his job with utmost courtesy. Has to argue that the accident of a war or the foreign policy that makes a war inevitable can change the nature of one's religious duty. Though Jesus says you must forgive your enemies, you really mustn't; you must kill them instead. ...After about half an hour, looking very grave he announces, "I am afraid I shall have to ask you to come ashore."

"Are you arresting me?" I enquire, immensely interested as a detective fan must be at finding herself the centre of the play.

"Oh, no!" he says, disclaiming such crudeness.

"Then, supposing I say I won't come, what happens?" I ask.

"Er—in that case—er—I'm afraid—er—we would have to find means to induce you to do so."

Taken down by two policemen and a police matron to pack; told I can eat dinner in peace and then will be escorted off the ship.

After dinner, Lester was taken ashore and placed temporarily in a hotel room, given instructions that she was confined to the grounds, and then was left for the night.

After being under supervision it was good to be alone. How solid a foundation to life God is! How glorious to discover that cosmic earthquakes do not occur! Ours are always only terrestrial. Reality is dependable. The ground of our being is unmoved. Little surface changes entice one to laugh with delight at the richness of life, at the joy we have inherited. When some part of your body is hurting, rigid, or inflamed, when your consciousness has become obsessed with the pain, what a blessed sense of wholeness creeps into every tissue when a hot water bottle is suddenly applied! The tangled knot of pain does not have to be unravelled, it serenely vanishes. One's tempo is no longer jerky but rhythmic. Once more the body feels it is an entity, an organism working harmoniously in every part. Such is the process when one can get alone, remembering God. It is His universe and He is in it.

I cleared up the scattered newspapers, put away the redundant ash trays, rearranged the room, unpacked, bathed, got into bed, tucked the mosquito net under the mattress, and slept.

*　　*　　*

[The next afternoon] the major looking very grave brings a large and typically beaming officer into my room and they hand me a warrant, saying I have offended against "Colonial Regulation number X.Y.Z." and am under detention. I wait for the formula that according to my detective novels generally follows arrest. But nothing comes. So I enquire, "Isn't something missing here? Oughtn't I to be told I may appeal or something?"

"You can," the major assures me.

Then I realize that I know no one on the island, and as it is very small, it will probably be more official ridden even than other parts of the Empire, where I have found that folk feel it is pretty hopeless to stand out against the government. So I say, "D'you think it'll make any difference if I appeal?"

They say, "No."

I say, "All right. I won't." The cheery one says he will be glad to drive me over to the internment camp after dinner. This seems to be the British pattern. I suppose it protects the officials' feelings. They are so bland and charming. He invites me as though he is escorting me to a picnic or a party.

*   *   *

It is quite dark when we reach the camp. ...Negro guards with fixed bayonets are stationed at the gates and at each corner of the camp, where towers and powerful searchlights are placed. Miles of barbed wire reinforce the three fences that surround us. We pass many huts before the second gate is unlocked and we enter the smaller enclosure for Aryans. Seated round the wooden steps of a hut under the brilliant lamp are the leader, her fifteen-year-old daughter and a couple of other women. I am introduced and taken to my room. It measures nine feet by five and contains a canvas stretcher bed, a chair, and a twelve inch by eight inch shelf; an enamel mug, plate, cup, saucer, knife, fork, and spoon; two unbleached calico sheets, two pillow cases, two towels, and a blanket, the latter not too clean. The women's bath room is on the other side of a lot of rough grass.

First morning—On the way to the bathroom at seven o'clock this morning I receive a queer impression. Across the grass plot a group of men are digging with furious energy, stripped to the waist, sweating. One or two women are among them. A tall, broad, bearded man is setting the pace. They work in silence, looking neither to right nor left. "Russian prisoners under the Czar," is the caption automatically supplied by my imagination; then "Galley slaves chained to the oars." Is this how I shall have to work?

Rather intimidated I wash my dusty utensils and go into the common room for breakfast. The leader sits beside me and opposite is her husband, an overwrought, anti-Nazi Austrian. She offers me coffee. I have to refuse the precious stuff, magic, enticing, fragrant, the best drink in the world, because I am silly enough to have an inside that dishonours it. I take the large, limp, new white roll which constitutes our breakfast, but cannot tackle it with any spirit. Every tissue in my body, every thought in my mind, intensifies one integral craving for a cup of tea. A bright and wonderful being at the far end of the table notices my sickly pretense of eating breakfast, and when nostalgia is at its height enquires in a clear Irish voice if I "can do with a drop of tea." I gaze at her as at a goddess and reverently pass up my mug. It comes back full of the hot brown nectar, enslaving me to her for ever. Frank Cahill! What a lot of seeming miracles like that you have worked for folk! And what a rich variety of beneficiaries yours are! Negro coolies, Trinidad Indians, stranded Czechs, bad-tempered old business men, exploited white workers, friends by the hundred, Portuguese, English, Polish, French, and German.

Very soon Frank and I joined forces, put our daily allowance of one and eightpence food money together, and achieved an excellent menu in partnership. Our neighbours were a Polish stoker taken off a torpedoed ship, a German chef taken off a fashionable American liner, a watchmaking jeweller and his wife and their four-year-old boy, two Colonial business men, two German business men, an Italian tailor, a Czech who had fought in Spain and in France against Hitler, a Colonial woman journalist, a German music teacher, and three generations of a German family that had escaped from Hitler in '33.

These all came in to their three meals a day, ate them quickly, and went out to their several pursuits, but Frank and I sat on. Each meal took an hour or two. I'm daily ashamed of my garrulity but I wasn't while in camp. There it was "Frank telling *me.*" She introduced me to the happenings of a large family on a small Irish farm, their zest in life undisturbed by poverty. She described her passionate indignation as a little girl when served with one potato less than her brothers; their unfailing gaiety; the courtesy of neighbours; the poorest women's insistence on getting high-priced tea, whatever else had to be cut out of the shopping list; the thrill of Christmas and Easter and other holidays, when household cares were thrown to the winds and batches of tarts and cakes were baked; the Christmas Eve one year when the brothers and sisters could bear to wait no longer and at midnight raided the pantry and devoured everything; the marvellous mother who accepted such happenings with equanimity; Frank's own

210

appetite for books; her passing of examinations, becoming a teacher, and accepting a post in a convent school in Trinidad; her happiness there. The next phase was lived through with one of her fellow teachers, another brilliant Irish girl. They began noticing the conditions of the native worker, his need of education, organization, and leadership. Soon they identified themselves with the workers, coloured and white. They became too well known to be ignored by Authority. The Catholic school authorities told them they must choose between their teaching job and their wider educational work. They chose the latter.

With what looked like absurd faith they started a monthly magazine, *New Dawn*, and gained a thouand subscribers. They co-operated with labour leaders, held open-air meetings all over the island, visited workers in their crowded homes, became their friends. The text of each of their addresses was taken from the report of the Royal Commission. They carried it with them everywhere. It was their Bible. From its travel-worn pages I was instructed in the faith. They believed in it and deeply deplored the idea that America might take over the islands.

Those who compose the Chamber of Commerce could not be expected to be so wholly enthusiastic for the findings of this commission, and its advice about setting up more schools and founding or encouraging trade unions on the island. Perhaps it was inevitable that these two girls should be told to choose between internment and repatriation. They appealed against the order. It would be naive, however, to expect a court composed of folk who depend on the good graces of those in authority to flout their wishes, in a little community like Trinidad in war time.

So they were interned and after a few months Frank's friend killed herself.

Most of the other internees used up much energy in grumbling. Some made themselves ill with self-pity. Frank wasted no such emotion. She let her Irish tongue loose on any subject, but always with a raillery and a light touch. She kept herself conscious of her countless devoted friends all over the island, reminded herself that she was still their servant—that one day they would be together again. Meanwhile, laugh and sleep and study and think. She said she might be white-haired before the war was over. But she knows how to wait.

*　　*　　*

Fourth day—There are only about twenty of us Aryans and the part of the camp allotted to us is at the end farthest from the heavily guarded entrance. It contains two wooden huts. The Jews number a hundred and fifty and have set up an ordered communal life for themselves. They run the post office, a general shop, a library, a tailoring business, cobbling bench, and a laundry. They give entertainments and hold synagogue services. Our two domains are separated by a barbed wire fence but the gate leading through it is left open until six o'clock each evening. ...

Tenth day—It is difficult to find the right place in which to spend one's time. ... Most people seem to have staked out their claim to some part of the grounds. ... There is one tree, however, that no one has appropriated, probably because it is near both the women's lavatory and the barbed wire fence overlooking the Jewish huts. One of the gardening men assures me it's mine for the taking and he will gladly clear grass and weeds away from its trunk. ...

Twelfth day—I find my domain ready. The raked, smoothed circle round the tree looks personally inviting. Here is a private plot, a place where I can choose solitude, or invite visits from other campers; where I can keep a rhythm between work, play, prayer, and sleep; where I can leave books and papers; where I can play on my pipe and disturb no one. ...

Seventeenth day—Now that I have a shaded immovable place of my own I have invited Kurt, the other camper who likes set times of prayer, to join me. He's a tall, fair, typical Nordic of twenty-six. His family has suffered much from the *Führer* but he is of the cheery indomitable sort, with skill in his finger tips, a good brain, a creative urge, and an imperturbable temper. He meant to be a Lutheran pastor but had to earn money to enable his aunt to set up a home for them both in Trinidad. So he built boats and mended cars for a livng and in his spare time read and wrote poetry, made music, carved wood, and roamed over hills. He is beautifully detached. Whatever camp rows are boiling up, attracting backers on both sides, if Kurt strolls past with his look of carefree and understanding goodwill, the temperature cools a little. He and I decide to start the day with prayer together.

212

*   *   *

I had had a two hours' pass and gone out shopping, undertaking also a few commissions from various campers who hate being conducted through public streets by uniformed warders. No shame casts its sinister shadow over me. I am blatantly and complacently satisfied to be interned. It's the inevitable corollary following the A of war-resistance in the name of Christ and the B of preaching it all over America. Nevertheless I find I do get resentful and sometimes consumed with fury at the slights and rudeness inflicted by wardresses who have already deadened whatever imagination they once had. This scalding anger is, of course, undiluted sin, pure pride. I did not know how much of it I carried about with me.

*   *   *

Twentieth day—Most people envy Frank and me at breakfast and wish they could spend the daily allowance of twenty pence on honey and marmalade and raisins and whole-meal bread, but at dinner time when they consume hot meat and gravy and steaming puddings, and see us sitting down to salad and cheese, they no longer feel sorry for themselves.

The six o'clock communal meal is the same as breakfast with anything left over from dinner, or some fish paste, or a tiny piece of cheese each. Although ready enough to eat, I deplore the time of this meal now that I have discovered what happens to the world outside the hut during that half hour. At first, not understanding the climate, I gloried in the coolness of 5:00 p.m. but soon started sneezing or shivering or aching. At 5:00 p.m. I wrap up and take a walk. As the sun sinks lower, our trees seem to become alive—not dreamlike nor faery, nor visionary, but with something to say to us, something tremendously important. They are beseeching us to listen. Their huge branches stretch toward us with an almost personal urgency. Often we refuse to take their blessing. Soon the light is gone, leaving serene darkness. Perhaps Lady Julian, anchorite of Norwich, translated their message best centuries ago when she told us that God says, "I may make all things well, I can make all things well, I will make all things well, and thou shalt see thyself that all manner of things shall be well."

Later on, the trees are illuminated by myriads of tiny silver stars, fireflies whose intricate dance pattern is displayed over so vast a stage that it appears simple. At night while the whole camp sleeps, the universe shows itself as friendly as it is majestic.

Twenty-fourth day—This morning I saw the security officer. I wanted to know the maximum sentence which could be imposed on me by any British court for the crime described on my warrant as "An offence against Colonial Regulation XYZ." I asked him if I was supposed to have committed treason by offending against Colonial Regulations XYZ. He blinked and said he thought not. To the question, "What is the worst punishment I could get?" he replied, "Perhaps to be detained like Sir Oswald Mosley until the end of the war." "What do you have to do before you get hanged?" I asked. "Set fire to a Royal Naval dockyard, commit murder, or assault the body of the Princess Royal," he answered with an amused look. He then enquired after my comfort. I told him I was enjoying myself but thought I ought to have my books back. I had not even a Bible. He was sorry but only pressure of time kept me bereft of them. Is there anything so convenient as this excuse? Or so unprovable?

*   *   *

Fortieth day—We have spent a good many evenings reading plays. Only Shakespeare's are available in sufficient numbers. The tragedies go well. They purge us by terror and pity. Being King Lear for an evening or two substantially relieves the swelling passionate misery of one internee. As soon as we turn to the comedies the interest collapses. Four or five of us carry our chairs across the dark garden to the place by the barbed wire fence which separates Jew from Gentile. We get as near each other as we can. Kurt gets a very long flex and fixes up a powerful lamp. I cast the parts. I am not good at the job but they think I distribute fairly the gloomy speeches, the imprecating utterances, the rich personal insults. We decide to become still more classic and bring Job's miseries into our purview. New readers join us to take the parts of the comforters. I find few know anything of Jonah's poignant psychological situation. His name only brings to mind a funny story about a sea monster. So we act him out and his recurrent bad temper, expressed in the language of his several borrowed Bibles, helps our own.

Forty-third day—Obviously our Jews are a well-knit community. Their intellectuals, writers, and scientists join with their rank and file on special festival days. I fancy that other Aryans besides myself would like to turn up at the synagogue on these occasions, but they don't, not being so convinced as I am that the devotees of any religion love to welcome to their prayers people who owe allegiance elsewhere. At the penitential services of the Day of Atonement, the sounds of public worship, solemn mourning, and corporate confession, that are wafted to us through the barbed wire fence, bring something that steadies and strengthens even the most callous among us.

I keep wondering why we have no visits from public-spirited citizens of Trinidad. The code seems to be, "Keep in with the authorities. Don't do anything noticeable. Stick to the conventions. Excess in drink, vice, or gambling won't draw attention to you but thinking independently will. If it leads you to act generously, to identify yourself with the poor or the prisoner or the foreigner or the Negro, the vested interests will be displeased. They can always get at the ear of the governor. They outlast each governor. They control the police. The police outlast all other sections of the imperial machine."

Forty-seventh day— ...Kurt's aunt took me to her room for a talk this morning and afterwards ushered me into his, next door, to see the Christus he carved out of a bit of camp firewood. It is armless, necessarily. The face is strong and understanding. Stuck behind Kurt's small, cracked shaving mirror are the words, "Father, forgive them," in German.

After ten weeks' internment, Lester was informed that she was to be released and would return to England by ship. She supposed it was because "someone at home had evidently stirred things up. After being granted permission to inspect housing, schools, and other institutions on the island, she was ready to go.

...leaving the campers was a woeful business. However, there was something I could do for most of them, once I had got home. They gave me a grand supper the night before I left.

Camp-grown radishes, slashed about by the chef's skill to represent swans, and tomatoes cut into other designs.

I got permission to sit up all night in the commandant's office, as I wanted to write a good many letters, just in case. ... Crossing the Atlantic in 1941 might take me anywhere.

The campers were up early to see me off. Kurt's aunt suddenly asked me if I would like the Christus he had carved with a penknife out of a bit of firewood. No gift could have pleased me more. It is always in the centre of my mantlepiece.

So I left Trinidad.

The ship went the northern route, landing in Scotland. As her passport was checked by immigration officers, Lester learned that she was not yet free:

Immigration Officer (I.O.): Where were you before embarking?

Lester (M.L.): Trinidad.

I.O.: Staying where?

M.L.: The Internment camp.

I.O.: Before that?

M.L.: Buenos Aires.

I.O.: Staying with whom?

M.L.: A German friend, Isobel Reinke.

I.O.: A German, did you say?

M.L.: Yes, an anti-Nazi who went to South American before Hitler got power in Germany.

I.O.: There are no anti-Nazi Germans.

M.L.: Really? Do you mean to say that all the money we're spending on propaganda among German folk to detach them from Hitler has been wasted?

I.O.: I must send examiners down to your cabin to go through your papers. Will you please wait here while I see to other passengers?

Soon I saw a soldier come up with my diary and painstakingly study it. It's a five year's diary—so that there's only a line or two for each day. After a few hours he had found three entries worthy of notice and stuffed wads of paper in the pages to mark them.

At my next examination after many other questions the immigration officer enquired if I spoke German. I answered "No."

I.O.: You've used a German word in your diary.

M.L.: Have I? Which?

When the word *Zeitgeist* was pointed out to me I couldn't help laughing, and the I.O. also agreed that it didn't really go against me.

*   *   *

The questioning continued:

He looked at me rather searchingly, "Don't you resent my detaining you?" he asked.

I considered a little. "I don't think I do. Evidently you think you've got to do it. So I suppose you must."

He swung round on me menacingly again. "Does that mean that you don't blame Hitler for doing things *he* thinks right?"

By this time I felt I had answered him enough and suggested the question was irrelevant.

When the questioning ended, Lester was taken in police custody to the Glasgow police station to spend the night. Her repeated requests to send a telegram to her sister Doris to let her know she was safe were denied. The next afternoon, she was put on a train to London.

No word was said about our destination, but it was obviously Holloway jail. ... I had been in Holloway before, but as a guest lecturer, the wardresses deferring to me, the porters obsequious. Now we were told to carry our baggage up the stone stairs, addressed by our surnames, told to take off all our clothes, made to wait in little wooden compartments until the reception officer was ready. Meanwhile young girls were noisily flinging about as much pertness and bad language as they could while awaiting examination. The remarks they kept shouting at one another showed they knew the ropes; the petty thefts, the unlucky soliciting, the blunder that had landed them into this place were only clumsiness; they'd be more adroit next time. The reception officer weighed me, enquired my age and my health record. The doctor asked if I'd had V.D. and searched my hair for lice. The result being satisfactorily entered into the prison book, she looked up at me as I dressed, and in an interested tone enquired, "Would you call yourself a healthy woman?"

"Most decidedly," I retorted.

217

The officials exchanged surprised glances. I looked at them wonderingly. One explained, "It's pleasant to get an answer like that; we generally are treated to such a long description of ailments. ..."

Dinner was brought round, stodgy and starchy. Sleep followed. Then my name was called. "Lester, Lester, Lester."

The wardress conducted me to an office where they wanted to know my religion. I swiftly decided that as they'd done all they wanted to me, and I'd obeyed all orders, I'd vary the monotony and have a little fun.

Officer: What religion?

Lester: Trying to be Christian.

O.: Church of England?

M.L.: No.

O.: Roman Catholic?

M.L.: No.

O.: What sect?

M.L.: None.

O.: What then?

M.L.: Trying to be Christian.

They couldn't find a fitting column and wanted to put me into one of the niches provided but as they had to get my consent, that didn't work either. Looking a little worried they said I could go.

Hours later I had a special visit from a wardress asking if they might enter me under a certain category, I forget which, but the game had gone on long enough and I agreed.

After a few days at Holloway, Lester was allowed to telegram Doris as to her whereabouts. Doris immediately began badgering the Home Office until Lester was released. After a time of rest, she threw herself into her work again. The IFOR lent her to the British section and she traveled all over England, Scotland and Wales. When the war ended, she resumed her travels abroad, especially on the war-ravaged continent, going from country to country, meeting with survivors of the war and members of the Resistance. She thought her role was only to look and listen, and to try to reach the deep places of faith in God that sustained these brothers and sisters.

In March, 1946 the IFOR was able to meet once again, hosted by the Swedish branch. Forty people

from fifteen national branches were able to attend.
They shared their wartime experiences.

Jacques Martin, a French member, was introduced as
worth precisely one thousand sheep. That was the price of his
life when in the hands of the Gestapo, and condemned to
death for giving so much strength of spirit to young Resistance
people who were hidden among the hills of the Cevennes. That
same week the Gestapo was trying to induce the local farmers
to deliver more food, especially sheep, to the occupying authority. But the French farmers know how to hold back
supplies. This time, they made a bargain—"Give us back
Jacques Martin, alive and well, and you have have your
thousand sheep," they said. And it was done.

We heard more of the ordeal Holland had gone through
during the last winter of the war. The possessor of a candle
stump was lucky. There would be reading aloud in his home.
All Shakespeare was thus re-read by one family. But often bed
was the only place were cold could be staved off, even as early
as 6:00 p.m.

It was reported that Japanese and Chinese students had
held a common day of prayer in each of their eight years of
war. They had found means of arranging a joint programme,
choosing the theme, the reading and the prayers. Just before
the atomic bomb fell they had selected for the following year's
subject the rather terrifying warning that "if you do not forgive
those who sin against you, you cannot expect God to forgive
you."

*   *   *

Pastor Wilhelm Menshing of Petzen, Hanover, the leader
of our Fellowship in Germany, had been under the disapprov-
ing eye of the Gestapo for 13 years but nothing could induce
him to make the Hitler salute. He gave us news of our many
staunch members in Germany. Some were untraceable. Numbers have been in prison and concentration camp. One at least
has been tortured to death. By making the Fellowship illegal
Hitler thought to abolish it in Germany. But he failed.

A young Norwegian pastor was with us, a huge person
both in body and in spirit. As a student leader he was tortured
in concentration camps both in Norway and in Germany
during four years, but never gave away the names or where-

219

abouts of other young leaders wanted by the Gestapo. He was wearing YMCA uniform, and was on his way back to Germany to serve the Gestapo men in the very same camps in which he had been imprisoned.

The Czech delegate told us how our members in his country, humble, simple people for the most part, had got permission from the government at the moment of liberation to take over four big castles in Prague and fill them with children from the various concentration camps. When they had nursed these small fellow-countrymen back to health and sent them out to good homes, they filled the castles up again with the children of the collaborators now inhabiting the camps. When these also were cared for, comforted, and sent to homes, they adopted another group, this time the children of incarcerated Germans. ...

From the three United States delegates were heard of the fifteen thousand men who went to civilian public service camps because of their resistance to war, of others who were imprisoned. ... It was reported from Britain that sixty thousand had refused to give war service, some going to prison and others into agriculture, forestry, or social work. ... Our Swedish and Swiss members told us of their work during and since the war in caring for refugees and feeding the hungry. ...

We came to the last session. There we sat in silence and prayed. Nathanial Beskow, our 83 year old host, artist, poet, and founder of Berkgatan Settlement in Stockholm, made us join hands in one huge circle while he summed up the conviction of us all in his parting words—"Nothing can divide us." We had known it all through the war, but now we'd had physical as well as spiritual assurance.

Epilogue

From the end of World War II until she was in her eighties, Muriel Lester continued her traveling, writing and speaking in the far corners of the world. Nine round-the-world tours took her repeatedly to North America, China, Japan, India, then also to Burma, Ceylon, Pakistan, Hong Kong, the Philippines, Indonesia, Kenya, the Middle East, New Zealand, and Australia. In the 1950s she played a vigorous role in FOR's effort to get clemency granted to the remaining Japanese war criminals imprisoned in Burma and the Philippines. She visited over ninety imprisoned Japanese and hand-carried scores of letters to their relatives in Japan. In 1950 she went to South Africa to establish an FOR and also to visit Manilal and Sushila Gandhi at the Phoenix Settlement. Probably no other person was as significant as Lester in spreading the worldwide witness and organizing the International Fellowship of Reconciliation.

In 1954 she began partial retirement as she left Bow with her sister Doris and settled in Kingsley Cottage at Loughton in Essex. In 1955 she made her eighth round-the-world tour and in 1958, her ninth. Her last trip to the United States was in 1966: this time, there were no speeches, just a farewell visit to her many friends across the states.

She remained an inveterate correspondent right up to the end. She wrote weekly letters to her friends, Elizabeth and Allan Hunter. In each letter there would be a concluding "overflowing of the heart" such as

> I sit on one of the big old trees that lie conveniently and comfortably about and say my prayers for our human race— poor, foolish people that we are *but* going ahead, bravely and in some way successfully in our attempts at understanding.

I often visited Allan Hunter when I was in Los Angeles. The last time I saw him before his death (Elizabeth had died earlier), he showed me the last letter from Muriel. She had written it the morning she died—Sunday, February 11, 1968.

221

She was in her eighty-fourth year. Thinking of the raging war in Vietnam, she wrote

> How can the world recover? Is it nearing its last trip around the sun? I know God has other worlds and probably wonderful beings are managing it better than we do, to preserve it from the absurd super-sensitivity and pride that start us grumbling and pitying ourselves and *resenting* (what a damnably dangerous habit that is!) and it eventually leads to the murder and tortures of children via war.

> I will interrupt the letter while I get ready for church. I must not hurry *at all, ever*, or else I get a pain (what a lot we learn as our bodies grow older and more stubborn!). But what a wonderful increase of *joy* and *Serenity* also occurs *very* often. Thank God...

Thirty minutes later Muriel Lester died. Her nurse mailed the letter, adding that she had passed on "to be with the saints."

Chronology

1884 Birth of Muriel Lester.

1915 Lester co-founds Kingsley Hall, Bow with her sister Doris Lester.

1923 Lester co-founds the Children's House, Bow with her sister Doris.

1926 Lester travels to India, stays with Mahatma Gandhi and Rabindranath Tagore.

1929 Lester co-founds Kingsley Hall, Dagenham and the Children's House, Dagenham with her sister Doris.

1930 Lester makes her first visit to the United States.

1931 Lester entertains Gandhi at Kingsley Hall, Bow for ten weeks during the second Round Table Conference.

1933 Lester makes her first visit to Japan and China.
Lester becomes Traveling Secretary for the International Fellowship of Reconciliation (IFOR).

1934 Lester travels through India with Gandhi to view the earthquake regions in Bihar and campaign against untouchability.

1941 Lester travels through Latin America.
Lester is imprisoned by British authorities in Trinidad for not supporting the war. Ten weeks later, she is released, although her passport is suspended until the end of the war.

1945 Lester resumes traveling the globe as Traveling Secretary for IFOR, including trips to Europe, New Zealand, South Africa, Burma, India, Pakistan, North America, Austria, Kenya, Ceylon, China, Japan, and the Philippines.

1958 Lester makes her ninth and last world tour.

1968 Death of Muriel Lester.

Bibliography

Brittain, Vera. *The Rebel Passion.* Nyack, NY: Fellowship Publications, 1964.

Lester, Muriel. "A Way of Life." New York: National Preaching Mission Committee (Federal Council of the Churches of Christ in America), undated.

_____. *Bond or Free?* Shanghai: Christian Literature Society, 1935.

_____. *Dare You Face Facts?* New York: Harper & Brothers, 1940.

_____. *Entertaining Gandhi.* Strand, Great Britain: Ivor, Nicholson & Watson, 1932.

_____. *It Occurred To Me.* New York: Harper & Brothers, 1937.

_____. *It So Happened.* New York: Harper & Brothers, 1947.

_____. *Kill or Cure?* Nashville: Cokesbury Press, 1937.

_____. *Let Your Soul Catch Up With Your Body.* London: Independent Press, Ltd., 1942.

_____. *The Prayer School.* Nashville: The Upper Room, 1942.

_____. *Training.* Nashville: Abingdon-Cokesbury Press, 1940.

_____. *Ways of Praying.* London: Independent Press Ltd., 1932.

_____. *Why Forbid Us?* Shanghai: The Christian Literature Society, 1935.

_____. *Why Worship?* Nashville: Abingdon-Cokesbury Press, 1937.

Schur, Norman W. *British English A to Zed.* New York: Facts on File Publications, 1987.

About the Fellowship of Reconciliation

Formed in the earliest days of World War I, the Fellowship of Reconciliation is composed of women and men who recognize the essential unity of all creation and have joined together to explore the power of love and truth for resolving human conflict. While it has always been vigorous in its opposition to war, the Fellowship has insisted equally that this effort must be based on a commitment to the achieving of a just and peaceful world community, with full dignity and freedom for every human being.

In working out these objectives the FOR seeks the company of people of faith who will respond nonviolently, seeking reconciliation through compassionate action. The Fellowship encourages the integration of faith into the lives of the individual members. At the same time it is a special role of the Fellowship to extend the boundaries of community and affirm its diversity of religious traditions as it seeks the resolution of conflict by the unitied efforts of people of many faiths.

Fellowship of Reconciliation
Box 271
Nyack, New York 10960
United States
(914)358-4601

International Fellowship of Reconciliation
Spoorstraat 38
1815 BK Alkmaar, The Netherlands
31. 72. 12. 30. 14